Llyfrgelloedd T.
Libraries

Please return/renew this item by the last date below
Dychwelwch/adnewyddwch erbyn y dyddiad olaf y nodir yma

Encounters
Jason Wallace

Also by
Jason Wallace

Out of Shadows

Encounters
Jason Wallace

Inspired by true events

Andersen Press

Published in 2017 by
Andersen Press Limited
20 Vauxhall Bridge Road
London SW1V 2SA
www.andersenpress.co.uk

British Library Cataloguing in Publication Data available.

ISBN 978 1 78344 528 8

Typeset by Palimpsest Book Production Limited, Falkirk, Stirlingshire
Printed and bound by in Great Britain by Clays Ltd,
Bungay, Suffolk, NR35 1ED

For Hugo –
treat life well X

FROM THE AUTHOR

Where I grew up you could really see the stars. Layer upon layer, so thick and so rich you felt you could just reach out and make ripples in the night. Like the night sky was this living veil that emerged at the end of each day, and if you didn't hold on tightly enough you just might fall in.

But then, it is alive. Right? The universe. A vast ocean of hundreds of billions of galaxies, each galaxy a seemingly frozen whirlpool of hundreds of billions of burning dots that we call stars. Suns. Being born. Being unborn. New suns from old. New light. And warmth. Whole solar systems, perhaps much like our own and playing home to countless planets and moons that have been spinning and orbiting for a time longer than our brains can grasp.

The universe is the stuff of life. A far-flung expanse of mystery and wonder, a mind-blowing wilderness of both creation and destruction on an unimaginable scale that they say exploded out from a single point no bigger than an atom, so abundant with energy that it's still accelerating some fourteen billion years later. Today, we are seeing and discovering more and more about the universe, which is pretty impressive considering how insignificant our place in it is, and yet the more we know the less we understand.

What we don't know, and what we'll never know, is what the *full* story of Out There is, and why Out There exists. Or, for that matter, if there is a *why*, so if you're expecting to find it in this book I'm afraid you'll be disappointed.

So what is this book about?

That, I can tell you.

It's a story about life, inspired by actual reports of an extraterrestrial encounter at Ariel School in Ruwa, Zimbabwe, in September 1994 – when sixty-two kids aged between five and twelve ran screaming back to their teachers because of a craft they claimed to have witnessed landing beyond the playground, from which alien creatures emerged.

The reports of that encounter are well-documented through interviews and video footage, taken by investigators and experts around and after that time, and you will have no problem finding these and a great deal more about this intriguing event online. However, although I have studied this material during my research, and even looked to contact some of those former pupils of Ariel School, you will not find any real person in these pages – not the children, not their teachers, and not the investigators who visited the school. Nor the school itself, for that matter. None of the people in my story are real. If I have somehow ended up using someone's real name – someone who was at the school, or associated with it, or even near it at the time – I can promise you this is purely coincidental. While those reports of an alien encounter did trigger this writer's imagination and form the bare bones of this story, my book is complete fiction from beginning to end.

Or rather, it is six separate fictions. A tale of six lonely young people, aged between eight and eighteen, who discover they are in fact far more connected than they could ever have thought possible.

Six *extraordinary* lives, because if you believe we are alone in the universe then you must believe all lives are extraordinary. Because when you think about it – when you really think about it – we must live on an extraordinarily lucky little planet.

If, on the other hand, you believe the universe is shared, then this book will mean a whole lot more.

Do I believe intelligent life exists elsewhere in the universe? Emphatically, yes. I find it impossible to consider that it doesn't, because the universe *is* life.

Did those children actually see an extraterrestrial craft descend into the trees on that September day in 1994, and two strange figures emerge from it? I don't know. I would like to think they did. I do, however, believe they saw something, because why would they lie – about the same thing – so convincingly, and for so long?

And if that's the case – for me, at least – the question that remains isn't simply, *What did they see?* but also, *Why did they see it?*

Jason Wallace

The aliens came just after the children had gone to the playground for their breaktime. There was much screaming and noise, and at first I did not know why it was so, but later some of the children said they did see something land in the trees. It lands in the trees, and there was this person there, and after it leaves there were some burn marks in the ground.

ELIJAH 'BABA' NYAMUNDA
Head Groundsman, Leda School

I'm fully aware of how children love a tall tale, but I've seen the pictures those kids drew. I've heard them talk about it, and looked into their eyes. And I'll tell you this for nothing: after over twenty years of living in this school I know kids, and they saw something. They did. I don't know what it was, but they saw something that day and it really got under their skins.

PATRICIA HYDE
Member of Staff, Leda School

'*When did you first realise something was there?*'
'When the wind started to blow. It was blowing really hard.'
'*And what did you see?*'
'I saw an object hovering over the trees. It was silver and had lights all around it.'
'*Tell me what happened next.*'
'The object started to come down, closer and closer to the ground.'
'*Were you scared?*'
'Yes.'
'*Of what, exactly? Scared that it was going to land?*'
'No.'
'*Because of the noise it was making?*'
'Because there wasn't any noise. That's why I was scared.'

GARY

When those sad-sacks at my school started screaming and yelling about bright lights and creatures in the trees, I was in the tuck shop. So I didn't see any of that stuff. Not that I would have seen any aliens or their dumb spaceship even if I *had* been out there because those kids made it up, so as far as I'm concerned these ET-hunters are wasting their time. And to think they came all the way from America for this . . . ? Nuts.

On Mondays we get tomato sandwiches at breaktime, and who the hell likes tomato sandwiches? So I'm in the tuck shop again, trying to get something decent to eat, when everyone starts rushing out to catch a glimpse of the Yanks. Personally, I don't see what's so special about a bunch of cowboys in our school, but little Chloe Pryor keeps staring and making me feel guilty, so I give her a shove and head out too.

And I'm right. Big bloody deal. I was kind of expecting to see the *Ghostbusters* crew marching across the grass with a load of cool hi-tech stuff, but instead it's this tall skinny guy, his OK-wife (if she weren't so bloody old), and this pale chick who I guess must be their daughter, who's completely gross with this bright ginger hair and a pair of bug-eye sunglasses that cover half her face. There is one guy with a camera on his shoulder, but only one, and he's got this floppy eighties fringe and looks like a complete chop to me. Plus he must be cooking in those trousers. Why do Americans always come to Africa dressed like they're on safari?

'Check these jokers out.' I slap the person nearest to me on the arm, and it happens to be Tendai. Just my luck. 'Your UFO crazies are here. Happy now?'

Tendai gives me this face like I've offered him shit on a plate. Or one of the tomato sandwiches from the break tray. Same diff.

Old Man Hyde is leading the visitors across the grass with his stiffest I'm-the-headmaster rod up his arse. He's pissing me off so much without even trying that I almost don't notice who's tailing at the back like a cabbage-fart. Only Karl Hyde. Karl bloody Hyde. Equally as pathetic as his old man. He was head boy here when I was too small to reach my dick over the toilet seat and now he's head boy down at Edelvalk, not to mention captain of wet-wipe cricket firsts. *Edelvalk.* That school's right down at the arse-end of the bloody country, so Christ on a sinking ship knows what he's doing here in the middle of term.

> *My name is Charmaine.*
> *I come from Spain.*
> *I eat sugar cane.*
> *What sugar? Brown sugar.*
> *What brown? Sand brown.*
> *What sand? Sea sand.*
> *What sea? Blue sea.*
> *What blue? Sky blue.*
> *What sky? Up high.*

Girls' games are so gay, so *thank you, God* when they stop to look up. The little kids quit screeching too. Everything's gone quiet.

'Look like a bunch of poofs to me,' I tune. 'What do they know about anything? They're not even from here.'

The Yank chick with the Fanta-head looks up like she heard. I don't care. She gives me the finger. I mimic crying then catch it like a kiss, arsehole my mouth, and blow it straight back.

I fake a sigh.

'Our love is like a red, red rose, and I am a little thorny.'

I hope she can read lips. That's Jim Carrey, that is, from *The Mask*. My brother Brad recks *The Mask* is one of the best movies ever, and that Cameron Diaz is a hottie, man. Like, seriously worth it. That Yank chick doesn't even come close. She might not be so bad if she didn't have the bushfire on her head, but she does, so she is. Cameron Diaz, though . . . Brad recks she's a one-out-of-ten chick, man, as in, *I'd give her one*. He says it all the time. He's such a gas, I wish I could be as funny as him.

Out on the grass, Old Man Hyde leads the Yanks all the way down to the line of rocks. Their feet kick up clouds as they go because there's no rain in winter and the playground's turned to dust.

That's the place, he points. *In those trees. There. That's where they saw it.*

We can't hear him but I can tell it's what he's saying, even though he doesn't believe it any more than I do, because Old Man Hyde isn't stupid. I could have explained what *really* happened that day on a torn-out page of my exercise book, spat on a fifty-cent stamp and saved the Yanks a trip. That is, explained what *they say* happened, because nothing did really. It didn't. I swear.

The tall Yank gazes out, the Yank woman makes notes on a pad, the Yank girl glares. I bet she fancies me. The Yank with the boy-band hairdo just films. Check the way he rolls his jacket sleeves up – so gay. Tendai starts showing off and tuning to me about the snazzy camera that guy's got like we're still friends, and how he's got one just like it, and about this tech guy his dad knows from overseas who works for Sony who's inventing a video camera that's so small it can fit into a mobile phone.

'If a camera's that small then where's the tape going to go, *stupid*?' I tell him.

Brad says you can always tell when a black's spouting shit because his lips move. He'd also call Tendai something else, but you're not allowed to say names like *kaffir* out loud. Mum used to really shout at him for saying racist stuff like that, but she's not around any more, so now, as I watch Tendai's big African face flap flops up and down, Brad's voice is all I can hear. Besides, Tendai's one of the idiots who recks he saw the spaceship so I guess he must be a liar about everything else. I wish he'd get the hint that I'm not his friend any more.

Brad's taught me loads of ways to wind a black up without getting in trouble. I throw a Korn Kurl at Tendai's hair springs and laugh at the way it bounces off, but he completely ignores me, and now little Chloe Pryor's giving me ice stares across the grass. I tell myself it's just because she's pissed off with me for pushing her in the tuck shop but maybe it's not. Maybe I should have helped her – back then, on that day. But how could I have helped her? I couldn't.

I turn so I can't see her looking. I wish she'd disappear and stop making me feel so guilty.

'I think your girlfriend wants to beat me up.' I slap Tendai again, though harder this time.

Tendai looks angry. Good.

'Stop calling her my girlfriend,' he says. 'She's not my girl-friend. OK?'

But then he turns and huffs off, and teasing's no fun when the other person won't let you do it. Jeez, I can't wait until the end of term when I can finally leave this place for ever. So long Leda School. *Adios* Tendai – luckily for me he's going to St John's next year, while I'm heading to Churchill. Goodbye the lot of you, it hasn't been a pleasure. Give me senior school over this dump any day because this is a dead-hole full of dead-beats. I hate it. Churchill's right in the middle of town, it'll be a gas being there. It will.

Old Man Hyde and the Yanks and Karl are heading back now. Woman Yank and Camera Poof peel off to collect Chloe and the rest of the Year Threes from in front of their classroom and let them lead them down the slope to the shady tree between us and the rocks. Old Man Hyde is heading back to his study on his own, and Aren't-I-So-Bloody-Perfect Karl escorts Tall Yank to the empty classroom opposite so I guess that's where the interviews are going to take place.

'If you need anything, Mr Jefferson, if I can help in any way at all, please let me know,' he tunes, and kind of bows his head like a Nip.

If you need anything else, Mr Jefferson. Can I put my tongue down your trousers, Mr Jefferson?

Such a sloosh. They sure as hell don't teach that at Edelvalk, because Edelvalk's a good school, they beat you up just for putting a parting in your hair. Brad says. Maybe there's a cricket match in town or something because, seriously, how does Karl get to be here? Edelvalk's eight hours away and the teachers there are Nazis, so how?

Break's nearly over. I clock Mr Greet come out of the staff-room and Schwarzenegger towards us. He's such a psycho. The tuck shop's clear so I quickly duck back in with my two bucks for some marshmallow fish and a tin of condensed milk. Ma Hyde's so gormless she won't notice I don't have quite enough money until it's too late. But now that Yankee chick with the ginger nut and the stupid shades is in there too, and she doesn't seem very pleased to see me, so I give her shit and clear out as soon as I can. I don't care.

School is finally done, and it's been a crappy day. I need to get out of here.

The road outside the main gate is dirt. Turn right and you're in town in twenty minutes, turn left and you get to the Eastern Highlands, if you've got all day and a car that can take it. No one uses the back road except the army. Brad reckons troops go up to Nyanga all the time on it because the North Koreans are giving them special training there so they can kill anyone who doesn't like our glorious leader, Robert Mugabe. They use it so that no one sees them going and so Mugabe can lie and say they're not, but anyone who's lying must be hiding something. Right?

We're not actually allowed to step foot outside the gate because of all the trucks, but Brad won't drive in because when he was here Old Man Hyde beat him almost every day and Brad reckons he won't put one toe back on the school grounds ever again.

As soon as school's done I whip off my shoes and sprint across the turning circle where parents' and Lift Club cars have to queue. The brown grass crackles under my feet. Man, it's hotter than a curry man's fart, yet I still almost trip over Tendai as he gets ready to run home. Crazy *munt*. He reckons he's so special just because his brother was this really good runner and was trained by Wilf Kennedy, who's Chloe Pryor's grandad and used to be the best athletics coach in the country. Tendai's always showing off because his old man buys him the latest trainers from overseas. His old man gets him anything he wants. Tendai's such a chop, I can't believe we used to be friends and that my mum liked him.

I look at him. At the sun. At him. Psycho Greet made us read *Rogue Male* all afternoon, which is bor*ring*, while Tendai got to go and have his interview with the Yank. I swear he lied about seeing the UFO just so he could skive.

'You going to run home?' I tune. 'In *this* heat? You'll sweat like a baboon's armpit.'

He shields his eyes from the sun.

'Well at least it's Nike sweat,' he tunes, cool as you bloody well like.

What's worse than a *munt*? A *munt* who thinks he's funny. I used to think Brad just said things like that because he hated blacks but right this second I see he's right. Since Mum left, I'm starting to see a lot of things differently. If we weren't in school I'd shove my fist into Tendai's face, I swear. I would.

Tendai stands. He's taller than me but I don't care.

He looks at me for a long time like he's going to speak. Is he going to start talking about my mum again? Is he?

'Why are you like this now?' he tunes.

No. He's not.

'Like what?'

'Like an idiot,' he tunes. 'We used to be friends.'

He's the idiot, not me.

I hate him.

'I don't need friends like you any more,' I tell him. 'I don't need anyone but especially not you.'

I think he's going to tune something else but in the end he realises what's good for him and runs away. I was this close to decking him, I swear.

I think about going after him and decking him anyway, but then Psycho Greet's voice grabs me from the steps of the admin block.

'Gary Marston,' he tunes, as if I don't know my own name. Like I'm scared.

But I have to be careful because Psycho Greet isn't called that for nothing. He's mean. Meaner than Dad and Brad put together. He went to Haven School, and everyone knows what happened there. They're all *Lord of the Flies*. I reckon he got really badly beaten up once because his jaw isn't straight and he talks like he's chewing a rubber band and has a long scar on his face, but no one dares ask. No chance.

He takes a long drag and eyeballs my bare feet. Psycho Greet hates me. Everyone hates me these days, but I'm glad.

'Shoes on. Now.'

I sit on the grass and start to pull on my socks. That's how you do it: look like you're giving in then the moment his back's turned . . . Brad taught me. I'm a good liar.

Suddenly a shadow falls across me and for a second I think Psycho Greet's on a mission. I look, and the sun's flashing in my eyes, but already I can tell it's not him.

'I'd do as Mr Greet suggested, if I were you, Gary.'

It's just Mr Stamps, Megan Stamps' dad. And he's with that bloody Yank chick who's so pale I'm scared I'll go blind. God, she just keeps turning up like a bad smell – why can't she keep her big beak out? 'Hi, sir. Good to see you.'

'You don't have to call me sir, remember? I'm not a teacher. Besides, it makes me feel old.'

'Sure, *John*,' I tune and check towards the Yank to make sure she's impressed and that she knows I wasn't really blubbing in the cricket pavilion when she caught me earlier. But she doesn't even crack a smile. She's one angry, nosy chick.

Mr Stamps is right. He isn't a teacher, although he does kind of work here. He supervises school trips, helps out on sports days, saves cats from trees, frees the streets of crime, walks on water . . . you get the picture. He even runs the music club after school because they're so crap none of the real teachers will touch it with a pole, not even Miss Roberts and she's the music teacher. And he does it all for *free*, if you can believe that, which must make him an idiot wrapped up in a moron, but I don't mind because if you're not a teacher you can't beat the kids so I can get away with anything around him.

'Let's not get too carried away.' He hands me one of my shoes. 'In the school grounds at least you should probably stick with good old-fashioned *Mr Stamps,* we don't want the other kids getting jealous, hey.'

Yank Chick smothers a laugh. Great, now she thinks I'm nothing more than a sloosh-bag, like Karl Hyde. Why's she even here? Now, with him? No, don't tell me, Mr Stamps has volunteered to show her around, just like he volunteers for everything the teachers don't want to do. Gee, lucky us.

I snatch my shoe and shove it into my bag. I'm no teacher's pet. I'm not anyone's pet. Not me.

'Whatever you say, John.'

I stand and turn the other way but he grabs my shoulder before I can get away. Not hard, but hard enough.

'I wasn't joking about Mr Greet. You know as well as I do he doesn't tolerate troublemakers of any kind, so I'd be very careful if I were you.'

I push his hand off.

'Whatever.'

He doesn't even blink, just leans in, and for a second – a very long second – I smell coffee mixed with danger on his breath. He's wetter than bog roll in a bog though, anyone else would have hauled me off to Old Man Hyde's office by now, but not him.

'There's no need to be like that,' he tunes, all caring. Like sure, he really cares about us kids. 'Look, I heard about your mother. I can see why you'd be angry. But you're also inches away from leaving this school with a dark mark against your name just like your brother, so you really have to watch that temper.'

I try to look away.

'I don't mean to be hard on you. If you ever want to talk . . .'

I'm crying again. Bastard! I hate crying.

I blink the tears out of my eyes.

'You want to hear a small piece of advice?' he drones on.

I shrug. I'd rather he whacked me with a stick and left me alone, it would hurt less.

'Not really.'

'Well, you're going to get it anyway. Just because you think something today, doesn't mean you'll think it tomorrow. Nothing in this world is for ever, not even how you feel, so don't do anything you'll regret. Please, don't, because once it's done you can never make it go away. You were a good lad, and underneath you still are. Don't spoil that. Don't let your mother down.'

What, like she didn't let me down? I want to scream at his stupid face, but then he opens two buttons and peels open the top of his shirt like a complete weirdo. Now I'm kind of scared. Even Yank Chick's checking him out like he's a freak. Then I see them – three dull stars on his left tit.

'You have a *tattoo*?' I tune louder than I mean to. Maybe there's more behind this drip than I thought.

'When I was in the army I got inspired by the night sky while out on recce in the bush once. I thought this was the best idea in the world.'

He turns briefly to Yank Chick.

'When you see your first African night tonight, Holly, you'll understand why,' he tunes.

Then back to me.

'Now when I look at them I just see a bad mistake.' He starts buttoning up his shirt again. 'You know I'm always around, so come find me if you need to get something off your chest . . . like I wish I could.'

I think that's a joke.

'Right, time for me to shut up before I start sounding like a teacher. Have you had your interview with Holly's dad yet?'

Yank Chick's looking at me again. She's not grinning but underneath she must be having a right laugh at my expense.

'I'm not having an interview.'

'How come?'

'I didn't see the spaceship.'

'You sure?' He sounds surprised.

'Positive. And, if you ask me, no one did.' Yank Chick's eyeing me hard, so as I walk away I add, 'They ought to spend a little more time trying to make something of themselves and a little less time trying to impress people.'

That's from *The Breakfast Club*, or pretty close, another one of the best movies ever made – much better than *The Mask*, although I'd never admit it in front of Brad. The line flies way over Mr Stamps' head but Yank Chick obviously gets it, so maybe she's not all bad.

Brad's waiting for me in the Renault 4 Dad's just had mended after I had a go and reversed into a tree. He acts all cool and stares out with a toothpick in his mouth – Brad Marston, my big brother.

He turns and looks me over without starting the engine.

'What the hell's wrong with you?'

I check I'm not still wearing any tears.

'Nothing,' I tune. 'Why?'

'Because you've got a face like a slapped arse,' he tunes from behind his shades. 'You said you were over her.'

'I am.' He means Mum.

'You better be, because I'm not having you moping all the way home again.'

I hate that he knows when I've had a bad day. And today really got to me, I don't know why. Some days are worse than others.

Something's on his mind though, I can tell. Has he been thinking about Mum today too?

'Jesus, this place is a hole.' He gazes out. I wish he'd just drive.

I put on the deepest movie trailer voice I can.

'"Out here, no one can hear you scream."'

'It's *in space*, Jerk-off. Not *out here*.'

'Sure, Brad.'

He's right, of course. *Alien* is one of his favourite flicks and I should have known. Brad made me watch it once and it was great, *plus* this astronaut chick strips down to her vest and panties at the end with no bra. Looking out of the window I am sort of right too because our school is in the middle of nowhere, but I won't tell him that either.

I put my feet on the dash and Brad's hand whips my thigh.

'You're not in Mum's car now. How many times? Make yourself useful and light me a smoke. And don't you dare try to inhale, you're too bloody young.'

I wipe my toe prints away and reach for his lighter. He has Madison, of course. They're the hard smokes, he reckons only poofs smoke Berkley. Sometimes he breaks off the butt and smokes right up until the end and has got yellow fingers to prove it even though he's only nineteen. Cool, man.

I get the tobacco glowing and pass it. He sucks and scratches his chin. He could grow a beard now, I reck. He blows smoke in my face then notices someone on the admin block steps.

'Well, look who we have,' he tunes. 'If it isn't little Karl Hyde. Why isn't he away doing his gay thing down with the queens at Edelvalk? Did he hear about your little green friends and think he might get a bit of extraterrestrial butt action?'

'Good one.'

'I'm serious.' He is too. He's waiting for me to give him an answer and my stomach knots like a wet towel because I don't know what to say.

A convoy of five troop-carriers rips along the road and kicks up red dust. The car rocks but Brad hardly moves.

'That's just stupid stories, man. No one actually saw anything.'

'That's not what you said before.'

'I was joking. There's no such things as UFOs.'

15

He checks me out, real slow, and the heat in the car is crushing my bones. Then, thank God, he smiles.

'Say, you know what they call a Quarter Pounder in France?'

'Royale with Cheese,' I tune back.

Brad turns the ignition and pushes the car into gear.

'Royale with Cheese.'

We've seen *Pulp Fiction* six times. It's such a gas. If we ever got caught saying *nigger* we'd get arrested but in that movie they say it a million times and it's allowed. Mum would never have let me watch an eighteen film or say *nigger* so I'm glad she's gone. I am.

'Dumb frogs,' he tunes.

'Ja. Stupid French frogs.'

Another army truck rushes by and then we move off. Brad accelerates around the first bend, and up ahead I see Tendai jogging along the side of the road.

'Go on, run him down, Brad,' I lean into the windscreen. 'Run him down.'

Brad laughs, and I'm so relieved I pull open my window and lean right out.

'"Run, Forrest. Run!"' I yell, and Tendai has to jump clean off the road. 'Jeez, I crack myself up.'

We have to pick up some parts for Dad in town before heading towards home along the Borrowdale Road. Brad drives as fast as he usually does, and as usual I grip the seat and wonder if today is the day I die. He's quiet again though. I know he's probably pissed off with me for dirtying the dash so I'm surprised when he parks at the Dairy Den and buys us both a Choc 99.

'Light me another *gwaai*,' he tunes, so I do, and he rubs the dent I made in the car as he smokes and eats. I subconsciously rub the bruise he gave me on my arm after I did it. It's one of those really deep ones that's going to try every colour of the rainbow before it goes – the bruise, not the dent. He said he won't ever give me another driving lesson after that but I hope he will.

'Have you noticed how many Chinks there are these days?' he tunes at last.

Brad hates Chinks. He hates Bunjies and Pakis, and Nips too, and he loathes Pommies – especially now that Mum lives in England – but he says Chinks are just *munts* in a yellow skin.

'Ja,' I tune.

'When?'

'What?'

'When have you noticed?'

'All the time.' I have to say something. Anything will do. 'In town. There were at least five of them in AgriCo earlier.'

It's a complete lie, I hadn't noticed any at all.

'I counted eight. They're bugs, man. They're all over the place. Mugabe's getting real cosy with them. You watch, they'll be stripping this country clean before we know it.'

'Ja,' I tune.

He punches me one on the leg.

'Quit being such a sad-sack follower and agreeing with everything I say. I'm serious. They'll ruin us, and Mugabe doesn't care.' He peels off his shades, but to my relief he doesn't look angry, just tired. 'Want to know what we can do about it?'

'What?'

'Nothing,' he tunes. He drags and exhales. 'Sweet . . . pissing . . . all. And speaking of arseholes . . .'

Brad fishes into the back pocket of his shorts and brings out an envelope that's creased and folded in three places.

'. . . I've got something for you.'

'What is it?'

'Are you trying to wind me up? It's a piece of folded paper in an envelope that's got Mum's handwriting on it and a Pommie bloody stamp – what do you think? It came for you today.'

He dangles it in front of my face and straight away I recognise the big loops of Mum's Gs and Ys. They look like hugs. I feel a burning in my throat.

I go to take it but he snaps it out of my reach.

'Really?' he tunes. '*Really?*'

'You said it was for me.'

I go for it again, but again he snatches it away.

'I wouldn't,' he tunes.

'Why not?'

'Give me strength. Didn't you listen to anything I told you?' He slaps my face with the envelope. For a second I smell Mum. 'Only because she left. Buggered off to Pommieland without even a thought about you, me and Dad. I'm sure this here is full of poor-little-old-me crap, but nothing she says can excuse the fact that she abandoned us. She doesn't care. But you're a limp dick like her, so I know if you read this you won't get angry like you should, you'll just start blubbing like a baby and I'm not putting up with all that again. *That's* why not. She's gone because she doesn't give a shit, but that's life all over. Deal with it and move on, and quit giving a shit about her because she doesn't deserve it.'

I start to shake my head to let him know he's wrong, but

his nostrils flare and I stop. I won't get upset. I won't.

'So what do you want me to do with it, then?' Brad tunes. 'Tell me.'

I think.

Brad teases with the letter right in front of my face, only this time he'll let me take it. I could read what it wants to say. Is it to tell me she *does* still love me? Or to explain why she had to leave so suddenly and go so far? Because I sort of think I know why. Or is Brad right – she doesn't care and she never wants to see me again?

I chew my lip. And he's staring at me. His eyebrow cocks slowly like a gun.

'OK. I won't read it,' I tune.

I grind loose stones into the road. Brad pats me on the back.

'You know I'm right.'

And before I can change my mind he takes his lighter and sparks a flame that's almost invisible in the sunlight and holds it under one corner. The flame catches. I can tell because a brown scorch mark rises up, and he drops what's left before the heat bites his fingers and we just watch the envelope and the paper inside and the words that Mum wrote disappear for good.

Do words mean anything if they haven't been read?

'There.' Brad King Kongs the ash away. 'You made the right choice, little brother. Now why don't I score you a Coke? Just don't spill any or you're walking home, you poof.'

Twenty minutes out of town we hit our farm road. We're home, though it's another ten minutes to the actual house. I've seen old pictures of it when it was a green oasis of grass with the building hiding in the shade of a tall acacia. Even during the war it was like that; Dad wasn't scared of the *gooks*. But a year or so after I was born the next farm to ours apparently got invaded by *munts*, and Old Man Hascott decided to sell up quickly to the Government and head Down South for good. Too quickly, Brad reckons. Officially, Old Man Hascott was a willing seller but Brad always says he was about as willing as a prisoner on death row and that the *munts* who invaded his farm were paid by someone in the Government to scare Old Man Hascott away. Anyway, that's when Dad put up a five-metre-high fence right the way around our house.

It hasn't for Brad, but for me the fence has been there for ever, and it always used to make me feel safe. But then Mum confided in me that the fence was just as much Dad's way of keeping her in as it was to keep the blacks out, and a few days later she was gone.

We drive into the yard and unpack the car, and the dogs jump all over us to say hello. Once we're done with chores and sure there's nothing Dad can yell at us for, we change into our cozzies and head down to the bottom of the garden for a swim. It's still hot outside but the water is October cold, and when Brad dives in he comes up and yells and says it's icy enough to freeze a bloke's *kahunas* off so it's a good job I don't have any. He's so funny.

We mess for a bit, then he puts me in goal for some water polo practice because he was the water polo god at school. The sun is sinking fast, though, and I can't really see, so he gets me with some really good stingers and only stops when we hear the dogs barking because they've managed to coax a cobra out and are playing like cats with a ping pong ball.

Brad swims to the edge of the pool to watch, resting his chin on his hands and lying on the water. His shoulders are big. Have they always been that big? He's almost a man now, and I wonder when that happened.

He's got this blank gaze all over his face. He looks kind of . . . thoughtful, and Brad hardly ever thinks.

'I'm going to miss this place,' he tunes.

I'm not sure I've heard him right. Stars are breaking out over us. I'm bloody freezing but I better stay in the water.

'Then don't put it somewhere you'll lose it,' I tune, but carefully, in a Dad voice so he doesn't hit me.

Brad opens his mouth to say something but whatever it is gets stuck, so he turns on me instead and ducks me under the water, and when I come up I'm coughing water out of my nose.

'Shit, you're strong, Brad. My teeth hit the bottom that time,' I just manage to tune.

'Poof.'

We eat supper on opposite sides of the table. Dad's place is set but he's still out on the farm, or maybe he's down at the country club, drinking. I've hardly seen him since Mum left.

Our forks clatter. Our maid Nomusa made us lasagne tonight, but Brad leaves half of his on the plate and calls it disgusting so I do too, even though I like it. I remember the marshmallow fish I bought at school and get them from my room, then follow him into the lounge where he's watching Mulder and Scully on *The X-Files* with his hand buried in his shorts for warmth. I love *The X-Files*, it's the best show on TV by far.

'Noise!' Brad barks. 'You're chewing like a heifer.'

He whips the last fish from my hand and crams the whole thing into his mouth. I laugh and sit down.

I haven't noticed until now that Pale Yank Chick today is actually a bit like Scully. It's hard to say how exactly, because Scully is a total babe and a *boner fidey* magazine chick while Holly is only real, but maybe it's her smile.

'Make yourself useful and get my smokes,' Brad tunes. 'A fresh pack. And they're by my bed, not under it. If I catch you checking through my glad-mags again, I'll whack you.'

'Sure, Brad. Hey, you want to hear a good joke?' I tune, but he glares to make me shut up then turns back to the TV.

Brad finished with Appleton last year but his room still smells like it belongs to someone who goes to boarding school. Sort of . . . empty, like he's not really there. Which he wasn't. For as long as I can remember it was just me and Mum, feeling safe because Dad was always out on the farm and Brad was just this empty room that reeked of floor polish. I used to come in here and lie on his bed in secret because he would have killed me if he'd known, wondering what he was doing and what boarding school was like and glad that I didn't have to go too, and counting down with dread the weeks, days, hours until he was next home because back then I never wanted him around.

He has an illegal Rhodesian flag hanging on his wall, and his favourite books – about the war, and how we should never have lost to the blacks – are on a shelf. I've read them both. They don't feel like real books though and even some of the really easy words are spelt wrong.

The flag and books are as they always are but now he's got these posters of chicks up too. One's on a tennis court with her hand scratching her bare arse, and one's working out with a chest expander only she's got her vest caught in the spring so that she's showing a nipple. Brad's such a gas. No one else I know would *dare* have pictures like that on their walls because their folks would just tell them to take them down. I'm not sure Dad even knows these are here but even if he does Brad can do what he wants because he's left school.

'What the hell,' Brad's suddenly behind me, 'did I tell you?'

I feel the need to crap in a hurry.

'I wasn't snooping.' Sometimes I hate the sound of my voice. Do I sound like that all the time?

I wait for a thump, but instead he moves to the poster with the tennis chick and starts peeling the corners off the wall. The Sticky Stuff has left greasy marks on the paint.

'Here,' he tunes, rolling it up into a tube.

'Huh?'

He mimics my *huh* then starts taking down the exercise chick as well.

'You're nearly thirteen. I remember what I was like at your age, so I know your need will be greater than mine. They're yours. But only after you give me the juice.'

'About what?'

'About Karl Hyde, you idiot. What was he really doing out of school?'

'I don't know.'

'Sure you do.'

'Really, I don't know. He was just there, showing the Yanks around. Old Man Hyde never said a word about it.'

'Then maybe Old Man Hyde has finally realised his son is a little faggot and is too ashamed to let him stay at a school like Edelvalk.'

'Do you really think that's why he's not where he should be?' I tune. 'Because he's a gay?'

When Brad grins his top lip turns inside out and almost touches his nose. His eyes are dancing.

I have a bad feeling.

'Probably not. But, whatever it is, Old Man Hyde obviously doesn't want anyone to find out, and that's good enough for me. Speaking of faggots, who are these Yanks you're talking about?'

'The ones who came to school today,' I tune. 'To interview the kids. Psychiatrists or something. Remember I told you? They're filming it and everything, it might even be on TV, but they're not from here so what could they know about anything?'

'About what?'

'About what happened.' Suddenly the air feels tight, like it's running out. 'That stupid story about the spaceship.'

'Oh, ja.' He moves across to his bed and breaks the seal of his fresh pack of smokes. 'The spaceship. Tell me again what it is you saw, I could do with a laugh.'

'Not me. I didn't see it.'

'Just tell me.'

'Well, apparently there was this wind . . . but so what, right? Then these silver things floating up in the sky, not very high. They said one of the big ones had lights all around the edge and it landed in the trees, but it didn't make any sound, and then a door slid open and this shiny black creature came out.'

'What do you mean, shiny? How can a creature be shiny?'

'I don't know. Like it was wearing a sort of a suit. And he had big black eyes and hardly any nose or mouth.'

He's listening, but I don't tell him any more. Nothing about the pictures everyone drew, or the burn mark in the trees, or the scary flying dreams I've had every night since that day happened. Does anyone else have those?

'But it wasn't me,' I tune.

'What do you mean, it wasn't you?'

'I mean, I didn't see it. Any of it. Because it didn't happen. It's all cow crap.'

'You sure?'

'It was just a light in the bush. You know, like a reflection glinting. It must have been. The younger kids saw it and got scared and made up the story about aliens.'

Brad eventually backs off.

'Good. Because if *you* tell gay stories like that when you're at Appleton, you're dead. Might as well dye your hair pink and change your name to Gary Nail-My-Arse-ton, and no brother of mine is going to get done for being a bum bandit. I don't care about anything else you do while you're there, just not that.'

I laugh.

'Ja. Good one, Brad . . .'

Then it hits me.

What he said.

My ears are ringing. The bulb over our heads seems to be getting brighter and dimming at the same time.

'Appleton?' The name lumps in my throat.

'Your ears are working, then.'

'But I thought I was staying here,' I say. 'I thought I was going to school in town. To day school. To Churchill. Mum said I didn't have to go to boarding school like you did if I didn't want to, I could go to Churchill. Remember? She said.'

'Ja, well Mum's not here now. Dad's changed the plan, and a good thing too because taking you to school and picking you up every day is doing my brain in.'

'But . . .'

'Besides, day school's for poofs.' Suddenly the floor's tipping like I'm on a boat. 'Don't look so worried, everyone was scared of me at Appleton so they'll be too chicken to do anything to you. Or maybe they'll beat the crap out of you for everything I did to them, I don't know, but you'll get over it.'

'But . . . but . . . can't I just stay here? I want to stay. Why can't I stay here like Mum said, with you?'

'Because I won't be here.' Brad won't look at my eyes. 'I'm leaving.'

'Leaving?'

'To Australia,' he says. 'This country is wanked now and it's only going to get worse. The *munts* will ruin South Africa so I can't go there, Australia is the next best place.'

'. . . leaving?'

'It'll be just you and Dad after I'm gone, so you *have* to go to Appleton.'

'But . . . I don't want . . . to . . .'

'Appleton's a gas, you'll see. After the first few years. Besides, it's about time you stopped being such a Mummy's boy.' Brad lies on his bed and spreads his arms. 'I think Mum leaving is the best thing that could have happened to you.'

He takes out a cigarette. He lights it. He breathes out smoke and lets it close in around him. I can't see him clearly any more.

'You know what they call a Quarter Pounder in France?'

I say nothing, and he looks at me.

'I said, do you know what they call a Quarter Pounder in France?'

'A Royale with Cheese,' I tell him.

'That's better,' he says, and breathes more fire. 'You're not going to start blubbing, are you?'

'No.'

'You look like you are.'

'I'm not.'

'So you're not upset with me?'

'No.'

'Good. Because you'd better not be. Now get out.'

See? Told you I was a good liar.

Later that night, and I'm in my room alone. Very alone.

The two chick posters Brad gave me are still rolled and leaning against my chair, there's nothing about them I want or even like any more. There's nothing about anything that I want. The thought of Christmas, and Brad leaving, and next year, and going to Appleton, and everything after that moment is a ticking clock and I can't stop it from getting louder so I'll just stand here in the dark and hide.

I stand at my window. There's no moon, and all I can see is a load of sweet bugger all. Only stars. So many stars. They're like a cloud that's smashed and scattered across the sky, and the pieces fill me with a sadness I can't understand. I touch the glass and it's cold and reassuringly hard against my head. If it wasn't there, a thought comes, I'd fall. Not down, but up. Or that's what it feels like. I'd fall up into the stars and into all that loneliness for ever, never landing.

'Mum.'

If she was here still nothing would have to change. If she was here she would take me to school each day and everything could go to how it was before. So why can't she come back? Please? Come back.

I squeeze my eyes and I see the letter we burned today. Curling. Turning brown. Turning to ash and disappearing under

Brad's feet. I could have stopped him. I should have stopped him. I should.

'Mum?'

But deep down I know she's never coming back. I didn't need to read that letter to understand what she was trying to tell me.

A silver line cuts across the sky. I jump back into the room.

I know it's just a shooting star but *Alien's* baby's about to burst out of my chest. I'm cold. I'm hot. Breath punches from my mouth.

I blink and look again, and outside is blacker than ever. A strange place, not our garden any more. Swirling and making nothing shapes and hiding things that I don't want to know about. All that blackness beneath the stars, but in it there are things moving about, I swear. Short legs and long, swinging arms. Quickly then slowly, quickly then slowly. Stopping to turn and look. Hurrying again. And now . . . *now* they're stepping out and I can see the outline of whole bodies, because that's what they are – bodies. Figures. But not human. I see their heads, and I see the not-quite-invisible glint in huge, unblinking eyes the nearer and nearer they get.

And it's them.

They're here.

The monsters.

Waiting. For me.

I yank my curtains together then leap onto my bed with my arms around my knees. I hear a noise, but it's from inside the house, not out. A light clicks on and a shadow sniffs around the bottom of my door. I'm ready to scream for the first time ever in my life but then I hear Dad's dry cough and I'm so happy I could cry. I wipe my face, ready to see him. *Wanting*

28

to see him. But the door stays shut and now he's sliding his feet down the wooden corridor.

The light clicks off.

From my bed I hear the soft ping of the telephone down the hall, and Brad's voice talking like he's got a cigarette in his mouth. I can smell Madison. It never has before but this morning it makes me feel sick.

I haul my heavy body up and draw the curtains, and to my relief the garden is as it's supposed to be. Like after a storm has passed. The stars have gone, the sky is still and blue, the cold is lifting and the sun is pushing misty spears through the trees. Firefinches chatter, hoopoes *whoop* and a lourie tells them to *go away*. The African day is starting, and all is good again.

Then I remember. What Brad said last night.

He's already at the breakfast table, chewing with his mouth open and shaking his head and tutting as he turns the pages of the *Herald*. I think, I hate you.

I sit and pour myself some Cerelac, only this morning it's like wet paper so I just make mounds with it in the bowl until Brad gets up.

He stands by the door, flipping his keys.

'Well? Are you coming or not?'

Brad drives with one arm hanging out. Even before we're off the farm he tells me to light him a smoke but I don't, I act like I haven't heard and he has to do it himself. When he puts his shades on I stare at them because it's like they're suddenly too small for his face, or his face is just fat, or both.

And I think, How did I ever choose to like you?

'You looking at me?' he Robert De Niros me. 'You looking at *me*?'

Is he just saying it to be funny or is he really saying it?

I don't know. I don't care.

I turn away, and we're all the way on the Borrowdale Road before he speaks again.

'So? Do you want to know or not?' he says.

I stay staring out of my window and at the racecourse off to our left, where someone's out training their horse and a car's following it. I've no idea what Brad's talking about and I don't want to know. Then the sun catches the windscreen of the other car and light daggers into my head, brilliant and sharp.

See? A reflection. Just a reflection. *That's* what I saw that day.

I quickly turn away.

'What?' I ask.

'Our friend Karl Hyde. Why he's not at school. I phoned Matt Davey this morning, his little brother's still at Edelvalk, and you want to know what our favourite head boy and hot-shot cricket captain and general arse-licker did?'

'What?'

He Popeyes his cigarette.

'Only got himself expelled.'

Now Brad has my full attention. He flicks his shades up and down with his eyebrows.

'Expelled?'

'You heard it. E-X-P-E-L-D. Spells *toast*. Spells *outta here*. Spells *his-tor-y*.'

Karl Hyde? Expelled? It's not possible.

'What did he do?'

'That's the best bit. You ready?'

I nod up and down. Brad grips the wheel in both hands.

'Bullying!' He almost shouts.

'No way.'

'Way.'

'But, how . . .?'

'How? Where? Who? When? Why? I can't give you any of those answers, little brother, only Karl can do that. Maybe the pressure of being a lick-arse just finally got to him and he cracked, he was a soft cock when I knew him at Leda and soft cocks don't change their spots. But I can tell you the *what*. Our *Karl* took his bat and ball and instigated a bit of catching practice with another boy.'

'What's so bad about that?'

'Because the poor guy he was hammering balls into was about three feet away and pinned against the side of the cricket nets. Karl just flipped, apparently, he was like a cannon gone out of control and it took five teachers to take him down. The other guy's going to be wearing bruises for months. Matt's baby brother saw the whole thing and swears to it.'

Brad sort of laughs.

'Jeez, who would have thought? Little Karl Hyde turning out to be a complete psycho bastard. Maybe he's not so bad. You have to hand it to him, he's got one serious set of *machendes* swinging between his legs considering . . . well, considering everything, but considering his dad especially. Old Man Hyde must be shitting through a straw about anyone finding out. I mean, picture his face if they did. Now *that* would be something worth sticking around for.'

He starts to tap his fingers on the wheel as he imagines what it would be like, and suddenly, in that moment, I see there's hope for me yet.

'Do you mean that?'

'You bet I do.'

'You'd stick around?'

'I'd give my right testicle to see it happen.'

I lean forward to the dash, pick up his box of Madison and light him a smoke that he wasn't expecting.

'Thanks, little brother,' he tunes.

'Sure,' I tune back.

The sun's pretty strong now. I pause at the school gate, and Brad's already turned the car and is heading off down the track. He swerves before the corner and then this big army Crocodile comes out of his dust with lights blazing, and when it reaches me I have to step back from the hot air and dirt. The troops in the back all sway. One of them even offers a wave but no way would Brad want me to wave back so I don't.

There's this new Pommie movie about a guy, Hugh Grant, although that's the actor's name, who goes to all these weddings and a funeral with his friends, and in the end the wedding is his own but he doesn't really want to marry the chick he's marrying because he really fancies this other chick who's a Yank. Brad reckons the film's gay but I remember the end bit really well now because Hugh Grant is being asked if he wants to marry the chick with the big beak or does he love someone else, and even though it's his wedding day, and even though he's in the church and everyone's watching him, including his duck-chick, he says he does. He does love someone else. He doesn't want to marry duck-chick, he wants to marry the Yank.

The duck-chick screams and whacks him on the nose.

Brad's right, the film *is* gay, but I have to be like that Hugh

Grant and do what I have to do to get what I want, which is get Brad to stay. And I want him to stay. I do. Even though he's like what he's like. Because who else will I have if he goes? Only Dad, and Dad is Brad but without the nice bits and with much bigger fists. Mum used to assure me I'm nothing like my big brother, but I am, because we're both scared of Dad – just like Mum was – and I'll do anything to keep him because it's better to have something than nothing. Isn't it?

So why does the little piccaninny kid staring at me from near the school gate make me feel so guilty before I've even done anything? He's only a black from the local village. So why?

'Hey!' I tune. 'What the hell are you looking at?'

He's about nine or ten, and such a lightweight his shadow's probably heavier than him. That's when I realise it's that Sixpence kid, the one who's always checking out all the stuff he can come and steal. I bet he's the one who stole my calculator last term. He's a black, isn't he? And all blacks steal according to Brad.

'Get here!'

He comes, but slowly. Like, cocky. He's got this stupid grin that's too big for his face, and Christ knows how he gets his teeth so white because he wouldn't know one end of a toothbrush from the other. Like a typical *munt*, he wears shorts that are held together with dust, his shirt is a rag, and forget shoes.

He's pushing one of those wire cars made out of coat hangers and old tins for the wheels. All the village kids make shit like that.

'What are you doing?' I tune.

He shrugs.

'I am not doing anything, mastah Gary,' he tunes back.

How the hell does he know my name? He *did* steal my calculator, he must have done.

'How the hell do you know my name?'

He shrugs again. I should clock him one right now for being so bloody cheeky but he'll just blub and Old Man Hyde or Psycho Greet will get me before I manage to carry out the plan that'll change Brad's mind about leaving the country, so I just step forward and put a heavy foot down onto his stupid wire car and don't stop until my shoe's on the ground and two of the wheels have snapped off. Bugs and insects cheer me on from the tall grass. I notice Elijah the gardener stopping his strimming across the way to look but he knows his place, he won't tell me off.

'There,' I tune. 'Now bugger off. And next time, treat me with some respect.'

I can't wait to tell Brad about this too. He'll be so chuffed. This whole day's going to be so great he'll *never* want to leave.

I keep on walking, through the arch of the admin block and to the classrooms.

Everyone else is out playing on the grass and I'm the first to go in. I'd kind of hoped to do this with someone watching because it's easier getting into trouble with an audience, but never mind. I go up to the blackboard and take a long bit of chalk, think about how far I should go, then stretch to write in big letters: KARL HYDE USES THE E—

—delvalk boys for batting practice. That's what I was going to write, but then I hear someone behind me.

'What're you doing?'

Great. It's Freckle Face Holly again, blinding me with her invisible tan. I swear, this chick's like a jack-in-the-box from a horror flick or something because she keeps turning up when you really don't want her.

'Leave me alone, Yank.'

But she just starts tuning off about my mum and is that why I'm making trouble, like she understands, and gay stuff like *feelings*. She says I should talk to her dad. Just because she caught me blubbing up at the cricket pavilion yesterday.

'I told you, Copper Top, I didn't see the spaceship . . . Tell your dad I wasn't anywhere near the trees. I was in the tuck shop when it came . . .'

How the hell would she know what I feel, anyway? She doesn't know me or my mum or anything about my life, other than what she heard coming out of Mr Stamps' big, stupid mouth.

'Shut up, Yank,' I tell her, but she won't.

I rush for the door, but she doesn't get out of my way either so I push her, and she just bounces off and falls down between the desks, red hair flashing out to the side. Metal shrieks against concrete. The shriek turns into Holly's voice, but it doesn't last long because her head connects with the back of a chair and her sunglasses clatter away, and she rolls to the floor covering her face with her hands just as Psycho Greet appears.

Now what do I do?

I'm outside Old Man Hyde's study, and Mrs Greenacre is shooting me with a look from behind her desk and shaking her head but without actually moving. I stare back at her, not blinking because I don't care, I don't, but inside I'm screaming at her, and Holly, and myself, because I only managed to get half the message written and no one's going to know what the hell it means. No one will know what Karl Hyde did, and they won't believe me if I just tell them. And Psycho Greet will just rub it off, and no one will know, and Old Man Hyde will beat me for pushing Holly, and Brad will still go to Australia, and I'll be stuck in a hell of Appleton School each term and home with Dad in the holidays.

The roof clicks. The clock on the wall drips loud seconds of time. Old Man Hyde isn't actually in his study, he makes troublemakers wait like this on purpose and is probably having a cup of tea in the staffroom right now. Mrs Greenacre sighs and gets back to her typing, because she's so stupid and doesn't know how to use a computer yet. She rolls in a fresh sheet of paper and clacks away, and when she's done she rolls it out again and leaves her office to pin whatever it is on the notice-board before coming back.

And *that's* when I see what I should do. And it's better than my lame idea of writing on the blackboard. *Heaps* better, Brad's going to love me for this.

I study the clock again. Gone half past nine. Old Man Hyde could get here any minute, so I use mind control on Mrs Greenacre to go get a cup of tea from the staffroom because I need her to be gone. It doesn't work.

Nine forty.

Nine fifty.

This is Old Man Hyde's longest wait ever, but Mrs Greenacre won't stop clacking her stupid typewriter keys.

Just before ten, someone passes the door and I'm sure I'm doomed, but it's not the head. I'm not sure who it is but Mrs Greenacre sees them too.

'Chloe?' She stands. Walks over. 'Chloe Pryor, was that you? Why aren't you in class?'

Then, miracle of miracles, she leaves.

'Chloe?'

I hear her voice getting thinner. Tendai's little *girlfriend* couldn't have skipped class at a better time, I'll have to thank her when this is all done.

I move quickly around Mrs Greenacre's desk and jump into the stationery cupboard and grab the thickest marker pen I can find and some paper.

KARL HYDE USES
EDELVALK BOYS FOR TARGET PRACTICE.

I haven't left myself quite enough room for the -ICE of practice but it looks sort of OK.

On another piece of paper I write,

KARL HYDE GOT EXPELLED FOR BULLYING.

I wasn't going to write any more, but suddenly I come up with,

KARL HYDE ISN'T WHO YOU THINK HE IS.

I'm not sure where that came from but it's brilliant because it'll freak them all right out. It's a good enough line for a movie trailer, Brad'll love it.

There. Done. Now for the tricky bit.

I creep back out of the stationery cupboard. Still no Old Man Hyde. I can hear lesson noises murmuring from the classrooms and the piano playing in the music room. I duck into the head's office. The Xerox machine is there in the corner, because the school gets charged five cents for every sheet you copy so only he's allowed to use it.

I open the lid, slap down the first sheet on the glass, close the lid and hit the big green button. The machine thinks, whirrs, thinks, then slides a white light under the lid.

A copy of what I wrote spits from the tray on the side, but only one, because I've forgotten to tell it how many I want. I tap in *20* and then hit the green button again and the stupid machine thinks for even longer before it finally starts retching up all those copies of my handwriting.

It feels like years have passed when I put the second sheet onto the glass. Through the murky light of the office I spot Old Man Hyde's cane leaning behind his chair. If he comes in now, that cane's on my arse for sure.

There's a soft knock at the door. I hadn't closed it and that Mr Jefferson Yank is standing there.

'Oh. Hi,' he tunes, like he's the kid and I'm the adult. Doesn't he know what I did to his stupid daughter?

He comes in a bit.

'I was looking for Mr Hyde.'

His voice is soft shapes with round edges. No, he doesn't know. He can't do.

He's got a whole bunch of stuff in his hands and when he holds it up I see it's a pile of card from the art room. I think about running, but if I do that then Brad's gone to Australia for sure.

'He's not here at the moment, Mr Jefferson,' I tune, all friendly.

'Hey, call me Rex,' he tunes, smiling. 'Mr Jefferson is my father. Heck, you guys are so polite. Wish I could pack some of your manners into my suitcase and take them back to the States.'

The photocopier is churning out KARL HYDE ISN'T WHO YOU THINK HE IS one by one.

'Sure, Mr Rex.'

He acts like I've told him a joke. He walks into the room

and puts the stack of art card on Old Man Hyde's desk.

'If you see Mr Hyde, let him know I've had a good look at the drawings.'

'Yes, sir.'

'Rex, please. And I'd like to talk to him about them, soon if possible. One or two are very . . . interesting. Can you do that for me?'

'Yes, sir.' I nod, perhaps for too long. 'I'll tell him, sir.'

'As soon as possible. Thanks, erm . . .'

He narrows his eyes for my name. I could lie, but he's being so nice that I forget to.

'Gary.'

'Right. Gary. I don't remember meeting you yesterday.'

'No, sir.'

'Maybe today, then?'

'No, sir. I didn't see anything,' I tell him.

The Yank pulls a surprised face then looks like he's about to say something else.

'Oh. OK. Say, can you tell me anything about Chloe Pryor?'

'Who?' I act like I've never heard the name.

'Chloe Pryor. One of the junior girls, I found her drawing particularly intriguing. I'd like to hear her story again but she's not in class. Do you know her?'

I pretend I'm thinking, then shrug.

'Not really. We don't really talk to the junior kids,' I tune. It slips out so easy. So calm. 'But I think she was outside a moment ago, you'll probably find her there.'

He studies my face a moment, then smiles his big, American smile.

'Sure,' he tunes. 'Well, I'd better go look. I appreciate your help.'

39

He goes and I breathe easy again. I'm going to do more than just thank Chloe, I'm going to give her a present!

The photocopier's finished the second lot and I quickly swap in the last sheet and hit *go*, certain Hyde's going to walk in at any moment.

I wave at the paper to go faster. Time seems to slow down. I feel like I'm being watched, and gradually I start to drift across to the drawings Mr Jefferson just put on Old Man Hyde's desk. The picture on the top is a young kid's version of a flying saucer in blue and yellow crayon that's sitting half hidden in red trees. A black figure with almond eyes is standing by the side of it while a second is close, stepping from the tree-line and getting closer. It doesn't surprise me because the kids who say they saw something – and some that say they didn't – have been drawing things ever since it happened. What surprises me is how similar the second picture is to the first. And the next, and the next. Not similar, but almost exactly the same.

Flying saucer. Trees. Figures. Eyes.

Flying saucer. Trees. Figures. Eyes.

Flying saucer.

Trees.

Figures.

Eyes.

Even the lights around the craft are the same colours, in identical order. Some drawings are OK, the ones by the younger kids are bad, but you can tell what they are and they're all the same thing.

They didn't see it, I tell myself. It didn't happen.

But *I* saw something.

Didn't I?

The Xerox skims light under the cover.

40

. . . and I remember light blasting through the gaps between the trees that day, brighter than anything I've known . . .

The machine whirs.

. . . I remember the sliding metal sound, like a door . . .

I squeeze my eyes tight.

. . . I remember . . . running . . .

. . . And I remember . . . Chloe Pryor, cowering in the tall grass, like she was hiding from something, and she was so, so scared . . .

When the Xerox beeps I almost fill my pants. The display is flashing PAPER JAM at me because this machine's an old pile of junk but I don't do anything about it because I don't know how. I've got enough anyway so I grab the piles I've made, snatch the chunky stapler off Mrs Greenacre's desk on my way through and head out.

There's no one around to see me, everyone's still in class but it'll be breaktime soon so I run around the classrooms punching my bits of paper onto every bit of wood I can find. Doors, notice-boards, picture-boards, walls, roof supports. All the way down one side of the classrooms, across the grass, then up the other. I manage to slap a few on staff car windscreens, and even get as far as the cricket pav before coming back to the admin block, but then someone's walking out of the staffroom and I don't even wait to see who it is. I gap it the hell away, back onto the grass and across the dusty playground.

I did it.

The hot air swirls in my lungs. Sun glimmers in the sweat over my eyes.

I *did* it.

So don't look round, just don't look.

We're not allowed past the rocks, but no way I'm stopping

now so I keep on running even though the dry grass is scratching at my legs. I'm approaching the trees, level with them. Deep amongst them. Now I finally stop and skid to the ground. I lie low on my front so the heat of the ground's pushing through my clothes and I peer back at the school through the grass, panting. I wait. And I wait.

And wait.

How long before someone notices? I wonder.

Something crawls over the back of my leg and I slap it off. More time goes by. I can't see much from here but I don't hear anything either. I reckon the breaktime bell should have rung so why can't I hear everyone as they see what I did? *Has* the bell rung? I didn't notice. The cicadas' screech rides in waves, I can't hear anything else. Now I start to worry that my plan hasn't worked. I've screwed up. Old Man Hyde or Psycho Greet or someone has seen the posters and taken them all down before anyone spied them. Crap.

The sun beats, and it's so hot it's like it's making me deaf. That's when I start to realise the cicadas aren't actually screeching any more. The air's still as death. I get hit with the feeling of being watched, of not being as alone as I thought I was. I push up on my elbows to check around, and when I do I see where I actually am and I'm on the edge of a big flattened patch of ground that looks slightly darker than everywhere else, like it's been burnt. There are spiders and bugs and beetles on the dirt but they're not moving, they're just legs-up and cooking where they died.

A shadow falls. I look up and I'm blind and I shield my eyes with my hand and a cannon ball jams into my throat. The figure stands over me, all black like a shadow. Tall and thin. Its head blocking the sun so I can't see its face, it has no features, just black.

It's leaning closer. Closer. Coming down. A long arm reaching out towards me. I can see who it is now – it's just Mr Stamps – but I scream all the same. I scream and push my legs like I'll die if I don't and now I'm moving away and I don't even stop to see if he's coming. I just twist onto my knees and my feet and up and I run and run and I run back towards the classrooms. I see all the other kids coming out, and I've never felt so relieved ever to see them but there's something wrong with the way they're coming out. Not normal. It's not right. Because they're hurrying . . . scampering . . . *afraid*. They're afraid too. I try to speak to one of them but they just rush right past like I'm a ghost. Like I'm a ghost to them. Everyone running in all different directions, out from the classrooms and towards the main gate, and now I hear crying and screaming filling the air, and all I can think is, *They're back they've come back the aliens have come back*

'I saw this silver thing flashing orange in the sky, and me and my friends were following it. At first we thought it was an aeroplane, but it had no wings and it was like a disc so we thought maybe it was a UFO, and we started getting scared.'

'Go on.'

'Then we saw it was a round shape, like a ball that had been squashed. It was one big spaceship with little ones all around it. They were moving around the big ship. They were just floating around in the air, they didn't touch the ground. They were flashing all sorts of lights, like orange, then green, then yellow and purple, one after the other.'

'And what about where the spaceship landed? Where was that?'

'Over there. In the trees. There were aliens coming out of it through a door, and after they went it left a huge black mark, and some of the older children said all the insects on the ground there were dead. My mum said there might have been a fire there but I don't think there was.'

'Did you go there to look?'

'We weren't allowed.'

'And why do you think the aliens in the ship came?'

'I don't know. The being I saw was just looking at me.'

'What did this being look like?'

'He had straight black hair.'

'*Were you close?*'
'*Yes.*'
'*How close?*'
'*Very.*'
'*Were you scared?*'
'*Yes.*'
'*Why? What made him scary?*'
'*The eyes.*'
'*What about the eyes?*'
'*The eyes looked evil.*'
'*What was evil about them?*'
'*He looked evil because he was just staring at me as if he wanted to hurt me.*'
'*Why would he want to do that, do you think?*'
'*I don't know, he just did.*'
'*Did you have nightmares about it?*'
'*I did. I do.*'
'*What do you dream?*'
'*I dream that the same one I saw, he comes into my bedroom and takes me from my bed. I wake up and scream.*'
'*Do you tell your parents about this dream?*'
'*Yes.*'
'*And do they believe you?*'
'*No. Nobody believes me. They just say it's a nightmare, they don't believe about anything I saw.*'
'*What's that like?*'
'*If you see something and no one believes it, it's like that thing can never be true even though it is, and they tease you and call you names, and it makes me really upset. That's what it's like.*'

CHLOE

Megan Stamps' daddy has a big Peugeot and it's the biggest car of all the Lift Club cars. It's his turn to take us to and from school every Tuesday and Thursday, and the car's big enough for seven children. Megan always sits in the front next to her daddy; me and Amanda Ray and Shaley Jacobs and Natasha Newell sit on the big seat in the back, and Cole and Dale Spencer go in the boot. Except of course when Megan's daddy drops everyone else off after school, even Megan, and there's only me left in the car because I live furthest away. Then Megan's daddy's eyes under his thick black hair look right at me from the rear-view mirror and he says I can sit in his daughter's place in the front because I'm his favourite of all the Lift Club kids but I mustn't tell anyone that because they'll get jealous, or that's what he says.

Today's Monday, though. I usually like Mondays because Natasha Newell's mummy drives us to school in her Honda, even though she sings really loud to old songs when they come on to the radio, and I have to sit squashed up next to Megan Stamps with Cole and Dale Spencer in the back, and the boys always fight quietly together because there's no space for them in the boot. But today smells of hate, and today hate smells like new shoes because when Megan got in she came round to my side even though she *knew* it was my turn to sit by the window and she pushed me into the middle with her bag. Then she looked down like she wanted me to look down, and she had these nice shoes on that she knows I wish I had with the buckles and the flower pattern made from holes across the top.

She said, 'My daddy bought me these. They're brand new, so there.'

I lost my shoes at school when I ran away and Mummy was really cross about it, and now I have to wear the old ones that pinch. I lost my cardigan too. And my hat.

Then Megan squashed her foot against mine so that it really hurt and left a mark on both our shoes and she glared at me like it was my fault.

She said, 'Look what you did! You've done it now, Chloe Pryor, we're going to get you for that,' even though it wasn't me it was her.

She's always saying stuff like that to me these days.

Cole and Dale Spencer are twins but Dale is one-and-a-half centimetres taller than Cole and he has a mole on his left cheek so it's easy to tell them apart.

Megan Stamps and Shaley Jacobs stand beside the sandwich tray at breaktime and won't let me eat any, and I like tomato sandwiches, and when I go to the tuck shop to buy something to eat instead Gary Marston comes in and makes us smaller kids move back so that he's at the front of the line. I don't think he's seen that it's me there.

I say, 'Hi, Gary.'

One time, I saw him crying down near the trees, and he told me not to tell anyone and I didn't. Now, he just ignores me like that day didn't happen, he just asks Mrs Hyde for a packet of Korn Kurls so that there are only two packets left and five kids in front of me, which is really unfair. When I get to the front only Flings will be left, and I don't like Flings because they're like eating Kaylite.

I see Tendai just outside the door, looking in but not looking at me. When you're a senior kid you don't talk to the junior kids. That's not a real rule, just a kids' one, but it's true because I used to be friends with Tendai even though he's much older than me and my gramps liked him too but now Tendai hardly ever speaks to me.

Gary pushes past me and laughs, and a bit later I hear him say to Tendai, 'I think your girlfriend wants to beat me up.'

I'm so embarrassed. Tendai isn't my boyfriend and I never once said he was – I don't ever want to have a boyfriend – but he pretends he can't even see me and won't do anything to help me.

After break Mr Hyde says we have to go sit under the tree because the lady American, Mrs Jefferson, would like to talk to us about what happened, and about the pictures of the spaceship that we drew, and already I think I wish I hadn't drawn mine now, at least not the way that I did.

'I heard this story about this guy, and he got kidnapped by aliens and they did all these experiments on him on their spaceship, and then they put him back where they found him but they come back all the time to do it again. And Mrs Jefferson?'

'Yes, Matthew?'

'Is he a pop star or something?'

And he points to the man with the camera who told us his name is Jason.

Sometimes Matthew McDonald is just stupid and he says stupid things. I want to tell him to shut up but I don't because I don't want to remind Mrs Jefferson that she was asking me questions about my drawing. The shade of the leaves is making patterns on my arm like holes and not-holes and I draw around the edges of them with my finger to make me look busy.

'Of course he's not,' some of the others turn around and tell him. They think he's silly too and I'm glad. Matthew, that is, not Jason. I don't know anything about Jason, only that he has the camera and hair that's long so that it falls a bit over his face.

'But, *noooo*. I mean, is he? Like, in America. Because he looks like one. Is he making a video with us in it for a song?'

Mrs Jefferson says, 'Jason is here to record our conversations with you, so that we can study them – if your parents are happy for us to do so, that is. He's not a pop star, but he does like listening to music. Right, Jason?'

She's really nice, Mrs Jefferson is. She has long brown hair that's completely straight and shines, and I wish I had hair like that but Mummy would never let me grow it that long. My hair's blonde anyways, and bumpy, especially when I wake up.

'Right now I'd like to hear about Chloe's picture. Chloe? You were saying about the figure. Do you always have dreams about him?'

I stop drawing on the patterns on my arm. Everyone is looking at me now and Mrs Jefferson is looking right at me too and I blush. She's waiting for me to say something but I mustn't make up tales. No one likes tales. He said.

I say, 'Are you and Mr Rex married, Mrs Jefferson?'

And she says, 'We sure are, Chloe. And Rex is his first name, he's *Mister* Jefferson.'

She laughs, but it's a nice laugh, she's not mean like Megan Stamps is to me now. Megan Stamps used to be my best friend but she isn't any more. We saw *The Lion King* at the movies together and afterwards she said it was her most favourite film ever, and we used to play it in the playground and *hakuna matata* was our secret word, but now she's just horrid and I don't know why but I think it's because of her daddy.

She's still waiting. I say, 'Where are you from, Mrs Jefferson?'

She says, 'From a little town in Texas you won't have heard of.'

And I say, 'Why?'

And she says, 'Because that's where I'm from.'

And I say, 'But why won't I have heard of it?'

And she says, 'Because no one has.'

'And is Mr Jefferson from Texas, too?'

'He sure is. Although we both live near San Francisco now. Have you heard of San Francisco?'

I nod and Shaley Jacobs puts her elbow in my ribs but I have heard of it too, I know it's on the left side of America. Shaley Jacobs is Megan Stamps' best friend now. She wears scrunchies to keep her hair up even though scrunchies aren't allowed.

I say, 'Why do you live there?'

And Mrs Jefferson says, 'To teach at the university.'

'Do you have children, Mrs Jefferson?'

'We have a daughter called Holly. You may have seen her, she's around somewhere.'

'How come she isn't at school?'

I wonder if it might be for the same reason as why Karl Hyde isn't in school but instead of telling me she says, 'It's my turn to ask a question. This picture you drew – is this what you see when you have your nightmares? Is this the figure?'

But I mustn't tell stories, even if they're true. I *mustn't*.

A red ant is climbing up Matthew McDonald's shirt and I flick it off for him in case it bites, and he turns around and looks at me with a cross face and says, 'Hey!' and Shaley Jacobs and Megan Stamps make a hiss.

By lunchtime I'm really hungry. I'm in the lunch queue and hoping it's something nice today when suddenly Megan Stamps' shoes are in front of me. I sort of smell the new smell before I see them. Megan and Shaley are standing there with their arms folded tight looking right at me. Megan's chewing gum and gum's not allowed.

Megan says about the interview we had after breaktime on the grass, 'Are you in love with Mrs Jefferson?'

And without even thinking about it I say, ''Course not.'

And Megan says, 'You are. You're in love with Mrs Jefferson *and* her husband, and you want their babies.'

My face goes all hot and Ignatius Rabbit is getting damp in my hand because I can tell everyone else in the line is looking at me. They're my friends, some of them, but I'm scared that Megan will make them hate me like she did with Shaley because she can do that.

Megan imitates me from before.

'Are you and Mr Rex married, Mrs Jefferson? Where are you from, Mrs Jefferson? Do you have children, Mrs Jefferson?'

She's not doing it in a nice way at all.

She says, 'Admit it. You love them.'

I say, 'No. I really don't.'

'Yes you do. And you're making all this up, you and your silly drawings.'

'I'm not.'

'Yes you are. I don't believe what you saw, you know. *We* don't believe you. You're a big fat liar, Chloe Pryor.'

She's looking at Shaley as she says it. Shaley says she was standing right by the boundary rocks that day the spaceship came and she told me she saw the figures coming out. She did. She told me. She said she was really scared. But now Shaley just nods her head like she agrees with everything Megan says.

'My daddy says you're a silly bitch and that you mustn't tell lies.'

And now I know Megan's the liar because Megan's daddy wouldn't say something like that, he calls me names like *poppet*, but I can't tell Megan that because he's her daddy and she'll get jealous. And she's taller than me, and I've got tears in my eyes, so instead I push past and run out of the dining hall and when I'm outside I keep going because I don't know where to stop.

The chapel is at the end of the long path that runs past the swimming pool and has a thick hedge with passion-fruit vine growing in it. I run in through the smaller door at the side, not the big double doors that they only use for special services when parents come and we have to sit on the grass because there's no room. It's quiet and dark and cool. No one comes in here during the day when it's not a service, only Rev Anderson and the cleaners, but at the moment they're probably having lunch too.

Rev means reverend, but I'm not exactly sure what reverend means, just that you work for God and you have to wear a white thing around your neck that's kind of like a slap bracelet.

I sit in the front row. It feels strange, being in here on my own. I'll probably be in trouble if a teacher finds me. I swing my legs and look at the big cross on the wall near the organ and wonder if I should pray. It'll look funny if I pray all by myself with no teachers to make sure I am, but it also feels kind of wrong being here and not praying so I bow my head and close my eyes and say, 'Thank you, God, amen,' just in case. I don't like closing my eyes any more, it's too scary, so I open them quickly and turn around to check the back of the chapel.

Just in case.

I have four Troll pencil toppers which I carry in my pocket. The orange one and the green one and the yellow one and the purple one. I really want the one with lots of different colours in his hair. Tadiwa Mbanji has that one and she says she'll swap it for three of mine. I don't understand why swapping's good because even though you get something you always have to give something away too so you never have what you want.

I take the Trolls out and stand them in a line. Then I take one of the hymn books and I put them on that with Ignatius Rabbit, and now the hymn book is an aeroplane and I fly them around but it's hard to hold all four Trolls and Ignatius at once without someone falling off so I fly Ignatius and just three of the Trolls and leave the orange one behind. I swish them to the end of the pew then back again. Then I take them up to the altar, but that feels *really* naughty because I'm not a reverend and God might get angry so I go back to the bench. I land the Trolls but in a way like the hymn book's a flying saucer now, not like an aeroplane at all. Straight down. I didn't mean to turn the aeroplane into a flying saucer, it just is, and the Trolls on it are staring at me like they're suddenly alive. Staring and staring and staring.

I look away because I know I'm being silly, the chapel is quiet so I know I'm alone and I'm only scaring myself by thinking it's not, so I should stop if I don't want more bad dreams. But then I notice the orange Troll I left behind isn't on the bench where I put it, it's gone, and now I'm *really* scared because who took it?

I hear the voice like a whisper, as if it's the *Trolls* who are talking to me and they stare at me with their oily eyes . . .

'Who are you hiding from, little girl?'

I scream, but only a bit because it's not the person I think it is. It's not *him*, it's just a boy. An African boy from the village, not one who goes to school – I can tell that straight away because of his clothes and he smells of smoke from a fire. He's the same height as me, too, so I don't know why he calls me little. He has bright teeth and his eyes are big and white and wide.

I mustn't tell tales so I say, 'I'm not hiding, I was praying. Are *you* hiding?'

He says, 'Yes, I am hiding.'

'Well, you don't have to hide from me, I won't get you into trouble.'

And when he says, 'It is someone else that I am hiding from,' I wonder if maybe he saw the flying saucer when it came, because if he did then maybe he'll believe other things too if I tell him.

I say, 'From the star people?'

But he shakes his head and puts his hand in his pocket like he's going to take something out.

'No.'

'But you do believe they're real, don't you?'

'No.'

And now I feel silly and small, and ashamed again, and I want to take the picture I drew of the spaceship back. Mrs Jefferson must think I'm really stupid for drawing it and I wish I could take my picture back right now. I wish I never said I saw what the others saw because it's just silly and no one will believe me. Mummy doesn't. Megan Stamps doesn't. Mrs Jefferson seems like she does but she won't in the end, I bet. No one does. I want to magic it all away like it didn't happen.

I say, 'Neither do I. And they've gone now anyway.' Then, 'I want to go home.'

He says, 'Is that why you are crying? Because you want to go home?'

I touch my face and it's wet.

I say, 'Yes.' Then I say, 'No.'

I wipe it harder but it won't get dry.

I say, 'And anyway, I was actually hiding from Megan Stamps.'

'What is this, *meg and stamps*?'

'Megan Stamps. She was my friend but she's not any more. She's mean. Her daddy takes the orchestra and does Lift Club for us on Tuesdays and Thursdays, and one time he let me sit in the front on my way home and I think the reason she hates me now is . . .'

His face doesn't move, so I don't finish, because he still

doesn't know her even though I've told him who she is. I wish I didn't know her either – her or her daddy.

I say, 'So why are you hiding then?'

And he says, 'Because I have been *ve-ry* very bad. Because I have stolen things.'

'Like what?'

He takes his hand out of his pocket and he's holding one of my Trolls, the one with the orange hair. I think he thinks I'm going to be cross but I'm not, I'm really happy because it means it's him who took it and not that other person I thought it was.

'That's OK, I don't mind really. You can keep it.' I won't tell Mummy about giving this Troll away because I lost those other things this term – my shoes, sun hat and cardigan – so she'll just get angry again and not believe me. 'It's OK. I want you to have it. Besides I have another orange one at home. What's your name?'

He says, 'I am Sixpence Chaparadza.'

'Hello, Sixpence Chaparadza. I'm Chloe Pryor.'

'Chlo-*weeeee*.'

I laugh.

'No, not Clo-*weeee*, because that sounds sort of rude. Just Chloe.' I spell my name out on the floor so he can see. 'Like that. Chloe. See?'

The boy's face is so black it shines. He stares at my name and wipes his face like he's scared of it. I wonder why, but also it's sort of nice knowing I'm not the only one who's scared because it's not nice being scared on your own.

I say, 'Sixpence?'

He says, 'Yes, Chlo-*weeeee*?'

'*Hakuna matata.*'

He makes his mouth into a shape with no sound.

He says, 'What does this mean?'

'It's from a movie called *The Lion King*. Have you seen it? It's really good.'

'I have not.'

'But you do have TV, don't you?'

'No.'

'You've never watched TV?'

'There is one in the village, I have seen it once. We watched it for football. Go Manchester United! Go David Beckham and Ryan Giggs!'

I say, 'Well, it means, no worries for the rest of your days. It can be our motto. Ask me what's a motto.'

'What is this motto?'

'Not like that. Like this. What's a motto?'

'What's a motto?'

'Nothing, what's a-motto with you?'

I laugh.

Sixpence doesn't.

I say, 'Never mind. But it can be our own special thing. A secret. You know, to help us when we're scared. That's what friends do.'

Now he looks at me surprised.

He says, 'We are friends?'

I say, 'Of course we are, that's why I gave you my orange Troll.' And then I say, 'I don't have any friends at the moment so you can be my best friend, if you like.' And then I say, 'Please?'

And I'm really glad when he says, 'Yes, I would like that very much.'

Because sometimes I get scared. Sometimes I get scared a lot, especially when I'm on my own. Like when I'm walking back much later, after Sixpence has gone and I'm alone again and there's no one around to see. And I hear a rustling in the bushes, and it's like Mr Stamps' eyes are looking at me through the leaves, and I can smell the *smell*. And even though I try to tell myself there's no one there it feels like there is.

I run really fast across the grass towards the cricket pavilion. But the cricket pavilion isn't safe either because the door is open so someone must be inside, and I cry, because I don't want him to do it again, I really don't, and I never did, but there's nothing I can do.

Then I see there *is* someone in there but it's only a girl. She's sitting asleep, but she's much older than me, and she has this lovely white skin and even more lovely orange hair that goes all the way down her back so she looks like she's an angel who's come to save me. Because if aliens are true then why can't angels be true as well?

I watch her for a bit until she starts to wake up and then I hurry away.

But I soon hear footsteps running behind me. She must have seen me and she's catching me up, and I don't know what to say.

She says, 'Hey. Did you want something?'

But I shake my head.

'It's OK. Don't be frightened.' And I want to tell her I'm not, even though I am sometimes. She says, 'What's your name?'

'Chloe.'

'And who's your friend?'

'This is Ignatius Rabbit.'

'Well, it's nice to meet you, Chloe. And nice to meet you

too, Ignatius. I'm Holly, the freak from another planet – at least, that's how I'm starting to feel because everyone else around here's either an idiot, or thinks I'm an idiot, or just runs away. Guess it's my accent and my stupid hair that does it. Suppose you don't see many redheads round here, do you?'

She's talking in American so I know she's just Mr and Mrs Jefferson's daughter, but maybe I can pretend she's an angel.

I say, 'I like you. And I like your hair.'

'You do?'

'You're really pretty.' She is. 'When I'm older I hope I'm as pretty as you.'

But I don't think she believes me even though it's not a lie.

She says, 'Did you see a little African boy around here? About your height?'

I think she means Sixpence.

'Skinny little guy. Had something in his hand. I think he might have stolen it.'

She does. She means Sixpence, my new best friend with my Troll pencil topper.

'He didn't steal it because I said he could have it.'

She says, 'You did?'

'Yes.'

'No way. Really?'

'I gave it to him. I did. I have a spare one at home so I said he could have it. He didn't do anything wrong.'

'*Really?*'

She laughs at me.

Why doesn't she believe me?

'*Why* don't you believe me?'

'Hey, easy, Chloe. I never said I don't believe you.'

'But it's true, you don't. Do you? No one ever believes me.'

I thought Holly might be different, but now I think maybe she's the same as Tendai because she thinks she's too old to be my friend. And it's too late anyway, because *he's* coming. Mr Stamps. I don't see him but I can feel him. And I know it's him. He's here. I look at Holly, and hope, but she doesn't do anything. No one ever does anything nice for me.

Hakuna matata . . .

On Mondays it's my mummy who usually picks us up because Natasha Newell's mummy works late, but today it's Daddy who's driving the car. He's parked in the turning circle with all the windows open because of the heat and he's staring out so hard that I don't think he hears us kids get in. Daddy's like some of the old folks are who live near Grans and Gramps because that's how old people stare out of windows.

When Cole and Dale pull the boot closed on themselves Daddy sort of wakes up and starts the car and drives. Nobody speaks the whole way back but I can feel Megan and Shaley making faces behind me so I just take out my Trolls and only look at those, and I'm glad when everyone else has gone and it's only me and Daddy left in the car.

I ask him, 'Did you and Mummy have another fight?'

He says, 'Hm?'

He looks at me while he's driving, not saying anything although he sort of is, just not out loud.

'I said, did you and Mummy have another fight?'

Then he smiles and strokes my hair. I used to like it when he did that. I want to like it still but I don't now.

Daddy says, 'I was going to ask you the same thing.'

'I didn't have a fight with Mummy.'

'Not Mummy, I mean with your friends. Because I don't think I heard a single word all journey. Are you OK?'

I'm not supposed to tell tales, and parents never believe what children tell them anyway.

So I just say, 'They're not really my friends.'

'What? But Shaley and Megan are your *best* friends.'

'Not any more.'

'Why not?'

'Because.'

Daddy looks at the Trolls in my hands.

'Did someone steal one of your pencil toppers?'

'I gave one away.'

'Gave one *away*?'

'Yes.'

'But you love those little guys, I thought you couldn't live without them.'

I shrug.

'Is someone being mean to you?'

I shrug.

I want him to ask me again, I do, and then maybe this time I'll tell him the truth, but he just tries to stroke my hair again and I just move again.

He says, 'I bet you and Megan and Shaley are still friends really. Of course you are.' Then he says, 'Are you sure you're OK?'

I say, 'Fine,' even though I'm not.

He's slowing the car down and we're not anywhere near home, this is still the middle of town.

I say, 'There is this one person.'

He's gazing out of the window again. Then he remembers me.

'Hm?'

'One person has been . . . sort of mean even though he says he's being nice.'

'Well, frankly I don't see any possible reason why anyone would want to be mean to a cupcake as nice as you.'

He chews his nails. He does that all the time these days, he's hardly got any left. He turns the car so that we move into a parking space on the side. We're in the road with all the jacarandas on it and it's like we're sitting under a big purple cloud.

He turns off the engine and everything goes quiet.

He says, 'Is it because of what you say you saw the other week? You know, the spaceship?'

'Lots of people saw it.'

'Cupcake . . .'

I say, 'Lots. It's true.'

He breathes in and his whole body moves up and down.

'I realise things can't be easy for you at home at the moment. Mummy and I don't want to fight all the time, we really don't, and we do both still love you. You know that, don't you, Cupcake? Our fighting isn't your fault, we do it because . . . when you get older things become complicated, and those complications get really big, and it's hard to get around them, and it's hard to know what to do, so we fight, and . . . and I'm not explaining this very well, am I?'

I shake my head.

I wonder what he's going to say next but he just smiles again but with sad eyes and then he opens his door.

He says, 'It must be great being you, being a kid's so much easier.'

I think, *No it's not*.

'Everything will be OK, Cupcake.'

I say, 'When?'

'Hm?'

'When will it be OK?'

'Later. In the end. I promise.'

But *later* is like a rainbow because it looks nice but it's always over there, never here, because Daddy stops talking with me and gets out of the car. The building he walks into has a square sign made of yellowy metal that says, Meake and Myles Solicitors.

I think, maybe *later* can be at home, then.

But when we get there the house stinks of silence and Mummy's burning onions at the cooker.

I take three-Romany-Creams-biscuits-but-no-more and sit at the table in the lounge with the TV on, but Mummy and Daddy stay in the kitchen and talk to each other over slamming cupboard doors.

Mummy says, 'I *did* try to ignore it, but she's not letting it go.'

Daddy says, 'You know what kids her age are like. It's just her imagination.'

'Have you seen those drawings, David? Have you? The ships, the alien creatures. Quite frankly I find the whole thing extremely—' she almost can't bring herself to say the word '—*upsetting*. Children her age don't create such wild stories and actually believe in them.'

'Children her age create such wild stories *because* they believe in them. It'll pass just as soon as she realises none of it's true. Don't you remember what it was like?'

'It's your fault she's like this, you know, because of what you did.'

And Daddy asks her, 'Can you hear how crazy that sounds?' Then he asks her, in a slightly different voice, 'I made a mistake. I felt lonely and I was weak, it'll never happen again. How many times can I say I'm sorry?'

And Mummy says, 'Well probably not as many as I have to picture you and *that woman* in my head. It is, it's all your fault.'

I switch the TV off and go to my room. Robina our maid's tidied it and made my bed, just like she does every day, but on my pillow is the pile of newer drawings of the spaceship that I drew which I hide under the clothes on the bottom shelf of my cupboard, and I wonder why Robina would have taken those out and left them where they are.

Mummy comes into my room suddenly and she's got watery eyes. Daddy's behind her.

She says, 'Listen, Chloe,' and her bracelet jangles sharply in my face so I listen.

And she says, 'You have to stop all this silly talk. OK?'

I don't know exactly what she means. Maybe Daddy told her about what we talked about on our way home, and I wish he hadn't, but then she points to all my crayon pictures on the bed. They're different to the one I showed Mrs Jefferson. There's no flying saucer in these ones, just the thing coming out of the trees. Just him and me and those stars.

So *she* found them.

I'm upset with her but I'm sort of glad too. I open my

mouth to tell her about them, but then I don't because Mummy's got her serious face on.

She says, 'If you want to discuss anything with your father and me, then please do, but all this aliens nonsense has to stop. OK?'

I say, 'OK,' while trying not to cry.

'I mean it. We've let this nonsense go on for too long and it's upsetting for all of us right now. If there's something on your mind, talk.'

So I open my mouth, but then in my head I want to scream, I'm trying to, because before I can say anything she says, 'Good girl. It's not healthy, all this silly talk of aliens . . . I don't know where you get it from. You're eight, Chloe. *Eight*. You need to start acting your age.'

I wake up and I don't know what the time is or if it's really late or really early but the light outside my door is off and the house isn't making any noise so I know it's that time of night where people don't belong. My room is full of dark and the only glow of anything is if I tilt my head like I'm looking up even though I'm lying down and look through the crack where the curtain doesn't quite touch the wall.

I see stars.

Lots and lots of stars.

I pretend there's a net that's covering the house to protect me from them, but the more I look the more the stars appear, and after a long time they start to look like they're breathing when I breathe, moving in the sky without actually going anywhere. Then some bits start to look brighter than other bits and gradually there's a patch that looks like the shape of a face, an alien with big eyes just like the one everyone else says they saw at school over in the trees only this one's not far away it's right outside my window.

I blink and the face becomes stars again. Stars everywhere, but always three brighter than the rest. Always. And then my curtain moves. I thought I asked Daddy to close the window before because it's too cold to have it open but it is open now and the curtain moves over the gap so that I can't see the stars any more. Now my room is even darker than it was before and the only things I can see in it are shapes that I know are there because they're blacker than the other shapes. I think I know what they are. My chair. My table. My wardrobe. My pictures on the wall. But then there's one that looks like it's in the middle of the room and I don't know what that is because I don't have anything in the middle of the room except my shoes and my *Beauty and the Beast* satchel but this is really tall.

I stare at it, because maybe then it'll go away. But it doesn't. So I close my eyes and hope *that* will make it go away instead but I hear a *hooshing* noise across the floor and when I open them it's close, right at the end of my bed. And it's moving even closer, and now I want to scream but I'm too afraid to because I don't know who will answer so I just stay as still as I can and try not to even breathe and maybe then it'll go.

I count to a hundred in my head. Your bones ache when you don't move for a long time, even when you're lying down.

When I look again the shape is right over me.

There's this dim-dim twinkle like a far-away flame but it's actually the light reflecting in an eye, because air's brushing against my cheek like someone's breathing really close. I hear it. I smell old coffee. I'm more scared than I was before.

Something heavy touches my foot, like cold fingers around my ankle, and then I'm starting to slip on my bed because it's pulling me. I hold onto my headboard. I don't know where it wants me to go but I don't want to go there. I don't. It pulls harder, so I hold harder. It pulls even harder still and its hands move further up my leg and I hold even harder still. My fingers hurt. My ankles hurt. My bed makes a sliding noise but I mustn't let go, I mustn't. I'm never going to let go.

Leave me alone, I try to say only I can't, it's like my voice doesn't work and nothing comes out. But it's also kind of like I did say it because just like that the cold fingers go from my ankles and my legs drop back onto my bed.

I wait.

The shape's gone. I wonder if it was even here in the first place and I dreamed the whole thing.

I pull my duvet back up on top of me and try to hide under it. I want to hide for ever. But my room's too dark so I get up and stand in front of my curtains and open them wide, and now I'm looking straight up at the stars. I almost can't breathe because it's like the sky is alive. This one . . . huge and enormous . . . alive thing. It wants me. It's sort of telling me what to do without words, and now I'm opening my window wider. I don't want to but I am, and my tummy does horrible flippity-flops like when Daddy drives over a bridge fast because outside the wind is blowing so hard it comes into my room and makes my *Tiny Toons* nightie go flap, and all the plants and trees are rushing loudly like a storm's coming even though there isn't one.

And the shape-figure is there again, looking at me from the garden.

I try to scream, but I can't.

I close my eyes again, but it's more scary *not* being able to see it so I say over and over in my head: *Hakuna matata, hakuna matata, hakuna matata, hakuna matata.*

And then, suddenly, the wind has stopped and I'm standing at my open window and the sky is just twinkling stars. I think I'm alone and as I wonder where the figure has gone I hear this noise behind me and I look round and then my room bursts open again with light—

—and Daddy is standing in his boxer shorts at my door, with his hair up in spikes. He's been sleeping on the couch again because he has a bad back. He told me his back was hurting at about the time he and Mummy started shouting at one another a lot.

He says, 'Hey, Cupcake. What's the matter?'

I say, 'Nothing.'

He's got a worried frown on. He looks out of the window but there's nothing there.

'You certain about that?'

'Yes.'

'You're not . . . you know . . . upset again?'

I say, 'Thirsty.'

'Oh good. OK. Well, hurry and get yourself a glass of water then back to bed, no point us both being tired in the morning.'

'Is it morning now?'

'Yes, I suppose it is.'

'But it's still the night?'

'Yes, it's still night too.'

'Are you sure?'

'Sure I'm sure. Look at my bags, I could go on holiday with these.'

Whatever that means.

'Daddy . . . ?'

'Come on, Cupcake, back to bed. You're too tired.'

'But, Daddy, I want to ask you something.'

'What?'

'Do you believe in the aliens?'

He thinks for a long time, then he moves his shoulders up and down like they're suddenly really heavy.

'I believe you think you saw something.'

'But do you believe it could happen?'

'That there are other people living in space who chose to come here?'

'Yes.'

'Space is pretty big, you know.'

'Do you, then?'

Because if he does believe that, maybe he'll believe me about the other stuff I wish I could tell him.

He makes this short laughing sound between his teeth that grown-ups sometimes do even though nothing's funny.

He says, 'Do I believe there's something else out there? Something more to life than this? I sure as hell would like to. But no, I don't. Now you get back into bed. You're far too young to be up all night worrying about things like that, you should enjoy your youth while it lasts. I'll get you that drink. And hurry up and close that window, it's freezing in here.'

I look down and want to cry.

I say, 'I'm not thirsty now.'

'Really?'

'Yes.'

He says, 'Suit yourself. Now you get some sleep, I don't want your mum blaming me because you're all crotchety in the morning.'

He tries to give me a kiss. I don't want to pull away because it's Daddy but I do, so he stops trying. I think he thinks I'm angry with him but I'm not, I'm really not, it's just . . .

I wish I could tell him why.

'I mean it, Cupcake, try not to worry. Everything will be OK, I promise.'

'But you said that before.'

'Did I? I must have meant it, then. See?'

But it's not OK, I want to say, and it never will be.

After he turns off my light I feel sick in my tummy again. I feel sick in my tummy because there's a faint glow of dawn from outside, and the birds have started to sing. Tonight's today now, and today's Tuesday, and soon I'll have to go to school.

As usual, Mummy and Daddy are talking with heavy voices to each other. The door slams, and when I look out the kitchen window I see the top of Daddy's car going in a hurry down the drive. I'm not tall enough to see Daddy, and I worry that I didn't because there's this other feeling in me that says I might not see him again.

Mummy's crying. She doesn't want me to see but she keeps on doing it so I put my hand on her arm to help her.

She says, 'Eat your breakfast, there's a good girl.'

But I don't. I can't. It's like eating wood. I think Mummy's going to be upset with me but she sits down and blows into the top of her mug so that her glasses go all steamy. I push my bowl away from me slowly because maybe she won't notice.

She says, 'Daddy told me you had a bad dream last night.'

I say, 'I don't think it was a dream, not all of it. It felt real.' Then Mummy gives me her look so I say, 'Yes, I did.'

She says, 'Poor thing. Nightmares are horrid, aren't they? I have them too, sometimes.'

'You do?'

Then she says, 'I'm sorry if I sounded stern last night, Chloe, I didn't mean to. Daddy and I are . . . very tired at the moment, and . . . Well, I didn't mean to. I shouldn't have done it and I'm sorry. But, Chloe?'

'Yes, Mummy?'

'About all those drawings you made.'

'Yes, Mummy?'

'They're very good, the colouring in is excellent and I particularly like how you've done the trees. But why so many?'

I'm not sure what to say, so I tell her, 'Because there are lots of trees when you step past the rocks.'

She smiles and blows more steam at herself.

'I mean, why so many drawings, but never mind. Is the little person meant to be you in them? And the figures are very strange looking, aren't they? Grans thinks you've an artistic eye. Did you copy them from a book?'

I say, 'No.'

'From the TV, then?'

'No.'

And she says, 'Well, you must have copied them from

somewhere. Chloe, sometimes nightmares can feel very real, but they're not. They're only dreams. They're in your head, they can't hurt you.'

'But I didn't dream it. He was there, I saw him.'

Mummy tilts her head, like she's saying, I thought we spoke about this.

So I say, 'Lots of us did.'

'And is that what you tell everyone?'

'Yes.'

'Everyone?'

'Yes.'

'Well, you know they won't believe you, don't you?'

Sometimes it feels like something really big is stuck in my throat.

Mummy watches me and taps her finger against the side of her mug like she's counting. She says, 'Don't worry, darling, I think I know why you're being like this.'

I look at her. She looks at me. Then she comes out of her chair to sit next to me and she puts her arms around me in a hug, and this time I let her.

I say, 'You do?'

She says, 'Yes. It's because you're afraid, aren't you? And I know whose fault that is.'

I want to cry, but a happy cry. The lump has gone from my throat. So she *does* understand. Now I can say it and she'll listen and she'll believe me, because she *knows*. Everything will be all right just like Daddy promised.

But then she says, 'It's Daddy's and my fault, so if anyone's to blame for your silly made-up drawings and your silly stories about aliens, it's us. We shouldn't . . . you shouldn't see all our fighting.'

But it's not. I don't know what Daddy did, but I know my drawings aren't his fault, and they're not Mummy's fault, either. But they can't see that, just like they couldn't see how upset I was when Mr Stamps started coming to our church one Sunday not long ago with Megan, when they have their own church miles away. I was really upset, but all Mummy could talk about was this Sally Stafford woman with the big bosoms, and how women who aren't married shouldn't be allowed into church because church is for families.

I want to tell her, I'm *not* making it up. Not really. But I can't.

She says it again, 'It's Daddy's fault. And mine. We've been going through a bad patch and we've let you see it all, and that's selfish and wrong. And I'm sorry.'

Outside, I hear a car coming up the drive. But it's not Daddy's sound. I look at the clock on the cooker and it grins back and says it's nearly time to go to school, which means it's Megan's daddy coming to pick me up, and I wish, wish, wish I could make time go backwards to make this moment go away, I *wish*.

Mummy takes her glasses off to clean them and now she can't see at all. She doesn't look like Mummy without them.

'We don't want to, but Daddy and I have made the decision to do the best thing for you. You know, until things get better. Because it's not fair on you.'

'But . . .'

'Parenthood is a duty, not a hobby, as you'll find out one day. Having children isn't just about buying you nice clothes and nice dollies and *Take That* CDs, it's about responsibility. You're our responsibility. You are, my girl, and we know we haven't been very responsible by letting you see all our fights and we're going to show you how sorry we are by putting you first.'

The car is stopping outside.

'But . . .'

'We've decided that Daddy and I should try some time apart. Just for a while, until things get better. I don't like that you're having nightmares, but I guess maybe it needed to happen to make us realise how selfish we've been, so thank you.'

Mummy puts her glasses back on.

'So maybe those aliens of yours aren't such a bad thing after all. In fact, the next time you have one of those nasty dreams say a big cheery thank you to them from me, I promise it'll make them seem less scary if you do. And you can get back to being the old Chloe we know and love, hey.'

Trapped smells like the exhaust fumes coming in through the window.

'That'll be Megan and her daddy. Go fetch your satchel, and *try* not to lose anything today. Did you ask Mr Stamps if he found your cardie in his car like I told you to? No, I thought not. Please do. He's so good with you kids, if anyone will take the time to help you find them, it's him.'

I can't see him but I can in my head – Megan's daddy, sitting in his Peugeot with his door wide open, waiting to take me to school, that straight smile on his face and his legs all horrid and hairy and bare and one foot slightly on the pedal so that the engine sort of chuckles. Megan watching me from the passenger seat, arms folded like I've done something mean to her so she's going to get me back. But *I'm* not the one who was mean, it wasn't *me*.

The petrol clouds sting my nose and throat and I want to

be sick but most of all I don't want to get in that car and I'm not going to.

I say, 'Mummy, I know you won't believe me but I really don't feel very well.'

Mummy looks a bit like someone just asked her a really difficult question like they do at school sometimes.

She touches my head and says, 'You feel fine to me.'

I say, 'I don't think I should go to school today. I really don't.'

And she says, 'Then it's a good job it's not up to you. *I* think you *should*. Come on, don't be like this. Daddy's and my problems are the last reason you should miss out on school. Now go get your bag.'

And Mr Stamps' car outside is revving and it's like I can't find any clean air.

'But I don't want to.'

'Chloe, please. I really don't want to fight.'

'I'm not going.'

'Yes, you are.'

'I'm *not*.'

I pull my arm from her like she's a crocodile's mouth and I run from the table and past Robina in the kitchen and then out into the garden.

By the time she finds me I think she'll be the angriest with me she's ever been because I'm late for school now, but she's not. She doesn't yell at me to come out, she just moves the leaves to one side so that she can come into the dim light with me and crouches so that she's looking at me in the face.

She strokes my hair. I make her stop by pretending I want to hold her hand but really I just want her to stop.

She says, 'OK, I believe you.'

I sniff.

I say, 'You do?'

I say, 'You really do?'

She says, 'Yes. You really don't want to go to school, I get that now.'

I say, 'Oh,' because I thought she meant about the other thing.

She gives me a hug.

After a long time she says, 'Here's the deal, then. And there's no comeback on this.'

I say, 'What's comeback?'

She says, 'It means, no argument. It's going to happen, OK?'

I nod.

'OK. Megan's daddy has gone now so I'm going to take you to school myself.'

So I say, 'Will you pick me up as well? Please?'

She says, 'Yes, I will. Just for today. Tomorrow it's back to Lift Club arrangements, you don't want your friends thinking you've stopped liking them, do you?'

'No, Mummy.'

'In return, I want you to understand that there are no aliens. There are no spaceships hovering about your school, no strange lights. So don't let me hear any more reports of stories about them. Clear?'

'But I didn't really see—'

'None of it happened. OK?'

'Yes, Mummy.'

'It's obvious you and your friends got a bit carried away. Fair enough, you're young, but the joke has to end now. If you're worried about anything – anything real – then ask me or your dad. Don't bottle it up.'

'Yes, Mummy. So what about—'

'I mean it. No more fairy tales and science fiction.'

She does mean it. I can tell.

I say, 'OK.'

'So, what were you going to ask?'

'Nothing, Mummy.'

'Good girl, that's more like it. Now get your bag and hurry, I've got to pop in and see Grans and Gramps on the way so we'd better start thinking about what we're going to tell Mr Hyde for being so late.'

We have to go quickly because Grans and Gramps are on the other side of town. The house where they live is really old, almost a hundred years, and *old* smells like grainy black-and-white photograph paper and creaky polished floorboards and a zebra-skin shield on the wall. It's right near the Mabelreign drive-in but they say when the house was built the drive-in wasn't there and the house was in the country-side with only bush around it. When we were friends Megan Stamps said she saw *D2: The Mighty Ducks* at the drive-in over the Easter holidays and she saw lots of older kids snog-ging in their cars because that's what they think drive-ins are for.

I like going to see Grans and Gramps. They have soft voices and a pantry that's full of fizzy drinks and these *lekker* choco-late biscuits from overseas, and when you have one on a school day they taste even better. After we get there I wish for the car to stop working and we'll have to stay all day or at least half so I can miss lots of lessons.

Gramps is really tall. He used to be a running coach and he trained Nelson Ndube, who was Tendai's older brother, before he died – before Nelson died, that is, not Gramps, because that would be silly. Grans is much shorter but she always tells Gramps what do to.

We all sit on the veranda but straight away Mummy tells me to go and play in the garden, which means they want to talk grown-up stuff, but I only go as far as the pomegranate tree and pretend I'm playing with Cecil-Jay the cat but really I'm listening to what they're talking about.

Grans asks how things are with me now, and Mummy says fine. Gramps says is she sure, because sometimes it's hard to know what young people are really thinking, and Mummy says that she and I talked about things that morning and everything's cleared up, and that my silly stories are over.

Gramps doesn't say anything.

Grans asks how Mummy is. Mummy sighs and says she and Daddy went to an *on-pas*, wherever that is, and Grans says she's sorry to hear that so I know it can't be good. Gramps still isn't saying anything for a while, but then he says . . . no, and *tells* Mummy that an *on-pas* isn't reason enough to ignore me, so Daddy and her need to work through it and work through it soon. Mummy gets a bit huffy and says she needs some clean air even though she's outside right now, and Gramps says, No, and he says that I should always come first. And then he says, Has Mummy really thought this through because a drift is hard to come back from? Mummy says, Frankly she and Daddy have been drifting for years and that's the swear-word problem, it's not just about That Woman.

Grans says Mummy and I are always welcome, and that we can stay as long as we like, and I get excited and wonder if that means I might be able to stay off school for the whole day. But then I feel sad because I realise they're talking about us actually living here in their house for ever, because Gramps says he doesn't think running away from The Problem is the right way of dealing with it though it sounds as though Mummy's already made up her mind. Mummy says she hasn't but I can tell Gramps doesn't believe her because he shakes his head, and Mummy asks Grans to Tell Him. And even though no one says anything for a long time now I know they're really talking about Daddy and Mummy not wanting to be together, and things never being like they used to be again . . .

All of a sudden Cecil-Jay starts to go crazy. Really, really. Like, super-cat-crazy. He's jumping and leaping like he's on a hot roof and his tail's gone all thick and bushy and he's making this horrid noise from the bottom of his throat. Then I see he's got a big baboon spider on the side of his neck and it won't come off. It's just holding on. Holding and clinging and hugging in a bad way and it won't let go, and Cecil-Jay is so mad and scared and he's making this growl I've never heard before.

I start to cry.

Then I start to scream. And it feels good and I never want to stop.

Mummy comes rushing over.

She grabs my shoulders quite hard and says, 'What is it? Are you OK? What's the matter?'

And I want to tell her, I really do, but all I can do is scream.

And Mummy says, 'What's the *matter*?' but stronger this time.

And I say, 'He's still here.'

And she says, 'Who?'

And I say, 'He hasn't gone away. He'll never go away and

he'll never leave me alone, and one day he's going to take me away where no one can find me for years just like Tendai's brother.'

And Mummy says, 'Who?'

And I almost tell her I mean Mr Stamps, but in the end I say, 'The aliens.'

Mummy looks *really* tired now. A small sob bursts from her mouth.

She says. 'What did we talk about this morning? I said, no more. *Please*. You have to stop this nonsense. Do you hear? I can't deal with this right now, I just can't.'

And now she's crying. Really crying. I've never seen her cry like this and I don't know what to do.

Then Grans is there and taking her away, and Gramps is putting his arms around me instead and his hands are so big and yet so gentle that I cry loads too and I can't stop.

His hair used to be brown and combed straight back with grease so that it didn't move because I've seen pictures of it when it was but now it's silver and wiry and much thinner and it sort of glows like a halo with the sun behind it.

We walk around the garden. He has his hand on my back the whole time. Grans and Mummy are on the veranda, but we stay right over on the far side where the bougainvillea grows over the garage like a roof.

In the end I stop crying and Gramps crouches down so he's as tall as me.

He says, 'Better?' A bit like he always used to when I was upset when I was younger.

I nod my head. It is, but *better* isn't as good as *gone*.

He brushes hair from my eyes.

He says, 'Now, why don't you tell me about these aliens.'

I don't say anything.

'What did they look like?'

Now he's stroking the skin on my arm, and even though it's only Gramps I still don't like being stroked any more and I pull away. I feel bad because he looks upset.

I look around the garden and say, 'I hope Cecil-Jay is all right.'

Gramps says, 'The cat will be fine, my dear, he's battled with a lot worse than that. I'm far more interested in hearing about the aliens. Can you tell me what they looked like?'

I don't say anything.

'Were they tall? Or short? Hairy? Ugly? Nice?'

I don't say anything.

'Did they look like anyone you know?'

I don't say anything.

'Did they look like Mummy or Daddy?'

I don't say anything.

'Like someone else, maybe?'

I *still* don't say anything, but I shake my head because I mustn't tell tales.

Gramps thinks about the answer that I didn't say and then he nods.

He says, 'I believe in your aliens, you know. I believe you saw them.'

I say, 'You do?'

And he says, 'Yes. And I also know how hard it is to have something that's inside you that you can't talk to anyone about, because it's hard to explain, or because you think no one will believe you. Lord knows I don't talk to anyone about the ghosts I see.'

'You see ghosts?'

'In this big old house? Plenty.'

'I didn't know that.'

'That's because I never told you. I don't want you being scared of visiting us – not that there's anything to be scared of. But I'm telling you now to show you that just because something's hard to believe, that doesn't make it a lie.'

He stands up and grimaces slightly. He used to be really strong because he ran in the Olympics when he was much younger, and he still is strong but doing easy things hurts when you're old. I wonder if that's what it'll be like for me when *I'm* old.

'And I'm telling you so that you know – if you want to talk, and when you're ready – you can talk to me.'

'About what? The aliens?'

'About anything you want, my dear. I mean it. Anything at all.'

And I wonder to myself if he sort of knows what happened really, because old people seem to know everything.

I don't want to go to school at all but there's no way I'd get out of it now. We drive through the school gate and stop and she gives me an I'm-sorry-I-yelled-at-you look, but before I have a chance to explain anything she tells me to hurry to class and heads off back into the dust cloud we made on our way in. I stand there and wipe my cheeks and I don't know what to do.

I look round and I see Mrs Jefferson coming out of the staffroom, walking quickly.

She says, 'Hi, Chloe, how are you?' Her *you* sounds like *yah* because she's American.

I back away even though I like Mrs Jefferson, because I'm late and I think I'm going to get into trouble, but she keeps on walking.

'Can't stop, I'm afraid, because Holly's got herself into a bit of trouble. It was great meeting you yesterday, though. I showed my husband your lovely drawing and he'd like to talk to you about it, if you wouldn't mind. Maybe later? He can come find you.'

She turns and trots across the grass.

Mrs Greenacre's typewriter makes typewriter noises. I hear teachers in their classrooms and the piano playing in the music room. That's where I should be now, and I imagine walking in and Miss Roberts stopping to look, and Megan Stamps nudging Shaley Jacobs, and Shaley Jacobs nudging Tadiwa Mbanji, who used to like me, and then Tadiwa Mbanji looking for who she can nudge.

School's not the same when you're late, like something's happened before you got there and everyone knows except you. From where I'm standing I can see Gary Marston sitting in Mrs Greenacre's office outside Mr Hyde's door, which means he must have done something wrong. Mr Hyde and Mr Greet are always picking on him because they think he's bad like his brother was but I don't think he is. He used to be nice to me before his mum ran away and left, and he was definitely scared that day the aliens came. I know, because I saw him.

Mrs Greenacre's typing stops.

She says, 'Chloe?' from inside her office.

I want to go home. I wish Mummy would come back and get me, but as I run back across the car park I spot another car there that I didn't notice before, and it's Megan's daddy's car. He's still here from dropping off because on Tuesdays he always stays in the school all day, and now he's getting out of the car and pretends he hasn't seen me even though I know he has because I'm the only one he ever sees.

He says, 'Hello, Chloe.'

I stop.

'I missed you this morning, poppet.'

He's smiling. Mr Stamps is always smiling.

He says, 'You look upset. Are you? I hope it's not because of yesterday. I didn't mean to sound cross, I just thought you should hurry back to class before you got into trouble with your teacher. I was just trying to protect you. Don't worry, you're still my favourite.'

He winks. I take a small step back and hope he won't notice.

'Chloe? If you're not feeling well I'm sure I can speak to Mr Hyde for you. I don't mind driving you home, to save your mummy having to come all the way back.'

I shake my head.

I say, 'I'm not unwell. Mummy's just angry because I lost my cardigan.'

And he says, 'Oh.' And, 'I see.' And then he opens the back door of his car and his long fingers invite me in.

He says, 'Maybe you left it in here. Let's have a look, shall we? You and me together. But if we find it, let's keep it a little secret between ourselves, because I reckon your mummy would be angry with the both of us. And we don't want her being angry, do we?'

I take another step back.

I say, 'I have to go.'

He says, 'It'll only take a moment.'

But I don't *want* to get into his car. I didn't want to go with

85

him into the trees that day either but I did, and he was horrible to me then even though he said he was being nice, so this time I turn and I run, and I keep running towards my class until I can't feel him watching. But also I don't want to have to see Megan Stamps nudging Shaley Jacobs about me, and Shaley Jacobs nudging Tadiwa Mbanji, so I go past the classrooms and round them to the back, and later, when I'm sure no one can see me, I run onto the path to the chapel and go there.

I hide right at the back. I wait, and wait. I'm crouching behind that big water basin you put babies in when you give them a name that never gets used because there are no babies at our school, even though sometimes Matthew McDonald acts like one.

The door at the front cracks open, and I'm scared that someone saw me and followed me here, and I'm going to be in big trouble. Or maybe it's someone much worse, maybe it's Mr Stamps. I think that wouldn't happen because chapels are meant to be safe places, but then I think maybe it would because the whole *school* is meant to be a safe place and yet what happened still happened before.

A voice says, 'Hey.' Then it says, 'Chlo-*weeee*,' and I'm really glad because I know who it is.

Slowly, I stand, and Sixpence smiles his big smile with white-white teeth. He has something in his hands.

He says, '*Hakuna matata.*'

And now I want to cry all over again because *hakuna matata* doesn't work. Not really. Because I'll have to leave the chapel sooner or later and be scared all over again.

I sit on one of the benches and hold my knees.

He comes closer.

I wipe my nose with my sleeve.

He says, 'It means, no worries.' In a proud way, because he remembered.

I say, 'I know what it means. I'm the one who told you it.'

He says, 'No worries for days.'

I say, '*For the rest of* your days, stupid.'

He says, 'But you have worries?'

I say, 'Loads.'

Sixpence walks slowly across to me because even he knows you shouldn't ever run in church.

He says, 'I made you this. A present for you.'

He holds out his arms and he's holding something made out of coat hangers and tins, only one of the wheels is a bit loose.

I say, 'What is it?'

He says, 'I made it for you.'

'But what is it?'

'It is a car. A boy tried to break it but it is fixed again. Number One! Baba says, *chisi hachiyeri musi wacharimwa.*'

I say, 'What?'

'It is meaning, the consequences of bad behaviour are not immediate, but they will come.'

I do cry now. I can't help it.

I say, 'Is that true?'

He says, 'It is.'

'When? If someone is bad behaviouring, when will the consequences come? Soon?'

But he just says, 'Maybe soon.'

I say, 'I hope so.'

I do. I really do.

'Why do you say this thing? Why are you here, my friend?'

'I told my mummy I didn't want to come to school today but she made me.'

'But why are you *here*? In this chapel again.'

I'm going to tell him why, but then I don't because no one believes what you say when you're me. They don't. They just say you're stupid or tell you off or make fun of you all the time. Even Mrs Jefferson and Mr Rex are probably laughing about my picture right now.

'I wish now I hadn't done that silly drawing.'

Sixpence says, 'What drawing?'

I say, 'The one I did.' Then I say, 'Never mind.'

He says, 'Are you here because you are scared?'

I say, 'Yes.'

'Of the big ship that came from the sky?'

And I look at him.

And I wonder, *did* he see it too, like all the others that saw it? I hope so.

So I say, 'Yes.'

'But you must not be scared. They are not the bad spirits.'

I think, Yes, he is. He is bad.

I say, 'How do you know?

'Because Baba told me. He says the bad spirits are already here.'

And I think, Yes they are. And I start to cry again.

'He wants to hurt me.'

Sixpence says, 'Are you sure?'

'Yes.'

'Did he tell this to you?'

He tells me he doesn't want to hurt me. He tells me I'm special, and he only wants to be nice. So I say, 'No, but . . .'

'Then how do you know? How does he want to hurt you?'

I can't explain it exactly, because he said he was being nice but . . .

I say, 'I don't know.'

'Baba says, problems come when we ask the right question in the wrong way.'

He keeps talking about Baba.

'That's silly, it doesn't even make sense. Who is this Baba?'

'If there was no sun, would we have eyes?'

I say, 'That's silly too.'

'If there was no wind, would the trees grow strong roots into the ground?'

He's not being like Sixpence now. He's teasing me and being like Megan Stamps.

'Stop it. I thought you were my friend.'

'A teacher cannot teach without pupils, and you cannot feel happy without first being sad.'

I wish he'd go away. 'You're being mean,' I say.

'The spirits who came on the ship do not want to hurt you, Chloe. Maybe they want to help.'

'Help?'

'From the struggle.'

'The what?'

'The struggle. The thing that is inside you and inside all of us. So you see, you do not need to be afraid.'

How does he know what's inside me? He doesn't. I thought he was my friend but he doesn't understand anything.

I cry harder.

And I say, 'But it's not the aliens I'm afraid of. I never saw them. I never saw the spaceship either, I just said I did because if so many others saw it and the grown-ups believed them then maybe the grown-ups would believe me too. I knew you wouldn't get it. No one gets it. Leave me alone.'

He says, 'Then if it's not the sky people who are making you scared like this, who is?'

And I start to say, 'It's someone else. It's Megan . . . It's Megan's . . .'

The door at the end of the chapel opens and light bombs in. I'm not sure who's there. Is it *him*? Is it? Even if it's not and it's just one of the teachers, I don't want anyone to find me because then Mr Rex will ask me about the drawing I did, and even if I tell him the truth he'll tell Mr Hyde and Mr Hyde won't believe me, and then he'll tell Mummy and Mummy *definitely* won't believe me.

'*Leave me alone.*'

So I'm running one more time. Out of the chapel, down the path, back towards the main part of the school even though there's nowhere for me to go. But then I think, there *is* somewhere. Not here. Not in school. I can go see Gramps. I want to see Gramps because *he* understands. I can tell *him*, I know I can. I can tell him what really happened because *he'll* believe me. He said.

I run down through the car park.

Then I'm running across the turning circle to the main gate.

Then I'm out of the gate even though we're not allowed, and onto the road, and I'm running there. And I can't *wait* till I see Gramps.

But then there's a wind blowing really hard around me.

And suddenly the light dims.

And all the sound in the world goes, everything is quiet.

And now I'm running so fast that my feet are off the ground, and I'm flying, and above me I see the stars. Lots and lots and lots, even though it's day. The sky is alive, like it's this living thing.

And I understand. I understand everything.

And I *want* to go up to the stars, I *do*. Because Sixpence is right.

'It looked like a disc.'

'Where was it?'

'Outside. There. Above the trees.'

'You say it looked like a disc. Are you sure it wasn't a helicopter or something?'

'No, it was a disc. A ship.'

'Why do you say ship? Was it more than just a shape?'

'It had a bump on the top, and it went out around the sides like this, like a platform.'

'Did you see it land?'

'Yes. After the bell rang I was walking up to class and I saw these strange flashes of light, so I stopped to have a look. It was silver, and the ring around it was orange and yellow and green and purple.'

'Did light come from the whole thing?'

'Yes, it was very bright, like the lights in a football stadium but if you put nine or ten on one spot. There was no shape behind the light when it was on the ground but I definitely remember seeing smaller yellow-orange lights at the base of the large white light. They were in motion. It was hard to tell if they were flames or actual moving lights attached to the main light.'

'What else?'

'That's when the man came. A thing.'

'*When you say "thing", what do you mean?*'

'*Well, it almost looked like a real person, but not quite.*'

'*What did you think it was?*'

'*At first I thought maybe it was a boy from the compound.*'

'*What's the compound?*'

'*The African village where lots of the school workers live. I thought it was some boy playing about, but its head was too big so it couldn't have been.*'

'*Could you see his face?*'

'*Not at first.*'

'*Why? Because he was amongst the trees?*'

'*Because he was like a shadow.*'

'*What did he do?*'

'*He walked towards us. He moved like when a film goes backwards, only he was coming forwards.*'

'*What did he look like close up?*'

'*His head was big and his face was long and his eyes were shaped like upside-down balloons.*'

'*Anything else? What about his mouth?*'

'*I couldn't see the nose or mouth. It was blank like a piece of paper.*'

'*What then?*'

'*Then we saw another one.*'

'*You saw two of them?*'

'*Yes, we saw the other one standing behind at the bottom of the ship. He looked small but we were a long way away.*'

'*Anything else? Anything you remember? About the eyes?*'

'*They looked horrible.*'

'*And what did you think at the time?*'

'*I felt . . . I felt that something bad was going to happen.*'

'*Like a warning?*'

'Yes.'

'A warning about what? Something that's going to happen to our planet?'

'I don't know.'

'And why do you think they came here, to your school, to give this warning?'

'I don't know.'

'But they didn't actually say anything?'

'No. They didn't have any mouths.'

'What did it feel like, when you felt they were warning you?'

'It felt horrible. It was a sort of dream even though I was awake, and I saw people were dead, and it was as though I was the only one left because I suddenly felt very, very lonely.'

'They told you all this?'

'Sort of. It was in their eyes.'

TENDAI

The light glows. Really glows. A sort of metal colour that's strong enough to fill a room and turn everything blue, like you're in space. It's good. It's *better* than good. It's the most powerful backlight LCD screen on the market – just like the advert says – and that's why they call it the G-Shock Illuminator instead of just the G-Shock DW-6600, which would be pretty boring for a name, only mine is even better than that because it's the Fox Fire special edition. My dad got it in New York.

It's been personalised so that it doesn't have a G sign when the face lights up, it has a T for Tendai. My name. It has an alarm, it has a countdown timer, and the battery lasts for ages. You can freeze it, you can wet it, you can hit it, and there was this guy who dropped his out of a jumbo jet by accident and it still worked OK. No lies. But now my G-Shock is gone. I was wearing it when I came to school and I put it into my Nike bag, I know I did, only when I get changed back into my running kit to go home it's completely gone.

Gary Marston's coming towards me across the grass. He used to be my friend – he used to be my *best* friend – but after his mum left we all stopped talking to him because he turned into his brother. No one likes him now. I bet a hundred bucks he knows where my watch is, but I hurry up and pull on my Js because he's been winding me up about Chloe Pryor being my girlfriend all morning and I don't want to hang around him any longer than I have to. I make sure no teachers are watching before I head through the school gates because we're not allowed, because of all the army trucks. The road's clear now, but Gary's brother is waiting for him as usual, and he's worse than a hundred trucks, so I turn quickly before he spots me and I run.

There's a lonely dust devil drifting along the road and I follow it for a while, I guess because it kind of reminds me of me. But as I get nearer it suddenly changes direction and turns on me, rushing and growing really big. I try to outrun it but suddenly I'm in it, and as the dust swirls and gets into my eyes I swear I check this boy in a tracksuit watching me from amongst the trees. He's not doing anything, just watching. Then the dust devil goes through me and moves on, and now when I look the boy has gone, but I definitely saw him. I swear I did. He was wearing a blue tracksuit. He couldn't have been someone from our school because Leda tracksuits are grey, and this one was blue.

Haven School has blue tracksuits. I know that because Nelson used to go there.

Nelson was my older brother. He's dead now.

I only have one really strong memory of Nelson, and it's of the last time I saw him before he died. I don't know if I've made it up or if it really happened, but I was three and he was leaning over me, dressed in his blue Haven School blazer so I guess he was about to go back for a new term. He was just looking at me. And he was crying. Not a little, a lot. Then he reached and took my hand, came in real close, and whispered, 'I wish we could swap places.'

Those exact words. I remember them.

Chloe Pryor's grandpa used to be Nelson's running coach for the national team. I guess my parents thought of him more as a friend than Nelson's trainer though because when Nelson went missing Chloe's grandpa started coming round to see us. Maybe it was every week or just every month, but it felt like all the time, and I know he came for years – a long time after Nelson's body was eventually found – because sometimes he brought little Chloe with him, and at the beginning she was just this tiny baby and towards the end she was coming to school with me at Leda.

Anyway, when Chloe came round once she told me this story her friend Shaley had told her about a house on the edge of town that's so haunted all the trees around it just died and grass won't ever grow in the garden. And if you spend even one night in there when you come out you'll be, like, thirty, because all the ghosts will scare you into old age. Chloe said Shaley swore it on her granny's grave, and when I told her Shaley couldn't do that because her granny was still alive, Chloe told me that just proved how much Shaley wasn't telling a lie.

Chloe was always saying things like that. She was funny. She cheered me up without even knowing it.

I never really believed ghosts exist but recently I've been thinking maybe they do, because ever since the aliens came I've had this bad feeling, and it's kind of like Nelson is watching me.

He's doing it now. Checking out my stride as I run, checking my rhythm, checking my elbows are tucked in enough. I can't remember what his voice sounded like but I can still hear him, telling me what to do, telling me I'm doing it wrong and that

I'll never be half as good as he was. The harder I try to get away the louder he becomes, and in the end I'm going so fast I just have to stop because I can't go any more.

I check the trees again. No one's there.

Because that would be stupid. Right? Nelson's gone. He died years ago, he can't really come back.

Gary might be acting like a total idiot these days but he was right about one thing – it is hot. The air in my chest is on fire. There's a rushing sound in my ears, and I think maybe it's the wind again only it's too loud for wind, so maybe it's an army truck coming. As I think that, a horn blasts and Gary's brother's Renault 4 *whooshes* by and I swear I feel the wing mirror brush my arm.

Gary's leaning out and yelling, 'Run, Forrest. Run!'

I hate him these days.

I jump off the road because last time I realised if I cut the corner to the back road and head through the bush I can shave a few minutes off my time. The back road's much safer anyways, the army trucks don't go down here. Not much does.

At first the ground's slightly downhill and there isn't much grass, apart from the scratchy stuff around the ankles. I can pick up a good bit of speed because when you're wearing shoes like my Js you don't have to worry about the thorns getting through. That's what you're supposed to call them, by the way. Not Air Jordans, even though that's what they are. Just Js. LA Gears are rubbish.

My Nike bag bounces on my back as I weave between termite nests like James Bond through a sea of snapping alligators. Then I'm zipping between the trees. I have to dodge a dead branch that could easily be a massive python, swerve to avoid a spider's web big enough to catch a car, and then have to skid to stop myself from falling down a hundred-foot hole.

I get up, pleased with my agility *and* my speed, then sit straight back down because it's like a knife's in my ankle and it won't let me stand. I check around for the dirt road I should have hit by now but all I see are trees. I can check something through the leaves, though, just over there, and I realise it's the back of the school. The classrooms, the playground, the line of rocks that look like footballs. I've done a big loop without realising. I'm no closer to home, I'm in the place where we checked the alien ship land that day.

I lift my wrist for the watch that isn't there. Cicadas make my ears hum real loud.

I wish I'd gone the normal way now. I wish I'd brought water, too. If you don't drink for long enough your tongue swells up so much it blocks your throat and you can't breathe, and one time this TV explorer guy got lost in the Sahara and had to drink his piss for a week.

I stand again and manage a step forward, and pain shoots up my leg. The dry ground snaps under my Js only it sounds like it's coming from somewhere else.

I swear I check something blue moving behind those trees.

I pull the low branches down. No boy in a tracksuit there, and no aliens either, just a large clearing. I limp through and the sky opens above me, and straight away I notice the ground, because the grass is charred and flat with new grass pushing through. Ants and bugs and beetles are all over the place – no living ones, all dead with their legs in the air – but if there was a fire then it burned in a way that's made a perfect circle. A big round burn mark with me at the edge.

'Hello?'

Now I definitely hear something, from the other side of the clearing. Someone running away across the brittle ground and a flash of long, ginger hair behind the leaves, heading back towards the school. The only person I know with hair like that is the American girl who arrived this morning, Mr Jefferson's daughter.

Now someone else is pushing through the leaves where the footsteps started. It's Mr Stamps. There's no point hiding, he's seen me. Then I wonder what made me want to hide in the first place. Mr Hyde's the one who'd beat you for going past the rocks, no one ever gets into trouble with Mr Stamps. Besides, it's not like I'm doing anything wrong.

He marches right across the burnt area. His face is like iron. I've never seen him look like this before.

'Tendai?' he says. 'What the hell are you doing here? You know Mr Hyde's rules.'

'Sorry, sir, I . . .' I shift the weight from my bad ankle and it makes me wince.

Then he smiles and it's OK again because he's just Mr Stamps.

'I just wasn't expecting to see anyone up here, that's all. You surprised me,' he says. 'What have you done to your foot? Want me to take a look?'

Before I can say anything he leans over and presses his fingers down the length of my leg.

'It's not sore,' I lie.

'Maybe not, but you still need to take care of yourself if you're going to make the nationals this year.' He looks up at me. 'You do *want* to make the nationals this year, don't you?'

I stare back. Is he teasing me? Of course I want to make the nationals this year, but my parents won't let me.

'I thought that's why you stopped turning up for orchestra practice. Too busy training. Your brother was a great runner, I hear.'

I nod. I don't like talking about Nelson.

'Such a tragedy. I assume your parents want you to follow in his footsteps, though.'

He gets up and checks me straight in the eye. I just stand there. Silent. He's been drinking strong coffee.

'I bet your parents are very proud of you. It's a shame about the orchestra though, you were the best saxophonist I had.'

I actually stopped going to orchestra because I wasn't any good, but maybe I was better than I realised. I glow and feel guilty at the same time. In that moment I even wonder if I should quit running and go back to the orchestra, because at least Mr Stamps thinks I'm good at something.

'How did you know about my brother? About Nelson?' I say instead.

'Doesn't everyone?'

'Not really, it was a long time ago. Did Chloe tell you?'

'Chloe Pryor?'

There's only one Chloe in school, yet he says her name like he doesn't know her but he does. He brings her to school in his Lift Club some days, I've seen them.

'Her grandpa is Wilf Kennedy, the famous athlete, and he was Nelson's coach.'

Only it's like Mr Stamps can't hear me all of a sudden and he just looks behind him, staring at the clearing and the scorched grass.

'Weird, isn't it?' he says after a while. 'Are you one of the ones who saw the spaceship, Tendai?'

At first I'm not sure what to say to him, because if I tell

him the truth he might think I'm stupid and stop liking me so much. But I did see it.

'Yes.'

'Is that a fact? I'm intrigued. So? What did you see?'

'I saw . . .' I have to think hard for a moment. It was only a few weeks back, but in some ways it seems longer ago than when Nelson was alive. 'I saw a light.'

'A light?'

I nod. He waits.

'And . . . ?' he says. 'Is that all? I hope you told Mr Jefferson more than that – our American visitors have come a long way to listen to your stories.'

'It was glinting in the trees, really bright. And then . . . there was this figure coming out. I saw him. Lots of us saw him. He kind of spoke to us.'

'*Kind of* spoke to you? How do you mean?'

Mr Stamps is grinning at me.

'Well, he didn't really have a mouth, so he couldn't talk, but I heard a voice. I think he was trying to warn us about something bad that was going to happen.'

One of Mr Stamps' eyebrows disappears up behind his fringe.

'Something bad? You mean like nuclear war, or pollution, or space monsters coming to blow up our planet for an inter-galactic highway? That sort of thing?'

But he just rolled his eyes as he said that so I'm not going to say anything else, because whatever I say will sound silly. It didn't when I told Mr Jefferson but now it does, and it's like Mr Stamps' words are all grinning at me too. I wish I'd just lied about seeing the spaceship.

'I don't know,' I say.

'Do you like science fiction movies, Tendai?' Mr Stamps says, like we've been talking about that.

I shut my mouth.

Mr Stamps is still grinning. He smiles all the time but this is definitely a grin. 'Don't be like that,' he says. 'I believe you, even if thousands wouldn't. And not because I love science fiction movies too, by the way, it's because I know you wouldn't lie to me as I wouldn't lie to you. Hey, I run a film club for my daughter and all her friends on Friday nights. It's just a bit of fun, really, but I'd love the chance to show some films for older people. You should come.'

'OK,' I say quickly because I'm so relieved he's not laughing at me now. Besides, a Friday night like that is better than one doing nothing on my own. Chloe and her grandpa used to come on a Friday sometimes but not any more. Not since my stupid parents told them to stay away.

'You'll need to clear it with your folks first, of course.'

'Sure,' I say, even though I won't, because they scarcely know I exist.

'And you can tell me more about the spaceship, if you like. I'm fascinated.'

'I can show you the picture I did for Mr Jefferson today,' I beam. I wish Mr Stamps was my dad – mine hasn't asked about it once.

Then I add: 'Actually, I think I just saw his daughter over there. Holly. Did you see her?'

Straight away I wish I hadn't because Mr Stamps glares and his mouth drops like a rock.

'You do realise what Mr Hyde would do if he found you here, don't you?' he says. 'I'd run along before your luck runs out.'

And from out of nowhere his hand gives me a push.

I find the back road easily, as if it was there all the time only I couldn't see it, and I jog free of the trees and into hot sunlight.

Does Mr Stamps still want me to go on Friday? Was he teasing when he said to tell him about the spaceship, because really he doesn't believe me at all? But I *saw* the ship, I did. And the figure. And now I've seen the burn mark, so I can't have been making it up. It definitely, definitely happened.

Did it?

I rejoin the main track and run right to the end. The Madondo Bottle Store is on the corner, which is usually the point I pick up the pace because here the dirt gives way to tarmac and I'm over halfway home, but I've already been giving it way too much and I can't go on. I limp off the road for a rest.

The store has a foosball table and broken chair outside and a fridge against the wall that isn't plugged in, and the whole wall has been painted to make it look like the label on the Castle lager bottles. Inside is too dark to check anything, but I can tell someone is in there because there usually is, and then this man comes out and he can't walk properly because he's been drinking too much. A local man from the village, because they're the only people who drink here. He has an old white T-shirt with the words *Frankie Says Relax* on it that used to be white but it looks rusty like the road. His trousers are full of holes, and his hair has a plastic comb sticking out of it but it hasn't been combed so it sticks out in bumps. He has red eyes and he's holding a carton of Chibuku that I can smell from here.

On his wrist, he's wearing a watch.

My watch. My G-Shock.

I've already half-forgotten about Mr Stamps.

'Hey!' I say, walking towards him. The limp's forgotten too.

But maybe he's not as drunk as I thought because he holds me pretty tight with those red eyes and his lips curl into a shape. I stop. He sees me checking the watch and lifts his arm. He looks pleased and pushes it out to me, like, You want it? Then he presses the button and even in the sun you can see the backlight come on, and the letter in the middle of it is clear, and it isn't a G, it says T, so it's one hundred per cent mine.

The man chuckles. It's what too many cigarettes sound like. His skin is much blacker than mine and he has yellow teeth.

'Eh?' He grunts and holds open his arms, like boys do when they want to fight each other. '*Eh?*'

It's my watch, but what can I do? He's a man, and he's sneering, and he stinks of danger and drink. I'm just a kid.

'Where did you get that from?' I say, like in a friendly way, like I'm interested, because really I'm going to call the police about him just as soon as I get home. But when I think that thought another man comes out of the bottle store, and he *is* the police because he's wearing the shorts and shirt and cap of a uniform. He's drunk, too.

The man with my watch takes a mouthful of Chibuku and doesn't lick the bits from around his mouth. He points a long finger into the air, straight up.

'It is a gift from God,' he says. 'In short and so to speak, I pray. I pray every day to God for nice things, and since God knows very well I am a good man he gives a watch that is *ve-ry* very nice and makes me *ve-ry* very happy. He sends the watch in a *bi-iig* flying saucer ship from the clouds in the sky, and he drops it into my house, and so now it is mine. From God.'

Their laugh is like a starter's gun and I am running again, and I don't stop till I reach home.

Sunset's shooting into my eyes.

We live right on the edge of town, and there's no fence at the end of our lawn, the grass stops suddenly and the bush takes over and the ground slopes down into a shallow valley that isn't ours. Mum's there, just staring from the edge of the garden. It would have been Nelson's birthday last week so Mum's been standing in the garden a lot recently. There's always an anniversary of some kind – Nelson's first day at school, Nelson's first race, Nelson's first medal, when Nelson went missing, when Nelson's body was found, when the crazy who the police reckoned killed Nelson went to jail . . . Once, after a few beers, Dad told me that every year's the same since Nelson died, because they're all just one big minefield of anniversaries.

The early summer's turning the grass all brown.

I say, 'Mum?'

Then, 'Mum?'

I *think* she's looking at me. She's smiling but that doesn't always mean she is.

'That's nice,' she says.

She moves her hand as though she's going to touch my face and then changes her mind, like she's already forgotten what she was going to do. She won't notice I'm not wearing my watch. I bet Dad won't either. Dad buys loads of things but he doesn't remember what they are, I'll probably just get a new watch for Christmas.

'I broke my record,' I lie. 'I ran home in nearly three and a half minutes less than my previous best. I didn't stop once, not once.'

She takes in this really deep breath, like the world is running out of air.

'That's nice,' she says. 'Why don't you watch some TV? It's that show you like.'

'Which one?'

It's as if remembering makes her head hurt.

'I don't know. You like lots of shows, don't you?'

There's a flash from the top of the garden, like sunlight bouncing off glass. I think maybe it's Dad back home from work early for once but as I jog back I can't see his car anywhere in the drive, and for a moment I think I check someone wearing blue looking out of the window. But that's stupid, there's no one in the house but me. I'm like that kid in the movie, completely home alone, the only difference being that he really was alone because his parents had forgotten to take him on holiday with them – my mum's here yet I'm still all alone.

The walk down the hall to my room is like a tunnel through Nelson's short life. It starts off, of course, when he was just a baby, and Mum and Dad are holding him in a black-and-white photo and Nelson is in a towel nappy and mittens and nothing else. Mum doesn't look like Mum because she's smiling and Dad's got this thin line moustache over his lip and hair that's bigger than a space hopper, which is funny because now he hardly has any hair at all. He's skinny then too, while now the space hopper lives under his shirt. They're standing in front of this really crappy house with no glass in the windows, but Dad says that's how lots of black people lived then because in those days everything was for the white people.

He also said the camera that took that first picture wasn't theirs, they couldn't afford a camera then, and that's why the next photo wasn't taken until Nelson was seven. It's colour now, although it looks sort of brown like it's been burned, and Nelson's already started running because in it he's beaming like a torch and standing next to a table with a silver cup on it that's smaller than an egg cup and if you look closely you can see a number '1'.

When Nelson was eight he stood with Mum and Dad in front of an old Toyota pick-up that was new to them. When he was nine he won more races, with bigger medals and a cup that's the size of his head.

When he was ten he rode on Dad's shoulders in the street as new Zimbabwe flags and pictures of Robert Mugabe waved behind them in the air.

When he was eleven he played water pistols with Mum in the garden we have now, and Mum's looking really big because she's got me in her tummy. She's happy. She's the mum I wish I had.

When he was twelve Nelson went to Victoria Falls and stood near the edge and got soaked from the spray. I don't know if I was there too because I'm not in the picture.

When he was thirteen he went to a new school. First he's standing outside our front door in his new blue Haven School blazer, then he's standing near the car – a different one, it's a Mercedes now – in an area full of other cars and a school boarding house behind them.

After that, all the pictures are of Nelson and his running. Nelson on a track. Nelson with medals. Nelson with silver cups. Nelson with more medals and more cups, and more, and more, and more. And at the end of the corridor, on the door that I'm never allowed to open – *Nelson's* door – a framed newspaper cutting reminds me every single day that Nelson, my big brother, was THE NEXT ZIMBABWE OLYMPIC GOLD MEDALLIST. The words scream into my eyes. There's a picture of Nelson, too, standing next to Chloe's grandpa, and it seems like he's looking down at me because he knows I'm not nearly as good a runner as he was – Nelson, that is, not Chloe's grandpa, who was always really nice even though sports coaches are supposed to be tough and mean. I remember once when he came round with Chloe he told me he'd be happy to be my coach too one day. I was so pleased, but afterwards Mum and Dad just laughed and said he'd been joking and hadn't really meant it. Not long after that he stopped coming round completely, Mum and Dad think I don't know why but I do.

Nelson would be twenty-four now. Twenty-*four*. That's really old. I try to imagine what it would be like having a brother of any age and I can't. I don't want to. I *never* want a brother because I don't even like the one I didn't have.

The Fresh Prince of Bel Air is on. It's the best show in the whole world, but I don't think Mum actually knew it was coming on when she said. I watch it then have a shower then dress into my overall jeans that are exactly the same as the ones the Fresh Prince wears. They're made by Guess and you can't buy Guess clothes anywhere in this country.

I watch the show again because I taped it on my own VCR and then play *Doom* on my computer. Dad got me my video camera *and* a Power Macintosh 6100 for my last birthday, and Apple computers are the best computers in the world. It's got a huge 700 MB hard drive, plus 72 bytes of RAM, and a floppy drive, and CD drive, and built-in speakers which make it the best for games. Dad knows somebody who knows somebody else that works for Apple in America, and *he* says that one day we'll all be walking around with Apple computers that are so small they'll fit into our *pockets*. Straight up. No one at school believes me when I tell them but it's true.

I don't know when Dad gets home exactly, only that it's dark when he does and I don't like the dark since I saw the spaceship. I also don't like it when we have food we have to cut, because that means there's only the sound of metal on the plates around the supper table. Mum eats her gravy with a fork and leaves the rest. Dad taps his fingers on the table and turns his beer glass round and round and round, sometimes I wonder if he'd rather stay at work when Mum's this bad. I just eat so the meal will be over quick.

Dad eventually picks up his glass and holds it to his face like he's looking in it for something to say.

'So,' he says. 'Isn't this nice? Sorry I couldn't pick you up from school,' he adds, as usual.

I shrug.

'That's OK,' I say even though it's not. As usual.

'I *tried* to leave on time, I really did, but . . . you know. Business is dollars, and everyone needs dollars.'

I nod. Yes, I know. I also know that he's always late back because he doesn't really like being at home with Mum either.

'Did you have a good day at school?'

I nod quickly.

'And I ran back and beat my record,' I say, because Mum's probably already forgotten. 'I didn't stop.'

'Well, good for you.'

'I beat it by almost four minutes.'

'You don't say. Could you pass the potatoes please?'

'I'm getting better all the time, so I was thinking . . .'

He glances at me. He looks worried about what I'm going to say.

'And the carrots, there's a good boy. Don't they look good?'

'I was thinking, maybe I'm good enough to try for the nationals like Nelson did? Mr Stamps reckons I am.'

Now he glances at Mum before putting his glass down. Maybe he feels guilty because everyone knows Mr Stamps is nice, he hangs around at the school to help out every single day while my mum and dad don't even pick me up and hardly know most of the teachers' names.

'Let's talk about this later, shall we?' he says, and I know that really means he's going to tell me I can't, because my running is just another mine waiting to be stepped on. Another thing to remind Mum about Nelson. That's why he feels guilty.

'Maybe when you are a little bit older,' he says. 'Next year, perhaps.'

'But I'm good enough now.'

'Or the year after.'

It's like he's punched me.

'The year *after*? But I'll be almost fifteen by then,' I say. 'It'll be too late. It's true. Nelson didn't have to wait that long. How come he didn't have to wait and I do? You always let him do everything but never me.'

Dad holds out a finger to *shush* me but Mum's already making a noise and putting her hands over her face. All I did was mention Nelson's name but it was enough, and now Dad's cross.

He stands up. I think he's going to escape outside for a half-hour cigarette like he usually does but instead he goes to his briefcase and takes out this box and slides it across the table.

'Here. I was keeping it for another time but you might as well have it now,' he says. 'Go and play with this.'

'What is it?'

'A game for your computer. It's called *Myst*. It's not even out yet.'

'Is it like *Doom*?'

'What is *Doom*?' he says. 'This is a puzzle game. You love puzzle games, don't you?'

'No.'

'Well, you should. They're much better than those silly alien shoot 'em games you spend all day playing.'

He does his crazy-waving-hands-in-the-air and tries to laugh, but Mum's not joining in. She's crying behind her fingers.

Dad's voice drops almost to a whisper.

'Go on, Tendai, give your mother a little peace. I'll come and see you later, OK? You are a very lucky boy, that game isn't even out yet.'

If I'm so lucky why don't I ever feel it?

I get down quickly from the table and head to my room, and when I get there Nelson's just glaring down from the picture on his door.

'I lost my watch today,' I shout back up the hall. 'Someone stole it. It's gone.'

Only no one hears.

No one ever hears.

Sometimes I really miss Chloe and wish her grandpa still visited us just so he could bring her round. She used to like hearing about my running and I'd tell her about me maybe making the nationals one day. She was actually interested. No one else is. She *listened,* and she sort of looked up to me, and that was nice because it made me feel special.

And then one day it all changed. All stopped. After years and years of looking forward to those times when they came, they vanished from my life.

On their last visit her grandpa had a very serious face when he arrived and he took my parents into another room to talk in private, but Chloe and I moved our game closer to the door so we could hear what was going on. He was asking them if they'd noticed anything different about me recently, and when they said they hadn't he asked flat-out if they'd ever realised how unhappy they were making me.

I was shocked. Not because he'd said it, but because until then I hadn't realised me being unhappy could be someone else's fault – not someone alive, only Nelson's – and I definitely hadn't thought anyone would ever notice.

My parents said I was fine, that Mr Kennedy was imagining things.

Then Mr Kennedy started talking about my running. He said I had potential and I could be good, they should let me train with him. It might give me a focus and an outlet to help me come out of myself . . . I'm not sure what that meant but I was pretty sure it had something to do with Nelson still.

My dad muttered something about wanting me to focus on school work, and to not be distracted by something I could never be great at.

'He *could* be great, he just needs to be given a chance,' Mr Kennedy told them. 'And he's only twelve, there's plenty of time for him to do both right now.'

I sat there. Hoping. Praying that Mum and Dad would listen to him. But Mum was crying again like she always did when anyone mentioned anything about running, and Dad's voice told me he really wished Mr Kennedy would just go away. I had no idea what Mr Kennedy was going to do next.

'You need to wake up, man,' he shouted at Dad. Like, really shouted. 'Nelson's gone. Stop living in the past, get some proper help for your wife, and start living for Tendai, because *he's* the one with the future. You still have a son. You lost something irreplaceable with Nelson – we all did – but you didn't lose everything.'

Mum was crying harder, and Dad was trying to make her stop, and getting angrier and angrier when he couldn't, and shouting back at Mr Kennedy about people not telling them how to live their lives or how Mum should grieve. I started crying too, but only because I knew Mr Kennedy was right and I could see now that my parents would never understand.

Chloe put her arm around me and hugged me until her grandpa came back through and left with her. He squeezed my shoulder as he passed me but I've never seen him since to say thank you.

Of course, once he stopped coming round it meant Chloe stopped coming as well. I saw her most days at school, but school's not the same, and when you're a senior you're not supposed to hang out with the younger kids anyway. It's like an unofficial rule. It's dumb, but it's still a rule. I missed her. I still miss her. I had a brother once and he got taken away before I knew him. Chloe wasn't Nelson, but for a short time in my life it was kind of how I imagined it would be to have a brother or sister – how it *should* be – only now I couldn't have that either.

Myst is an island and you're the Stranger who has to explore it through the different Ages and pick up clues along the way. It's more like a story, which sounds really boring and it kind of is, but I actually really like it too because you can play for hours.

I don't know what time it is when the power goes off, but I know it's late and that Mum and Dad must have gone to bed without telling me they have because everything is so still. We get power cuts a lot when there's a storm but there is no storm tonight, so as I sit in the dark I wonder what made this one happen. And it's *really* dark. I can't move. I just listen to the house as it ticks and groans, and I wish I had my watch after all because the backlight is like a torch, and despite the millions of stuff in my room I don't have one of those.

Slowly a glow makes the shape of my window, and when I pull back the curtains the stars are waiting for me. Just . . . stars. Stars that I could never count, I didn't know there could be so many. As if they're all one thing. A fog. A blanket. A pale reflection in upside-down water that's floating in the sky. People sometimes say that space is black and full of nothing, but it's not, because when I hold up my arm it's my hand that's black, a void in the shape of my fingers with the sky of stars all around it. I'm the nothing.

I quickly pull my hand away. The sky behind it comes back, and maybe I made a mark on the window or something because just in that place the stars seem thicker, brighter, and I can still see the shape of my fingers only they're shimmering and alive. It's as if . . . as if I've made a hole in the glass and now the stars want to flood in. They're coming in. They're *com*—

Something moves. It cuts right in front of me on the other side of the window. I stagger into the middle of my room and the blood in my ears is like thunder. My eyes yawn for light. I wait. And wait. Out there, the world waits too. I'm certain a figure will appear at my window and it'll be one of the aliens, because I know they exist, but in that moment I can't remember exactly what they look like. I saw them that day, I did. But no one else believes us so now all the details are blurred like a disappearing dream.

A rattle sound comes from behind me and I jump, and my door handle is moving up and down.

'Dad?'

But it's not Dad. I know it's not Dad, because the light that's suddenly pushing through the thin crack around the doorframe is burning white. The handle moves so fast I think it's going to break off and the door will fly open but then it just stops, and as suddenly as it came the white light goes and I'm alone in the dark again. The house is as silent as it was before.

A gentle *pop* and my door swings open, yet nobody's there.

A cold wind blows into me, and on the other side of the hall I can tell Nelson's door is wide open, and his door is always, always closed.

Tendai.

I hear it. From inside Nelson's room.

You think if that happened you'd scream but you don't. You just don't.

Tendai, it's me.

'Who?' my voice says.

But I don't need to ask.

And suddenly the cold air lifts me and I'm being carried by nothing, out of my room and across the hall, and I can't stop, and Nelson's curtains are wide open even though Mum closes them every night like he's still alive, and standing in front of his window and making a silhouette against the stars I see a figure. Not alien, but human. A boy, but one who's a bit taller and a bit older than me.

And he says, *Don't worry, I'm here now.*

I can't speak, and even if I could I wouldn't know what it would be.

Well, aren't you going to say something?

Is *that* why the aliens came? To tell me Nelson was coming back? Is that the bad thing they were trying to warn us about?

And the figure says, *What aliens, Tendai? There are no aliens, it's only me. It's only ever been me.*

But I *saw* the aliens. I did. I'm sure I did. And I don't *want* Nelson here, because if he's here then Mum and Dad won't want me, they only care about him.

They never wanted you in the first place, the figure says. *That's why I'm here. I'm going to swap places with you.*

And he drifts towards me.

Now I scream.

More light, exploding and burning into my head. When I can open my eyes again the figure by the window has gone but my dad is behind me with his dressing gown not quite fitting around his belly.

'Tendai?' he says, looking around the room. 'Are you OK? Who were you talking to?'

Then Mum appears, and *she* just rushes in to make sure all of Nelson's stuff is OK – that his running cups haven't been moved, that his hanging medals are all there, that his clothes and his shoes haven't been disturbed. And when she's sure of all that she turns round to me.

'What are you doing?' she says.

I start to say something, but there's no point because she won't listen. No one listens.

'You know you shouldn't be in your brother's room.' She's yelling. 'You *never* come into your brother's room. Get out. Get out. *Get out!*'

When Dad's angry he doesn't speak. When he's *really* angry he speaks quietly but it's so mumbly you can hardly hear what he's saying.

'I can't imagine what was going through your head.' He talks into the back of his hand and he's sitting in the seat like the car's not moving but he's actually driving really fast. 'You know what it's like around his birthday. You know how she gets.'

The words I want to say thump against the back of my teeth.

Dad sighs and turns into the school road, sharp. When we arrive through the school gate he just waits for me to get out of the car.

'She was doing well, it's been a good couple of months. You *know* how she likes to keep his stuff just so. You *know* she likes to have his room tidy for . . .'

He stops and pretends to check his wing mirror. He was going to say, When he comes back. He was. But he doesn't believe he actually will, it's only Mum who does.

'I'm sorry,' I try to tell him.

'It's going to take me weeks to talk her out of this slump.

We might even have to restart the medication, and I can't tell you how depressed that makes me . . .'

He stops suddenly.

'Tendai, where is your new watch?'

It's too late to lie now.

'I lost it,' I say. His lips go thin. 'Dad, please . . . I'm sorry, I really am. I'll get it back.'

He pulls away before I've even closed the door and the dust is like a parachute behind him.

I walk slowly to the classroom. On the way across the grass I see Elijah the gardener is sitting under a tree with a kid from his village. It's Sixpence. Everyone used to think Elijah was Sixpence's dad only he's way too old. Elijah's got this wire toy that he's pulling back into the shape of a car, and I wouldn't have noticed it except as he hands it back to Sixpence I spot Sixpence is wearing my watch. He is. It's right there, hanging loosely on his thin little wrist.

Did *he* steal it? But he's such a nice kid. Maybe he stole it from the man yesterday at the bottle store and is bringing it back.

I hang, waiting for Elijah to leave so I can go get it from him, but then the bell rings so I can't hang any longer, because Mr Greet crucifies anyone who's more than half a second late. In fact, he's already started, because he's got Gary by the collar and is half-dragging, half-lifting him all the way to Mr Hyde's office. He must be super-psycho today.

I don't want to but I leave Sixpence for now and hurry to class, and when I get there I realise Gary must have done something seriously wrong because there are blood drops on the floor and everyone's whispering about something that happened to that American girl and how her head was bleeding.

A few minutes later Mr Greet comes back and tells us to get on with some reading because he's too busy to teach us at the moment and all I can think about is what Gary must have done to Holly Jefferson to keep Mr Greet out of class.

That, and my watch. I need to get that watch back.

With no Mr Greet around, this is my best chance to find it. I stand up and walk back out.

School is like a different place completely when you're outside during lesson time, everywhere allowed's suddenly out of bounds. I move quickly, but Sixpence and Elijah aren't there any more, my watch has gone again and if I get caught now I'll be in trouble for nothing.

I tiptoe back towards class. I can hear Mrs Greenacre typing in the admin block, and as I pass the door I see Gary outside the head's office waiting for whatever he's going to get. I hear the noise of a door from somewhere else, and when I check across the grass Mr Jefferson is by the Year Three classroom with a whole bunch of the pictures we drew. I panic and gap it the other way along the path towards the chapel, if anyone catches me now I'm too far away from the main toilets to make it look like that's where I was heading.

It seems I'm not the only one skipping class, though, because when I check ahead I catch Chloe ducking into the side entrance of the chapel, and even from here I can tell she's upset. Is she in trouble?

I can't remember the last time I spoke to her. I just try *not* to speak to her, and that makes me feel bad. I'd better go and see what's wrong.

I run towards the chapel when suddenly Sixpence darts across the path. I want to see who's upset Chloe but in that moment I want my watch back more. It's like Sixpence's got these weird superhero invisibility powers that make him flash on and off and he might disappear again for good. Chloe will still be here later, I can find her then.

Sixpence vanishes behind a bush. I think I'm close enough to get him but when I jump round he's suddenly up by the cricket pav. By the time I get *there* he's gone again, and the only person I see is Mr Stamps coming the other way. I know it's only him, but I don't want to have to explain what I'm doing out of class and I jump into a ditch to wait. Then when he's gone I have to wait some more because now *Gary's* running past. He doesn't see me, just sprints with a load of papers flapping in his hands and staples one to the pavilion door before going off again.

The coast is finally clear. I climb out.

KARL HYDE USES EDELVALK BOYS FOR TARGET PRACTICE, Gary's notice says.

Whatever that's supposed mean. Probably nothing, just Gary being even weirder than what's normal for him these days.

I push the door open and go in.

'Sixpence?' I say.

He's not here. Someone is, though, but inside it's too dark to see who.

The shadow crouching in the corner shifts like it's been waiting for me, and I hear feet scrape on grit. I see it stand, its arms drop to its sides, and for one horrible moment I think it's Nelson again. Then my eyes get used to the light.

'Oh,' I say. 'It's only you.'

The American girl puts her hands on her hips.

'I'm sorry, I didn't mean . . .' Older girls make me nervous. 'You're Holly, aren't you?'

'That's my name, don't wear it out.'

'How's your head?'

I guess she must think that's a dumb question because she just shrugs, so I tell her, 'I'm Tendai,' even though she didn't ask.

I think about also telling her I spoke with her dad, but change my mind because she probably wouldn't believe about the spaceship either.

'I saw you up in the trees yesterday.' I say. 'Were you checking out the burn mark?'

Now she seems interested.

'That was you?'

'Yes.'

'In that case I owe you. Thanks.'

'For what?' I say.

She just looks around me and out through the open door.

'Has he gone yet?'

'Who?'

'That creep.'

'Gary? Yes, he's gone. He left this on the door, though, I've no idea what it means.'

I hold up the piece of paper and she checks it out. She nods like she knows.

'That's what he wrote on the blackboard this morning. At least, he was trying to before I walked in. That's when he . . . you know.'

She points to the plaster on her head.

'Does it hurt?'

'I'll live.'

'If it makes you feel better, Gary pushes lots of people around these days.'

'Yeah, he's a real jerk all right. But he's not a creep, I wasn't talking about him. I was talking about that guy.'

'Which guy?'

'You know. The one who took me up to see the burn mark.'

'Mr *Stamps*?' I'm not sure if she's joking or not. She must be. 'Why?'

But, if there is a why, Holly decides in the end not to tell me.

She sits down on the ground again and scratches around her plaster.

'Never mind. It doesn't matter,' she says. 'So tell me about Gary. Was he a jerk before his mom left or did he become one overnight?'

'You know about that?'

'Sure I do. I may be this dumb American chick to most of you lot but I have ears. Plus I caught him bawling his eyes out in here yesterday.'

'He was crying?' I didn't mean for that to come out so loud. I guess, despite everything, I feel sorry for Gary. 'In here?'

'You better believe it,' she says. 'I felt pretty sorry for him. At least, I did until he turned all *Street Fighter* on me. I'm guessing he doesn't have many friends, right?'

'I was his friend,' I tell her. 'His best friend.'

'Was?'

'We fell out.'

'How come?'

'He started calling me names.'

'Oh dear, you poor baby,' she laughs. 'So what? Kids slash each other with names all the time.'

'Not any old names. Bad stuff. Racist stuff, like *kaffir* and *munt* and *nigger*.'

She pulls a face like she's been stung. 'I take it back. That's pretty bad.'

'We've hardly spoken since.'

'Since when?' she asks.

'Four weeks yesterday.'

'Not that you're counting or anything. That's pretty specific, he must have really gotten to you.'

'I know it was then because it was the day the aliens came. We were down near the trees, and we'd just finished arguing when I saw the ship hovering above. It was coming down.'

Now Holly's head snaps up and she's looking right at me.

'You're one of the ones, then?' she says. 'You saw it?'

'Yes.'

I can tell she doesn't believe it. No one who didn't see it believes it. But as I think that, her face changes, like she's just realising something.

'Hold up.'

'What?'

'Gary said he was in the tuck shop when the aliens were supposed to have come.'

'And . . .?'

'Well, he wasn't, I know that for a fact. He lied. But now you're saying he was right here by the trees? Why would he make up a lie like that if all these kids who saw the aliens were just making up a stupid story?'

The sound, when it comes, is as if it's right over the pavilion. Not really a sound, more like a rushing wind only not. Then it changes and it's like a horn playing one note, on and on. Then it's a sort of crash, but a muffled crash wrapped up in cloth.

After a while, nothing. Then we hear screaming coming from the main part of the school. Everyone's screaming, like when the aliens came before only worse, just *screaming*.

*

It's been quiet for ages.

'What the hell was that?' Holly says, not too loud. I don't think she's realised she grabbed my hand.

'I don't know,' I tell her.

I check up at the roof, like maybe that's where it came from, then through the open door.

At first I can't see anyone. It's like the school's empty, like everyone's gone. Did the aliens just come and take everyone?

Holly lets go and we walk slowly across the grass, and when we get nearer the classrooms we spot some kids at last. There's a whole bunch of them standing around this cloud of dust, as if something's blowing hard from above, like a silent rocket, only there's nothing above them and when we get closer we see the dust's actually being kicked up by someone rolling about on the ground. *Two* somebodies. Scuffing and kicking and having a big fight.

One of them is Mr Hyde's son Karl.

The other is Gary.

Karl has Gary pinned down and is punching him. Blood's coming out of Gary's nose. Normally when there's a fight everyone comes rushing and cheering, but now they drift and gather round without saying a thing as if it's a dream. There's no one to stop it and I think maybe that's why this one's no fun to watch, and why everyone looks so sad.

It feels weird. Not real. Not right.

I ask a Year Five girl standing nearby what happened, and she just has this look on her face that's all waxy and pale.

'Didn't you hear?' she says. 'It's Chloe. Chloe Pryor. She ran out into the road and got hit by a truck, and now . . .'

She swallows and starts the words again.

'And now she's dead. They're ringing all our parents to come and take us home.'

Karl and Gary are still fighting on the ground.

From somewhere, Mr Greet yells and comes running.

The girl starts to cry. Everyone's crying.

There's no point waiting for my parents to come because they won't, so I just run, towards the rocks and beyond them to the back road because I don't want to see outside the front where the accident happened.

When I reach the bottle store the man who had my watch yesterday is there again, grinning and drunk, but I don't care about who took my stupid watch or where it is now. How could I ever have thought getting that back was more important than talking to Chloe? If I'd gone after Chloe when I had the chance . . . if I'd followed her into the chapel . . . if I'd asked her why she was crying . . . if I'd just called out her name, then she wouldn't have needed to run away from school and out into the stupid road. I could have stopped her. I *should* have stopped her. She'd still be alive right now. She'd be right here and everything would be normal, but she's not. She's dead. I should have gone after her and now it's too late and it was for *nothing*.

I run. And I keep on running, until I can't feel my legs and my chest is on fire, because I think Nelson's ghost is watching me again. I hear his scream. When I finally collapse into the dirt, though, I realise I'm the only one who's screaming. There is no boy in a blue tracksuit in the trees, there is no Nelson. I thought the aliens had appeared that day to tell me something bad was going to happen, and that something was Nelson wanting to come back and take my place, but they weren't. It was Chloe they were warning me about. It was her.

My mum is shocked to see me coming through the door. She stands up quickly and photographs spill from her lap onto the floor and they're all of Nelson. Only Nelson. Her son. But I'm her son too.

'What are you doing?'

I don't answer. I don't listen. I just run down the hall to the bedrooms, pulling at picture frames as I go and hearing them smash behind me.

'Tendai! Stop that! What are you *doing*?'

I charge into his room and I don't care. I sweep my arm through the cups and rip medal ribbons from the wall and *I don't care*. And when I've finished in there I go into my room and start on that because I don't want any fancy computers or cool games or snazzy sneakers or Nike bags or the latest jeans or expensive cameras and watches. I don't want them.

I don't want them.

I don't *want them*.

What I want is Chloe not to be dead.

What I want is Nelson to stay where he is.

What I want is . . . my parents.

What I . . .

want . . .

is . . .

is . . .

. . .

'We were all in the staffroom, there weren't any adults in the playground at the time it happened. The first we knew of it was when the children screamed, and moments later they were at the door, pushing to come in even though they know they're not allowed. When they finally calmed down we asked each one what they saw, and what they heard . . . and it was the same thing, over and over. I'm convinced it wasn't a prank because I don't know anyone who could get that many kids to lie about the same thing. Not a chance.'

KARL

'Your dad's a real jerk.'

And there it is. Bullseye. It's taken an outsider – this thirteen-year-old girl called Holly – all of two minutes to understand what I've had to endure for almost every one of my eighteen years, *plus* she's American so she has the guts to say it out loud.

Come to think of it, she's the first American I've ever really met. She's the first foreigner to come to the school for as long as I can remember, and as far as I'm concerned it's a good thing because she speaks and acts and thinks differently to anyone I know.

I could kiss her, I really could. Everyone might get the wrong idea about me if I did that so maybe I should.

'Did I say something funny?' Holly says.

'No, I was just thinking . . . it wasn't supposed to be . . .' She's five years younger than me but my words are coming out like I'm on a first date.

'Do you work here, Karl?'

'Don't be silly,' I laugh stupidly, forgetting for a moment, 'I'm still at school.'

'So why aren't you, then?'

'What?'

'At school. Why aren't you at school now? You're obviously way too old for this one.'

She's waiting for an answer.

'I . . . I'm not sure . . .'

I turn to the door, expecting to see Dad arching in to check how badly I'm already messing up the story he ordered me to tell. He isn't, but I can hear his voice rumbling as he talks to Holly's folks. They probably can't even tell he's angry, but he is. He's a like a volcano, Dad is, simmering under rock about a mile thick, and when he finally blows his shower of scorn's going to rain down right on me and me alone and it's going to be big. The biggest – I got expelled, how much worse could it get? I've been waiting for it all week, and now his bad mood lava's got hotter by about a thousand degrees because not only is he pissed off that these Americans have come to disrupt his school in the first place, but they were late.

'I . . . I . . . I mean,' I stutter hotly, 'I am sure, and I'm not there right now because . . . there's this cricket tournament in town . . . and I'm going to that . . .'

To my relief, she's not in the least bit interested in cricket tournaments, whether they're made-up ones or not.

'How come there aren't any animals around here? You know, like real animals. Elephants and lions and stuff. So far I've only seen a big-assed spider out in the parking lot and I hate spiders.'

I wipe drops of sweat from my forehead, each one like a spotlight on my lie.

'You've never been to Africa before, have you?' I say, and I laugh again, but now she gives me a look like I'm being rude, which I guess I am, and I don't mean to be. 'Do you like elephants? I spent a week of last holidays on a game reserve in the low veld helping to look after some.'

'Cool.'

'Yeah. It was, even though it was actually pretty hot down there. The best thing I've ever done in my life.'

And for a moment I'm back in the camp with Mark and happy to be there, but I realise she's staring at me so I change the subject quickly.

'Your parents wanted tea, right? Or did they say coffee? I can't remember. Coffee. No, tea. Coffee?'

Whichever one I choose Dad'll tell me it's wrong.

I decide it's tea and start pouring. I remember the super-sweet stuff they used to make with condensed milk for us kids when I was here. Do they still give that at break? They do. I glance out of the window and see the urn by the tuck shop door with a tray of half-eaten tomato sandwiches – a couple of junior girls seem to be picking on another junior girl by pushing her and stopping her from getting to them. I never much liked those tomato sandwiches when I was here, I figure they're probably doing her a favour.

It's weird being here in term time. This is my home, I've lived here all my life, but the school now and the school in the holidays are as different as seeing a movie at the flicks or seeing it on video in your own front room. It's definitely smaller than I remember. Did I really sit on those same chairs in class? At those desks? Was I really little Karl Hyde in that little khaki uniform and little floppy sun hat you could dress a doll with? Me with my best friend Toby, filling our days with running and jumping and making a load of noise? When I saw Toby a few months ago he was starting an office job at his dad's firm and had enough stubble around his lips to grow a goatee – when we were youngsters I thought being older was so far away that it would never actually happen, but it did. It tricked us.

The little girl who was being picked on is crying now while the other two laugh.

'*Chloe Ravioli.*'

'*Liar Pryor, pants on fire,*' they chant at her.

Just stupid, childish names, but I can tell they hurt because the Chloe girl is turning round and desperately looking for help. Anyone will do. She sees me watching through the window, and for that second her desperation turns into a vague glimmer of hope, but I'm not even supposed to be here so I pretend not to notice, and in the end she just runs away in the direction of the tuck shop.

A bitter taste starts to rise from my stomach so I swallow it down, and gaze at the pictures on the staffroom wall. Only I can't even do that because they're not actually pictures any more, they're scorecards from matches I've played that Dad's framed and hung around the whole room. I feel like tearing them down.

'You remind me of Johnny Depp,' Holly tells me, and I nearly spill tea over the table.

My tongue swells.

'I . . . I . . .'

'So what's the deal with the spaceship? It's a joke, right?'

'I don't know about that either.'

'Come on. It must be. A bunch of kids in the playground, and a ship full of ETs just drops in at the exact time when there are no adults around to see it?'

'I don't think the aliens would have known it was breaktime,' I say.

'Exactly. Kind of convenient, don't you think?'

'For who?'

'They're yanking your chain, man. Don't you see?'

'That's what Dad says, though in slightly different words.'

'And, for that matter, isn't it strange that practically the whole school was out there, and yet out of two hundred kids only a few actually saw something.'

'Fifty-three.'

'Huh?'

'The number of kids who saw something – fifty-three, not just a few.' But she grins like I've got *sucker* written on my forehead so I add, 'Dad says it's strange as well.'

She laughs. 'I can't figure out who's more stupid, you guys for listening to them or my mom and dad for coming all the way out here to record their crap. I'll call it evens. Hey, I've got Beastie Boys on my Discman. You wanna listen?'

Dad's fingers appear around the door and click. Not the rest of him, just his fingers.

'We're dying of thirst out here. What's taking you so long, boy?'

I scoop up as many tea cups as I can.

Outside, Dad spikes his eyebrow at me then rolls his eyes.

'Which part of *coffee* do you not understand?' he says. 'For goodness sake, can you get through at least one day without disappointing me?'

I wish he'd just hurry up and yell or scream or hit me for what I did. I reckon I could deal with that, it's the constant waiting for it that I can't take. But then, he knows that, doesn't he?

It felt like the middle of nowhere when our guide Mark told us we'd arrived and to start setting up camp. Anyone's entitled to stretch their legs for a bit after seven hours in the back of a Land Rover, but we were in the middle of a game reserve with night almost on us, and Dorfmann, Judd and Jumbe were still messing around over by the termite hills. No turd-trench had been dug, no firewood collected, and putting up a large bivouac on your own was impossible.

'Guys,' I called over. 'I could do with a hand.'

But the only ones listening to me were the vervet monkeys up on a nearby branch, and even they seemed bored of my voice. Flat and whingey. Did I always sound like that? I did, didn't I? I'd always thought things would have been better by now, because it was me who was at the top of the school. It was me that had won the prized position that every other boy dreamed of – head boy – which, in a school like Edelvalk, is as good as being a god. Me. So, two terms into my reign with only one left to go, why didn't I *feel* any better? Sure, the jokes, the teasing, the nudges, the hushed whispers had all stopped, my position of authority made me safe from all that, but in their place was something else. Another sort of loneliness, one I hadn't expected. I guess because almost overnight I'd stopped being one of the ordinary boys and become an outsider, and everyone started treating me differently because I *was* different, just in a different way from before.

I tugged at the bivouac, trying to make it tight.

Something snapped close behind me.

I spun round, hoping to find Mark, though he was still way over by the Land Rover organising his stuff. The bush was silent but that didn't mean there wasn't anything there. I could feel it watching, full of life that I couldn't see. Sundown is a time of the African day that belongs to no man, only animals, and right then that thought was both terrifying and exciting. Or at least it would have been if Judd and Jumbe hadn't ruined the moment by shrieking and running like a bunch of bloody baboons. Dorfmann was after them with a huge snake over his head, the sunset war-painted all over his face.

I reached for my rucksack to use as a weight and felt my damp sleeping bag. I sniffed it and smelled human piss, and straight away Judd and Jumbe's shrieks turned to laughter.

'Guys . . . that's not funny.'

Dorfmann had stopped too, the snake still over his head. He gave me a fuck-you shrug as if to say, Don't bloody look at me, I didn't do it. And I dare say he was telling the truth, but only because he always got the others to do his dirty work. I told myself he was jealous, he'd wanted the position of head boy for himself, and maybe that was true, but he'd always hated me and I suspected I knew why – because deep down he knew the truth about me and loathed me for it. He was Brad Marston all over again.

That's not funny, Dad echoed me in my head, only worse. Don't be so wet. Be a leader, take control. Stand up for yourself, for God's sake.

Maybe he was right.

Now Mark did come over and I jumped – I prayed he hadn't noticed. He was standing with a couple of beers in his hand and held one out as if he'd known me for years. I was eighteen and a long way from school grounds, but this was a school trip, so technically I was still covered by the rules. Wasn't I?

'I won't tell if you won't,' Mark told me.

I took the beer, and we stood side by side, watching the other three messing around like a show.

'Kids, hey.' He winked.

If Mark had been at my school he would have been given god-status of head boy without a doubt, only unlike me he would have been popular.

The monkeys chattered. I silently wished them away so that Mark and I could be alone, even though when I was around him I felt plain and clumsy and dull. I tried to impress him by opening the beer bottle with my teeth but he stopped me before I got the chance.

'Jeez, Karl, what the hell are you doing?' He remembered my name. I wasn't *oune* or *mate* or *man*, I was Karl. Did he remember all our names? 'In case you hadn't noticed, there aren't too many emergency dentists out here.'

Were the monkeys laughing at me?

'I've done it before, it's no big deal.'

'It's a very big deal.' Why do people refer to black people as *black*? They're not. They're brown, and Mark's skin was the richest, smoothest brown I'd ever seen. His braided hair made him look more like a pop star than a ranger. 'I once had this guy on a trip – a real Boer with a big belly and even bigger ego, you know the sort – who used to sit around the camp fire each night and prove how hard he was by eating glass. I warned him not to but what could a black person possibly know, right? Said he'd been doing it for years anyway. Sure, everyone else thought it was hilarious, but one night he woke up, pissed blood into a bucket and howled at the moon. And

I mean, *howled*. I called in a helicopter and probably saved his life, but by the time we got him to a hospital his kidneys were completely shot.'

'Oh.' The word dropped from my mouth. If only I could have thought of something better than that. Anything.

'Oh, indeed,' Mark said, 'but *oh* doesn't come with spare body parts. There's being cool, and there's being stupid. They're two completely different things. What people admire most is someone who knows the difference. OK?'

He grabbed my bottle and flipped the top off with the top of his in one easy movement.

Out over there, Dorfmann and Jumbe were in hysterics because Judd had somehow managed to find a pile of fresh elephant crap with his face and suddenly he wasn't having fun. He picked bits out of his ears and his nose and told them to shut up, but that only made them laugh harder.

'What are you staring at?' Dorfmann suddenly stopped when he noticed me watching with a smile on my face.

'Yes, Hyde,' Judd of course noticed too. He flicked a big lump of turd my way. 'What the hell are you staring at?'

I should have said something. I should. But nothing came. Mark was looking at me too, no doubt waiting for me to speak, and my cheeks glowed hotter and hotter. But just as I thought maybe I'd blown it I tipped my beer towards Mark's and clinked necks, took a long sip, and said, 'Over-tired.'

Mark laughed and clinked necks back. I'd never felt as high as I felt right then.

'Don't you want to join your friends?' he said.

They're not my friends, I wanted to tell him, only then he might have asked me why not so I simply said, 'I don't think so,' I told him.

'How come?'

'That's not really why we're here. Is it?'

I started back on the bivouac. He watched for a moment then gave me a hand. The two of us working together felt the most natural thing in the world.

'So if having a bit of a mess around out in the middle of the bush isn't the reason, why are you here, Karl?' he said at last.

I wasn't sure what he meant.

'I don't know.'

'You don't know much, do you?'

'I mean, I do know,' I laughed stupidly, 'but didn't the school tell you why?'

God, I sounded such an idiot.

'Oh, sure, I know all that – tactile experience, preparing for the future, healthy detachment from exam pressure. Blah, blah, blah. My school did the same. But why *this*? I'm sure you had a whole bunch of things to choose from, and you're the shit-hot cricketer of the moment, so why? And don't say you don't know.'

I only just stopped myself from shrugging.

'I'm not that hot at cricket.'

'I heard you have the second highest batting average.'

'Maybe.'

'*In the whole country*, forget the fluffy schoolboy stuff.'

The fact that he knew that made me glow but Dad's voice rushed in and chalkboarded in my head.

'Second is just the first of the losers,' I said.

'Bullshit. People know your name. You're hot, man.'

'I can play a bit,' I said.

'Bit, my arse. I heard you could turn pro tomorrow, so that's why I'm baffled.'

He'd heard about me!

'About what?'

'About why you're here in the middle of bloody nowhere when I know for a fact you could have gone to the cricket academy in town and shone like a star. That's where all the wannabes are, waiting for the international scouts to pluck them out, and yet you chose to come on an elephant conservation field trip with Alvin and the Chipmunks over there.'

Now Judd was running around in his underpants because somehow Dorfmann had got his shorts. He was wearing them on his head, but then he whipped them off and started playing piggy-in-the-middle with Jumbe.

'Well?' Mark still had his eyes on me.

I felt brave.

'Do you have children?' I asked.

He seemed to find that funny. Of all the idiotic questions, I had to ask that?

'Give me a chance, Karl. Twenty-six may be ancient from where you're standing but it's really not.' He slipped an effortless knot into a rope. 'To be honest with you, I haven't given it much thought. Elephants are my family and I guess I'm happy with that. The pay's crap, the hours are long, and every day holds the threat of a poacher's bullet, but hey, I like it. Besides, I'm not sure a wife and family life is really for me, if you know what I mean.'

Did I? Should I have known? Did I miss something while I'd been watching his mouth?

I made nothing lines in the dirt with my feet.

'Why'd you ask?' he said.

Because I bet you'd be the kind of dad all the kids wanted, not like mine – I'm here because this trip was the perfect chance to escape my dad for as long as possible over the holidays. And I'm here because I might not know much about elephants but I care less about the cricket academy.

I glanced up and he was looking right at me. *Into* me. My chest thumped. Could he tell what I'd been thinking? Shit.

A blur came crashing through the bushes.

Everyone stopped, nobody moved. Not even Dorfmann.

For a moment, in the dying light, I wasn't certain what it was I was looking at. Then it became clear. A huge, massive bull elephant emerging between the trees. Slowly at first, but as soon as he entered the clearing the great grey bulk moved his legs with frightening speed and his strong trunk rose like a cobra. His tusks were so thick and long they virtually met at the end to make a single, deadly point and he was driving them straight towards Mark and me. His skin rubbed like a saw. Dust kicked out in clouds. Sure, I'd seen elephants before, but never like this.

I stepped closer to Mark.

The elephant cut the distance in no time. Dorfmann and Jumbe were already halfway up a tree and Judd had taken refuge in the shallow crap-ditch that I bet he wished he'd finished off.

'He's charging,' was all I could think of saying.

Mark didn't even flinch. I would have given anything to be even half like him.

'Who, Ngara? Those aren't charging ears, he's just hungry. But we will lose our vehicle if we're not careful, and I don't fancy your friends' chances marooned in the bush for five minutes, never mind five days.'

And suddenly he ran – still calm, but fast – back to the

Land Rover, and when he got there he yanked open the back door and pulled out the others' backpacks.

The elephant was less than fifty metres away. Mark started tearing through the packs, but whatever he was looking for he couldn't find it.

'Which one of you brought the orange?' he shouted.

I shook my head. The others just stared.

Mark was lost behind a fountain of one of the other's clothes as he went from zipper to zipper.

'I don't give a shit about your illegal stash of cigarettes and vodka, just tell me which one of you brought the orange.'

Nothing.

Thirty metres now.

'Listen to me. I promise no one's in trouble, but we will be if you don't speak out because elephants will walk through fire if they get so much as a whiff of an orange. So please, before it's too late, just bloody *tell me*.'

Twenty metres.

From the shallow trench, Judd raised his arm like he was in class.

'It was me, sir.'

Mark was already there. He tore through Judd's things. Into each of the side pockets.

Ten.

The big pocket at the top.

Five.

At last, the orange dropped and rolled across the dirt, and Mark grabbed it and hurled it as far into the bush as he could. The bull elephant let out a huge trumpet, veered and went crashing out.

When Mark came back he picked up his beer bottle, swished a fly from the neck and took a long sip.

'I reckon we've got about ten minutes of daylight left,' he said. 'We need to crack on with that fire.'

I didn't think I'd ever laughed so much in my life, though whether it was because it was funny, or from relief, or from the other thing, I wasn't sure.

'Well, I wasn't out here at the time. My staff were in the staff-room and I was in my study. I heard the screams but thought that was just the children playing, so the first I realised something was up was when I spotted a large group of the children taking their teachers to where they'd apparently seen this thing in the trees. They were all standing over there.'

Dad points to the boundary at the edge of the area.

'That's when I became concerned. The children know they mustn't go beyond the rocks.'

The Americans make interested noises. Dad pushes out his chest.

He moves us down the steps from the admin block, across the grass between the classrooms and the main playground area. Kids make way like we're Moses parting the Red Sea and it feels like everyone is watching. Are they looking at me more than the Americans? They are. They're looking at me. Especially the ones who know me from when I was here. There's Tendai Ndube, whose older brother Nelson was this really hot runner but never made the big time because he was apparently murdered by some crazy while he was still at school; and Gary Marston . . . *his* older brother Brad was a mean bastard to everyone when he was at Leda but saved the best for me.

They're much bigger now, I nearly don't recognise them. Are they thinking the same about me, or are they too busy wondering why I'm not at school?

They wouldn't believe me if I told them, I think.

Does anyone believe their stories about the spaceship? I know Dad doesn't, but he wouldn't believe the sky was blue if you told him. I'm not sure about the Americans, though I guess they must do because why else are they here?

It's hot. Really hot. The grass is loud and crisp.

'Do you mind if *we* go to the trees sometime?' Mr Jefferson asks.

Dad scrunches his mouth. As far as he's concerned the rocks are the edge of the world, no one can pass them and live, but then he notices the Jason guy has got the camera pointed straight at him.

'If you must.'

'And I'd like to say sorry now for the disruption we're causing.'

'That's not a problem.' Grinning for the camera. 'Just as long as we can keep the school running,' he adds with a laugh.

That doesn't even rhyme with the things he was saying about them before they arrived.

'I promise we shall keep any interference to an absolute minimum,' Mr Jefferson assures him. 'The important thing for us is to talk to the children and listen to their stories. I'd also like to take a good look at the drawings you told me about, because sometimes drawings tell a lot more than what's being said.'

'Excuse me, sir?'

Everyone stops. The camera lens swings onto me. Suddenly

I wish I'd kept quiet because Dad's glaring at me and chewing on grit.

'Yes, Karl?' Mr Jefferson cocks his head, and he says it in such a way that I almost forget about Dad. Maybe that's because he's not actually the UFO idiot Dad's been calling him the whole time before they got here, he's a psychiatrist. Just by talking to me he's able to make me forget Dad's even there – for a few seconds, at least – because he's more interested in people than flying saucers.

Dad grumbles something under his breath and my bubble has burst.

'Nothing,' I say. 'It wasn't important. I've forgotten now.'

Mr Jefferson simply smiles. How do Americans always have such perfect teeth?

'Well, in case you were wondering what I believe the kids saw . . .'

'What they *think* they saw.' Dad pushes the camera lens down so that it's not on me. Later, he'll probably give me a lecture on how this is the kind of media attention that'll come back to bite me one day and ruin the career that I don't even have yet.

Mr Jefferson completely ignores him. He and his daughter are very different from one another. Holly's got a lot to say for herself, her dad's got very little, but there's something in the way that he doesn't say it that makes me think they've actually a lot in common, and I decide in that secret place I have inside me that I like him too.

'At this stage I wouldn't want to speculate because the simple answer is, I don't know. There was a Russian satellite that went up in August and failed, so possibly something came down from that, and there was also a well-documented meteorite shower over southern Africa last month, although neither of those would account for the two figures that were reportedly seen. Whatever the facts are, I think something has been going on.'

Dad makes one of his dismissive headmaster laughs, like he's listening to one of his pupils and not an adult, and the Jason guy slams the camera back on him.

'By that, I hope you're not telling me you're actually considering the notion that there have been visitors from another world,' Dad says. 'Here, in my school.'

Dad looks around the circle. Everyone looks back at him.

'I'm just saying I think we need to keep an open mind,' Mr Jefferson tells him. 'Don't you?'

Dad folds and unfolds his arms.

'But of course. I always do.'

Dad is so full of *crap*.

I cough into my hand like I'm getting rid of a bad taste. Dad's scowl tells me he won't forget that in a hurry, but right then, with Mr and Mrs Jefferson and Jason-the-camera-guy-with-the-floppy-fringe standing so close, I don't really care. When I was a kid here my dad had seemed like a giant, but he's not. I never realised until today how small he really is.

'Karl.'

I wasn't sure what time it was, only that it was still mostly dark. Mark's whisper was like a secret, and so close that my heart immediately started to pound because I thought he must have come for me alone.

Had he?

'We have to go,' he said.

Then I saw the others sitting up in their beds too, and I had to quickly disguise the disappointment in my voice.

'What time is it?'

'Early enough.'

'Where are we going?' I rubbed sleep from my eyes.

'You want to do something different with your life?' he said. 'Well, next stop: different.'

Then he hurried out.

The Land Rover's engine was already rumbling when I climbed in beside him.

Mark drove without speaking, eyes front, so I looked out and watched the night become a memory as dawn peeled across the sky. At this time of day the world was full of promise, I thought, dreams and hopes were made right here. They couldn't last, I knew that, because the reality of day would come and spoil it all, but for those few minutes I let myself enjoy the possibility of another life.

One of the other three started to snore in the back. The Land Rover hit a huge bump in the road and jumped, quickly followed by a muffled, '*Shit!*' in Dorfmann's voice.

'I know some of you might think this trip's a bit of a holiday,' Mark told us. 'Time away from the folks, smuggle in a bit of booze, have a laugh. I get all that. And you know what? You're right, it is a kind of holiday, so explore your freedom. But there is another, more serious side to it. Now, I don't want to sound like one of your teachers – I'm sure they're no better than mine were – but I hope you're clever enough to keep your ears open and listen to what it's trying to tell you.'

We waited. Mark kept driving, steering through trees and

scrub along the dirt road while the sunrise exploded in slow motion.

'What *is* it trying to tell us?' I said at last.

Dorfmann gave the other two a nudge. Jumbe flicked the back of my head while Judd hissed into my ear.

'Quit asking questions, brown-nose, or he might give us a test.'

Mark pushed up a gear and acted like he hadn't noticed.

'I can't answer that,' he told me, 'because there is no one answer, it's different for everyone. But what I can promise you instead is that very soon, after you finish your last exam and leave school for ever, life will grab you by the balls. Don't get me wrong, sometimes that's a pretty nice feeling, but as it is for most people I bet it – life – is always going to be the one who's in charge, not you, and every now and again the grip will get tight and have you flinching like you're squatting over a block of ice.'

Everyone laughed. I've never really understood why testicles and pain are so funny together.

Soon Mark pulled off the road and the ground was bumpy and grassy and there was no obvious way to go. The Land Rover slid in deep dust. I thought I saw flashes of grooves from another vehicle but then they were gone. After a bit the bush got thicker, and thorns and leaves scratched down the side of the car. A huge dip sucked us down and Mark had to fight the steering wheel to get us out again while the three guys in the back cracked skulls and I practically ended up in Mark's lap.

Of course, Dorfmann made like it was my fault.

'Nice going, bum-boy,' he said, and he was so pissed off that this time he punched one of the other two into action.

'Ja,' Judd rubbed his arm. He was trying not to let anyone see the pain. 'Stop messing with the driver, you idiot, we want to get there alive. Where the hell are we going, anyways?'

Mark ignored them all. I wasn't sure, but for a second I thought I saw him flash a smile my way.

The sun sprayed out. The cold vanished as quickly as a vampire and I pulled my window open for some dusty air. I was convinced we were lost, but then we rounded into a clearing and I saw another, bigger vehicle and three other rangers in the same khaki uniform as Mark's. They seemed to be standing around a huge rock just under where a line of acacia trees began but when a part of it moved I realised it wasn't a rock at all, it was an elephant lying on its side.

Mark was getting out of the Landy before it had even stopped.

'*Unjani?*' he called out. *How is he?*

The nearest ranger turned, the sweat already glistening on his black-brown skin.

'*Siyenze lucky isikati lesi, uzobvaright,*' he replied. *We were lucky this time, he's going to be OK.*

The elephant was small with young tusks. One of the other rangers looked like he was tying a piece of rope around its foot, but as we drew near I could see it was actually a wire snare that he was attempting to take off that had cut a red ring deep into the elephant's skin. The elephant was thrashing its trunk and let out a loud squeal.

I took a step back. Mark spotted it and called me closer. I was sure the elephant was going to leap up and charge now, and even a baby was big enough to hurt, but when I was there Mark took my hand, placed it gently on a spot behind its eye and moved it in small circles. The skin was rough, yet in some ways not rough at all, and almost straight away the young elephant rested its head back to the ground. Mark took his hand off mine to let me carry on by myself.

'You're a natural,' he told me. 'You've just made a friend for life.'

No cricket coach had ever made me feel that good about myself.

'You remember Ngara?' Mark spoke to all of us – especially Judd. 'The big chap you invited into camp with your fruit basket last night? This is his son, Zamani. And that,' he pointed to the loop of wire, 'is proof to you all, if you needed it, that a poacher doesn't give a crap about anything but the street value of the ivory he's trying to steal.'

'But why would anyone want to catch him?' Dorfmann wanted to know. 'He's just a baby. His tusks make Karl's dick look big.'

Sniggers from Judd and Jumbe.

'As eloquently put as I'd expect from someone with your intelligence,' Mark told him, and Dorfmann's grin dropped. 'To answer your question, they wouldn't want to catch him. To a poacher, Zamani is nothing, he's hardly worth getting out of bed for.'

'So I'm right then.' Dorfmann threw missiles with his eyes – some at Mark, mostly at me.

'Poachers are only interested in the big ones, and, at two hundred bucks a kilo, the bigger the better. But a snare can't tell the difference. Grab anything and hope for the best, is the way a poacher thinks, he doesn't give a monkey's about collateral damage. The AK-47 is usually his weapon of choice, but bullets cost money and a snare is cheap. Cheap and particularly cruel. This time little Zamani here was lucky, a snare can do far, far worse than this.'

'Jeez, thanks for the help, *Dad*,' Judd carried on playing to his audience, meaning Ngara. 'Good of you to help your kid out when he needed it.'

'If an elephant as big and as strong as Ngara had tried to pull this little chap out of a snare, trust me, Zamani wouldn't have a foot left to stand on right now,' Mark told him. 'Besides, Ngara doesn't live with the herd. He doesn't have anything to do with his kids.'

Dorfmann slapped my back like a friend, but he made sure it stung even through my T-shirt.

'And you thought *your* dad was a bastard, Karl.'

'He doesn't have anything to do with his kids because male elephants don't,' Mark carried on. 'The females don't want adult males in the herd and pretty much send them packing to live a lonely life on their own as soon as they can. As far as females are concerned, males are only good for one thing.'

Judd ringed his fingers and poked a finger in and out. Jumbe giggled. Dorfmann kept his hand firmly on my back.

I slid out from beneath it and carried on stroking Zamani. I could have sworn he was looking and blinking right at me.

'Poor little guy,' I said.

I hadn't meant for it to come out loud. Had anyone heard?

Mark had, but somehow I didn't mind. Dorfmann was the one I had to watch out for but I especially didn't mind if it was Mark.

'True enough. Elephants aren't the only ones to think like that, though, humans aren't much different. The female of the species . . .'

He gave a wink. Was that just for me? I was sure it was. Was it?

The ranger working on the wire managed to free Zamani's foot and Zamani trumpeted in pain or with gratitude, I couldn't tell which. I was sure Mark knew the difference and I wished I could too.

Zamani surged and rolled onto his legs and we jumped back. When he was up I was *certain* he would attack, but the rangers stood where they were. Little Zamani turned to look at each one in turn, raising his trunk. Then he looked at me. That face, those eyes . . . I could have sworn he was talking to me. Was he? Talking without speaking. Thanking me. It was the eyes.

But surely that wasn't possible. He was just an animal, and animals couldn't do that. Could they?

'We can't stand and stare all day,' Mark said. 'Zamani's still in danger, he needs to be back with his mum. If we're lucky the herd merely got a bit spooked by the poachers and isn't too far away. If we're not . . .'

Only he didn't want to finish that line.

Out of all of us, he turned to me.

'Can you drive?'

I nodded.

'Good. Hurry, get the Landy started, we have to be quick.'

Mark tossed me the car keys. Right then I would have climbed into the cockpit of a plane if he'd asked.

The theme music to *Melrose Place* kicks in. Mum's already fish-hooked by the flashes of perfect hair and perfect smiles and perfect teeth of impossibly good-looking actors.

'Your father would be having kittens if he knew I was watching this rubbish,' she tells me. 'But he's not here to tell me to turn it off, so I guess that's our evening's entertainment sorted.'

She laughs, but I'm not in the mood for jokes. I'm still angry with Dad – for everything, but mostly for the way he's still making me wait before he finally blows and gives me hell for what I did.

I can feel Mum looking at me. Eventually she thumbs the remote, and the screen blacks out and Heather Locklear disappears. I hardly recognise myself as the person in the reflection. I wish I didn't have to look at it. I wish I was back at school, because it's so much easier being there, I can hide behind my head boy door and my head boy walls and pretend that nothing's wrong. Or at least I could, because school's over for me now, I remind myself. For good. Gone in the flash of a cricket bat. My cricket bat. Just like I wanted. Remember?

'I know your father can be harsh sometimes but he really is proud of you,' Mum tells me without even a blink. 'He talks about your cricket all the time. Did you see the scorecards he's hung up in the staffroom?'

Is it true? Is he really proud of me? Or is she just trying to make me feel better, because I think it's more likely my dad hates me for what I did. He *should* hate me, it's what I deserve and it would be much easier all round if he did, but Mum . . .

She smiles, but it's a sad smile. And that's more than I can bear.

I get up and stand by the window. Something moves in the bushes by the tree. Is it Dad, waiting outside while I sweat? No, that's not his style, he'll be down working in his office.

Another thought prises into my head: Is it Robert Dorfmann, then? Or even Brad Marston?

But that's *really* stupid. I only think it because I spotted Brad this afternoon, picking his brother up outside the school gate. Enough years have passed but I knew it was him straight away, making me feel sick all over again because the face had changed but the cruel grin was exactly as I remember it. Does he know I still have nightmares about him? Does he know I still feel the punches and stings and taunts? Judging by the way he looked at me today from his car, him and his little brother Gary, I think he does.

I peer closer. No, definitely not Brad, or Dorfmann, or Dad. Not anyone. Just ghosts in the glass coming to make me feel worse than I already do.

The night is quicksand and I can't breathe. I realise this is my life now – here, existing as a sort of *nothing*, worrying about Dad, being scared of him. Worrying and being scared of everything, for that matter – for ever and ever – and that thought is too much to endure. I go to my room to wait on my bed instead, where I'm surrounded by old pictures of Madonna and Mariah Carey and whoever the hell else I'm supposed to fancy, and the George Michael *Freedom* poster I once ripped down in shame and then painstakingly taped back together. I only want to be alone now, but when Mum taps softly against my door and follows me in I feel I might explode. Because what if she's coming to tell me that I have disappointed her? Let her down?

'I know I shouldn't say this, only it's true: I'm glad that you're here,' she starts.

But there's more. I know there's more.

'Darling, about what happened.'

She touches me lightly. It hurts more than any punch from Brad Marston or any taunt from Robert Dorfmann.

I pull away. Sit up.

'I'm going out,' I tell her.

'But we've hardly spoken since you—'

What? *Smashed cricket balls into that boy?* Is that what she's going to say?

'—got back, I thought maybe we . . .'

'Maybe later, Mum, right now I need some air. I'm not feeling so good.'

She holds me with her eyes, and in the end she nods.

'Sure,' she says. 'I understand. I'll be here when you get back. It's not like I've got anywhere to go.'

When people describe a moonless night they say it's black. It's not black, it's *thick*. Thick with a black fog that stops me even seeing my hand in front of my face, and the sky is thick with stars. I can't see anything else, so I use memory to guide me around the cricket field and down past the chapel. As I near the swimming pool the path thins and I start bumping into the hedge and I wish I'd brought a torch. Noises rustle and scratch and I hope it's not Dad coming to remind me how stupid I am. I think I might have to turn back, but then a small light dots up ahead and guides me down towards the classrooms. It blinks out as soon as I get close so I figure it was probably just Dad finishing up whatever he was doing and now he's gone.

My eyes are slowly getting used to the night. The stars give everything an eerie glow as I walk on to the main part of the school. Dad's definitely not here, and I carry on past the classrooms and across the grass until I almost fall over the rocks. Dad's rocks, I think. Dad's boundary. Dad's rules. Stopping anyone going further. The older I get the more my junior school memories fade, but these rocks will always be with me.

Beyond, the bush is a frozen wave of shadows, and as I look out to it I find myself thinking about Mark again. No surprise there. I remember our camp. I remember the heat of the low veld. I remember Ngara, as determined as a straight-line bulldozer as he came looking for Judd's orange. I remember the baby Zamani, lying in pain on his side, and the sheer exhilaration I felt at not just seeing him freed from the snare but as he seemed to thank me for stroking him and helping to calm him.

Then I try not to remember any of it. I yearn for a time before this moment now with an ache, but only when it was good. I don't want the bad things.

Like when we went looking for Zamani's mother, Khethiwe, and discovered her hacked and mutilated body.

Like when I royally fucked things up with Mark.

Or like when I went back to school and deliberately fucked things up even more – by launching a cricket ball at Robert Dorfmann's vulnerable body as hard as I could, and again, and again, and again, until someone had to physically pin me down to the ground – because it was the only way I could see out of a dark, dark place. That moment can stay in the past too, thank you very much, and the further away the better.

I close my eyes, but the image of Dorfmann and his screams still haunt me so I quickly open them again. Up there, every-thing is stars. A dome of universe, endless and pure, and I long for it. I want it so badly it makes me dizzy. I want to be a part of it. To be *lost* in it. More than anything else, I want to be in that wonderful, tantalising place where I don't matter. Tiny. Insignificant. Anonymous. Where no one knows me. Because now that I don't even have a school to hide in – from Dad, from the truth, and from myself – I'm terrified, and it's always going to be like this. If I had the choice of staying where I am or floating up there into eternity, space would get my vote every time.

What if I begged the school? Would they take me back? If I promise I'd be anything Dad wants me to be . . . But then what? Won't I be where I started? Won't I just be lining myself up for the life Dad wants? Head boy, cricket captain, exam results to suit. Cricket. More cricket. Cricket, cricket, cricket. Be so good at it that I'm set for life, because that's what Dad says life's all about – being set, securing the future, having a bed of money to lie on when I die. Sure, I could use the game to help me get away from him. I could play for the country, break a few records and travel around the world, even become a little bit famous. But what about when I'm too old to play? What about if I get injured or if I'm actually not as good as they say? *Then* where would I hide?

So do I really want to go back? Do I really want to be 'normal'? Because my normal and Dad's normal are *definitely* not the same thing.

Something scampers through the dark and it's big. The shadows come alive. There are no dangerous animals this close to town but I can taste my heart in my mouth.

Less than a minute later, a torch swings from up by the classrooms down to where I am. Is it Dad? I think it must be, so I'm relieved to hear Mr Jefferson's American accent instead.

'Hey,' he says. He holds the torch beam straight up so that it catches both our faces. 'I was just going through some of the pictures and interviews from today and heard someone out here.'

'Sorry.' Why am I apologising? He's not Dad. 'I didn't mean to disturb you.'

'You didn't.' His teeth really are perfect. 'It was this little African boy, apparently, about yay high and skinny legs. No shoes. Holly must have startled him and he climbed out the back of the library, but I reckon she was more spooked than he was.'

'That was probably Sixpence.'

'Sixpence?'

'He's always hanging about.' Dad thinks he's behind the thefts around the school, but Dad would – I don't tell Mr Jefferson that.

'I see.'

I think Mr Jefferson is going to ask something else about it but changes his mind. He turns off the torch and stares up at the night sky with me.

'Quite something, isn't it?' he says.

'Is it?' God, I hate myself. 'I mean, yes. It is.'

'I've missed this. Makes me realise I don't get home as often as I should.'

'America?'

'Texas.'

'Why not?' I don't mean to sound nosy, but he's got a warmth that matches his accent.

'Oh, you know. This and that.' He's locked on the stars, turning a slow three-sixty. 'Nothing that's actually very important. The problem is, the older you get the more what you call life ties you down and keeps you away from actually living. You tell yourself you'll eventually get round to doing all those things you haven't done, but you don't. You know, I've never even shown my daughter the state I grew up in, never mind the street, and that's wrong. But standing here with you, looking at this free show, I think I might just do something about that when we get back.'

He pauses. Takes in a deep breath.

'What a sight. Is it any wonder how us humans came up with the notion of heaven, and God, and angels, and life after death? Because who wouldn't want to believe that's what's waiting for us. Who wouldn't look to that for the answers to everything here on Earth? I mean, look at that. Just . . . look at it.'

I find myself nodding in the dark. I used to believe in God too, once, until I realised I wasn't getting any answers to my questions.

We stand a while, almost shoulder to shoulder.

'Then again,' he says, 'when heaven was invented, the Earth was flat, the sun revolved around us, and no one had any clue that *that*, out there, is actually the most unimaginably violent, hostile, destructive, and yet equally creative force in . . .' He makes a small laugh. 'You know? I almost damn near finished that sentence with, *in the universe*. How's that for lack of imagination?'

He turns to me.

'You're still wondering, aren't you?'

'About what, Mr Jefferson?'

'Please, it's Rex. About whether I think the kids here really saw what they say they saw, or if they're just making it up.'

Are psychiatrists trained to read minds?

'Do you?' I ask.

'Do *you*?'

I hesitate.

'I think they believe they saw something.'

'That's your dad talking. What do *you* think?'

He waits.

'I don't know,' I tell him.

'I had a feeling you'd say that.'

'You did?'

'I bet it's your answer to a lot of things. Am I right?' I can feel him looking at me. 'Well, just so you know, I'm not going to make your life easier by giving you *my* answer, Karl, but I will tell you what I *know*. I know the universe is a big place. Real big. Full of a lot of space but also full of galaxies. Hundreds of billions of them. And to give you a sense of scale, our own backyard in all of it – our galaxy, the Milky Way – is a hundred thousand light years across. As in, our sun's light takes eight minutes to reach us each day, but it would take a hundred thousand years if we were at either end of the galaxy. If you were looking at our galaxy from beyond it, finding our Earth would be a lot like trying to spot the dot of an "i" in an area the size of the United States.'

He turns back to the sky.

'There are probably at least two hundred billion stars in our galaxy alone. That's two hundred billion suns, each with who-knows-how-many planets in orbit. Unfortunately we're not able to check those distant solar systems out very easily because even the nearest is a short one-hundred-and-fifty-thousand year trip by space shuttle, which is almost as long as humans have been on the planet. I don't know about you, but that's what I call one big backyard.'

He puts his hand on my shoulder.

'Got you thinking now, haven't I? There it is – Alpha Centauri. Draw a line through the crossbar of the Southern Cross and head west. Second star. Got it? The nearest sun to ours. Or as I should say, *suns*, because even though it looks like one it's actually a star *system* – a fact some ancient Egyptian, Chinese, even Australian people seem to have been aware of long before the first telescope was even dreamed up, so don't ask me how they knew because I have no idea.'

Once again, I'm nodding in the dark.

'Yes.'

'OK, so we have every star with at least one planet on average. Probably more, but for the sake of making a point let's just say it's one. That's still a lot, right? At least two hundred billion planets in the Milky Way. Sure, not all planets can sustain life, but even if our own Goldilocks orbit is one in a million, with at least two hundred billion planets out there the likelihood of one being like ours is pretty strong, wouldn't you say? Two hundred billion over a million – you do the math.'

He has a smooth, calming voice. A bit like Mark's. I'm hanging on every word.

'Definitely.'

'Glad you agree, but now that I've got your head wrapped around that figure I'm going to take you one step closer to insanity: that's just our galaxy. Consider the whole universe. Because when I said it's big, I mean *biiiiig*.' His accent stretches the word out. 'It takes light a hundred thousand years to travel from one side of our galaxy to the other, but that's nothing when you consider there are hundreds of *billions* of other galaxies playing around in all that space. Swirling. Floating. Crashing. Some smaller, some similar, some positively immense in comparison to ours. We're talking a stupid number of suns, and an even stupider number of planets. Even if life exists on a mere *few hundred thousand* planets in each galaxy, consider the billions of civilisations that might be out there.'

He pauses to let this soak in. The stars shimmer.

All of a sudden Mr Jefferson is close to my ear.

'Would they notice us? Earth isn't even a speck, it could disappear tomorrow and no one would know. And, if they did know we were here, could they get to us across such vast distances? Is it possible to travel at the speed of light? *Faster* than the speed of light? Because they'd need to.'

'I don't think so,' I say after a thought.

'I have to agree,' he says, 'but only because our advanced minds can't conceive of any kind of vessel capable of moving that fast, let alone transporting a living cargo. Ask yourself this, though: in, say, one hundred and fifty million years from now, do you think humans will still be driving cars and flying planes and sending rockets into space? Assuming we last that long, of course. Will we still be phoning each other, and telling the time on a watch. Eating food out of a can? Playing *Minesweeper* on Windows 3.1? Somehow, I doubt it.'

'One hundred and fifty million?' I ask. Just one year of my life seems too long, I can't grasp that much time. 'Surely nothing could live on Earth for so long. Could it?'

'It already has. Take the dinosaurs, because one hundred and fifty million's about how many years they were kicking around the planet. One-sixty-five, including holidays and weekends. Way, way, *way* longer than us. Who's to say species on other planets – and I'm talking intelligent species, not giant lizards – haven't lasted that long? Who's to say we won't? Who's to say a civilisation hasn't been out there for a *billion* years? It's possible.'

'It's Windows 3.2 now.'

Is that really all I can think of to say? God, I can be such a *gorm*.

'Well, there you go! My point exactly.' He laughs and moves away. I wish he'd come back closer, and then hate myself. 'I guess what I'm trying to say is, we don't know what's out there, and maybe we never will. But the thought that our planet might, against the odds, be unique, and that we might be the only living beings to marvel at a sight like this, leaves me feeling just a little sad.'

He takes in a deep breath. I watch his silhouette against the silver-crushed sky. The stars sparkle in his eyes.

'That's the first thing I know,' he says at long last. 'You want to hear the second?'

'I do.'

'In all my years of working with children, I've never come across so many to stick to the same story – any story – for so long. Usually one or two at least would have started to crack by now, but none has. They saw something, all right.'

His torch blinks back on. The stars shrink away and I jump. He's looking right at me.

'OK, lesson over. I've bored you enough. I'd better be heading back anyway or Holly will start to worry she'll get eaten by a giant spider. She hates spiders. Goodnight.'

'Goodnight, Mr Jefferson,' I say. Then, 'Thank you,' even though I'm not sure what I'm thanking him for.

'Pleasure's mine. And it's Rex.' He stops. 'By the way, do you know anything about Chloe Pryor?'

The name glimmers with vague recognition. Perhaps I've heard Dad or one of the other teachers mention her name.

'Is she one of the younger kids?'

'Second grader. Sorry, I mean Year Three.'

Then I remember. *Chloe Ravioli . . . Liar Pryor, pants on*

fire. She was the poor kid getting a hard time from her class-mates that I chose to ignore.

'I only remember the older kids,' I say. 'What about her?'

Mr Jefferson thinks about something then changes his mind.

'She drew a slightly unusual picture compared with the others'. But it's probably nothing, it can wait till tomorrow. G'night, Karl.'

His torchlight bounces back towards the classrooms. A minute later it's gone and it's just me under the stars.

And now I think, The universe isn't the lonely place I thought it was.

And I think, There *are* answers out there. Somewhere.

And I imagine those kids that day, standing where I'm standing, looking out and seeing . . . *something* . . . hovering above the trees, landing in the bush, emerging out of a door and coming forward, and I wish more than anything in the world I'd seen it too.

We found Khethiwe's body just a few kilometres away. Mark spotted her first, a lifeless mound of grey in knee-high grass. The sun was rising, the heat with it, the air was full of flies.

Bullet holes ran all the way along her side and glistened red. The canopy of her ear must have caught thorns or a branch as she'd fallen and lay ripped and tattered on her neck. Her eyes were still open, and it wasn't terror or pain or confusion I saw locked behind her long lashes, it was a sadness, crying out even in death. From there, there was nothing more to see, just a big, messy hole where her trunk had once been, the iconic symbol of this once beautiful creature hacked out with an axe and tossed into the dirt like a dead snake.

Of the tusks, there was no sign. Of course not.

Mark squatted. Was he was going to be sick? He stared at the body for a long, long time before he got up to follow a track I hadn't even noticed to a small fire that still glowed hot. Old baked bean tins for brewing tea stood in the ash, and cigarettes made from newspaper lay scattered around, not even trodden into the ground. They'd slaughtered Khethiwe, mangled her face and ripped out her tusks, but to me the cruellest image of all was them drinking tea and smoking after they were done.

Nobody said a word. None of the rangers seemed in any hurry to do anything.

'They'll be long gone by now.' Mark read the look on my face – the one that showed I wanted to go after the poachers, pin them down, and see how *they'd* like having the fronts of their skulls hollowed out with a rusty axe. I was sure, somewhere deep down, he was having the same thoughts.

He kicked dust over the embers.

'If they'd felt under any pressure they would have buried the ivory and come back when it was safe. This lot had all the time in the world. We failed.'

'But shouldn't we do *something*?' I said.

I sensed Dorfmann nudging my other two classmates behind me. One of them made a poor attempt at smothering a laugh.

'What, you going to teach them a lesson with some of your big words, Karl?' Jumbe snorted. 'Wave a pair of toe clippers in their faces? Ooh, scary.'

'Yes, *Karl*.' Now it was Judd's turn. 'When was the last fight you had, goody-two-shoes? When have you ever had a fight?'

Dorfmann whispered something into his ear and then he added: 'Besides, this is the bush, everyone knows you got to let nature take its course. You wouldn't stand a chance.'

Mark closed the distance in no time. His breath was shallow and short, and Judd cowered beneath it.

'Nature?' Mark said.

'Sure. Animal against animal. That's the natural way.' Judd was drowning in Mark's shadow. He turned to Dorfmann for guidance, but Dorfmann had stepped back into clear light like he had nothing to do with it. 'Isn't it? You know, man against beast, survival of the fittest, and all that crap. That's why we're us and they're just them.'

'Us?'

'Humans. Intelligent beings.' He checked for Dorfmann again, but now Dorfmann wasn't even looking. 'Better than dumb animals, anyway.'

'If you think,' Mark managed to control his words, but only just, 'that gouging out an animal's teeth with a blunt lump of metal while it's still alive is natural, then I pity you and anyone who knows you.'

He turned.

That should have been it. Judd should have left it there, but he didn't. He laughed to himself. Not brave, just stupid.

'Well, what is it, then?' he said.

Mark walked slowly back.

'Don't they teach you anything at that expensive school of yours? It's about money,' Mark spat. 'It's always about money.'

'But we've got too many elephants,' Jumbe decided to join in for some reason, and Dorfmann hadn't even told him to – he was just watching it all from a few feet away with that slit of a grin of his. 'They need to be culled or they'll die

169

anyway, any idiot knows that, might as well make some cash out of them and put it to something good.'

'Good?' Mark almost choked on the word. 'You think feeding a market that warrants the brutal murder of animals for Chinese hard-on pills and carved bloody trinkets is *good*?'

I thought he was going to hit Jumbe, I really did, but just then something rushed at us through the leaves. Jumbe and Judd ran squealing for cover like someone was going to start shooting but it wasn't a poacher that came, it was baby Zamani. He'd found us. He'd found his mum.

The young elephant fanned his ears out like he was on a charge, limping on his bad foot. The other rangers ran around him and tried to get in his way, and Zamani got annoyed and raised his trunk to make an immature warning cry. His feet stamped and hovered with indecision.

'*Limchiye aghambhe*,' Mark shouted across to them. *Let him go.*

The rangers backed off and Zamani's trumpeting stopped instantly, replaced by a low, sad growl. The young bull walked up to his dead mother and began to nudge her with his trunk, like she might wake. He brushed her skin. Stroked her ears. Sniffed the blood and the bullet holes. When he reached the mutilated hole where his mother's trunk wasn't, Zamani let out a sound I'd never heard from an elephant before.

I turned to Mark.

'What's going to happen to him now?' I asked.

Mark wiped his face. His hands were shaking, and when he spoke there was a crack in his throat.

'We'll have to take him in,' he said.

'Where?'

'To the orphanage, look after him until he's ready to be

released. If he will ever be ready,' he added. 'The orphanage is full of too many elephants like Zamani, if we're lucky one of them will take him under their wing. All we can do now is hope he gets over it, because some elephants never do. Sure, they might escape the poacher's bullet, but a sight like this kills them from the inside out. It's a slow death. The worst kind.'

He went over and touched Zamani on the side.

When Zamani turned to acknowledge him I could have sworn there were tears running from the baby elephant's eyes, and Mark put both arms and his face against him in a sort of hug. I suddenly realised I'd started to cry too. Not much, just a single drop drawing a line through the dirt on my cheek. I wiped it away but too late, Dorfmann had already seen.

'Poof,' he said, heading slowly back to the Land Rover, clipping my shoulder hard with his as he went by.

But I decided I didn't care about him any more, or Judd, or Jumbe. Not now. What could their name-calling and taunts and stupid childish games do to me that was worse than what had happened to Zamani, or his mum? They weren't important to me now, only the elephants – and Mark, and what he must have been going through – were.

By the time Zamani was on a truck and heading to the orphanage, the day was almost done. Mark drove us back to camp in silence, and when we got there he went straight to his tent. Dorfmann, Jumbe and Judd took the opportunity to break out their illegal stash of vodka and sat drinking and smoking over behind one of the termite nests, while I stayed by the fire until long after dark. Alone again. Always alone.

When the fire was nothing more than a glow I headed for bed, but there was another glow that came from Mark's tent, and I stood for a moment, watching it, wondering. The bush was buried in silence, and with my torch off there was a wall of darkness so close and so thick it felt nothing could get through. There was only me, and the stars – more out here than I'd ever seen before in my life – and Mark in his tent, everything and everyone else felt like they could have been on another planet.

I moved closer, heart thumping in my ears. Then I took a deep breath, took the clasp in my fingers and quietly unzipped the door.

Mark was sitting in the middle of his sleeping bag and not at all surprised to see me there, like he'd been expecting me. Like he'd been waiting for me to come. Had he? I could tell he was still upset by what had happened that day, and he rubbed his eyes.

'It's sad,' he explained. 'Days like today have happened so many times you'd think I'd be used to it by now, but I'm not. It's always like it's for the first time.'

At that precise moment there was no one else in the world, only us.

I leaned in to kiss him.

Immediately Mark pulled away, keeping the distance between us, and everything that had been in his face fluttered away and was replaced by something else.

'Hey! Karl.'

Shock at first. Then plain awkwardness – most guys would have hit me by now, but Mark wasn't most guys.

'I think you might have the wrong idea.'

Then the worst one of all: pity.

I felt sick. I felt dizzy. Cheeks blazed. I opened my mouth to say something, but what could I possibly say that could make this moment better? In the end I backed out of the tent and ducked under the cover of the stars.

Only there was no cover. Because standing to the side of a bush no more than a dozen feet away was Dorfmann.

'Well, would you look at that.' He spoke like he was giving himself an instruction because he did exactly what he said – looked past me, to where Mark was clearly silhouetted against the side of the tent, to me again.

He stank of cigarettes and was slightly drunk, and somewhere in the back of my head I figured he must have been for a piss because he stopped wiping his hands on his shirt to prod me with a hard finger.

'Take a deep breath, faggot, and enjoy the fresh air while you can. Because as soon as we get back, everyone's going to hear about what their head boy really is, and all you're going to smell for the rest of your school days is the shit that you deserve. You're going to wish you were dead.'

It's not so hard being cruel, I thought as I smashed the first cricket ball into Robert Dorfmann's shins.

He let out a yelp and fell against the cricket net. The net pushed him back again, there was nowhere for him to go.

'Jesus, Hyde, what the fuck do you think you're doing?'

But he knew what, and why, and that I fully intended to do it again so there was no bargaining on offer. He'd started telling the school about me, just like he'd promised he would, only this wasn't about revenge, or fury. It was me fighting to survive. I had no option but to make sure I got out of school, for good, and right then – in that moment – there was no other escape route that I could see.

I swung my bat and sent a second missile on its short journey. It smashed into his chest with a thud that made me feel sick but it was the only way, I had to keep reminding myself that.

He staggered and came forward. I fired off another shot that caught him square on the knee cap and he went down with a scream.

'Are you *crazy?*' he yelled, writhing.

At that precise moment, I think I was a little bit.

By now he was fighting genuine tears, but teachers were running across the field and they were the ones who had to see this.

I took another ball from the bag, looped it up high and took another almighty swing.

I wake up. It's morning.

I don't know what time it is, but I'm certain it's gone eight so at least Dad isn't here to tell me what to do. I can hear the thwack of a cricket ball being hit and I realise Dad's gone to work and left a cricket video playing really loudly next door. He does that sometimes when I'm home. He calls it 'subliminal coaching'. Once he recorded a whole five-day game on to a wall of audio cassettes and told me to listen to one every night at school before bed.

I bury myself back under the duvet.

When I do finally get up, any good mood I managed to scrape together is wiped out by the prospectus for a new school waiting for me on the dining-room table. A Post-It note with Dad's handwriting says, THIS LOT WILL TAKE ANYONE. Another says, MAKE AN ENQUIRY. TODAY! YOU'RE DESPERATE, REMEMBER?

I sit down with a sick feeling in my stomach. It's a fourth-rate cricketing school in town for no-hopers, so obviously Dad's plan is to get me into somewhere I'll look especially good. He'll probably make up a lie about my school not giving me enough playing time and that's why I left, and try to get away with what I did that way.

The back door swings. I assume it's just Rosie, our maid, but Mum's coming through the house looking more worried than usual. I check the clock on the wall and it's gone ten – breaktime soon, and she's not in the tuck shop?

'What's the matter, Mum? You didn't fancy school either?'

She's not in the mood for jokes today. Come to think of it, when was the last time I heard her laugh?

She sits quietly at the table and holds my hand like something really bad's happened. My stomach flips.

'It's your father.' She checks over her shoulder as though he might be there. 'He's not at all happy.'

'Dad's never happy,' I say.

'There are posters.'

'Posters?'

'Someone's made them on the photocopier, they're all over the school. About you. About what you—' she swallows '—did.'

I go weak. I feel the colour drain from my face. Does she know what I did with Mark now, or at least what I tried to do? Has the news gone beyond just the boys in my school and spread this far already?

I stand. Mum tries to pull me back down.

'Your father's furious, I'd stay here if I were you.'

And *Dad*? Does he know too?

I groan. A low, mournful sound.

'I have to go.'

'Where? I really think you should stay here. Besides, I'd like to talk to you. It's been so long since we talked properly.'

But she can't hold me and I run out from the house towards the main part of the school, taking a short cut across the middle of the cricket field. A piece of paper limps across my path in the wind, and before I've even picked it up I see my name written on it.

KARL HYDE USES EDELVALK BOYS FOR TARGET PRACTICE.

So *that's* what Mum meant when she said 'about what you did'. Smashing cricket balls into Dorfmann. Not the thing with Mark after all.

I'd laugh if I wasn't so ashamed.

I screw the paper into a ball, but there's another one on a tree at the edge of the field.

KARL HYDE GOT EXPELLED FOR BULLYING.

That smarts. Did I become a bully that day? Did I turn into Dad? I was only trying to find a way out but I guess I did.

Then another, stapled to a post,

KARL HYDE ISN'T WHO YOU THINK HE IS.

That one's the worst, because it's completely true, whether the person who wrote it knew what they were talking about or not. I'm not who people think I am. I'm a fraud. A liar. The real Karl Hyde is a secret who doesn't exist in the real world because he *can't*, people like him fill normal people with revulsion.

I rip into that one but the corners stay caught under the staples, and with a strange cry I try to pick the bits out of the wood but I realise I'll never be able to get rid of them completely, they'll be there for ever.

I shove the paper into my pocket and run on, but there are more. The chapel door. The swimming-pool gate. Hanging from bushes along the path. When I get to the car park Dad's ripping them out from under the windscreen wipers of every vehicle with huge sweat patches under his pits. As soon as he sees me he stands and points at me like a cannon.

'What have you done?' he says.

Like it's my fault. Like I was the one who put them all there.

'Someone's messing about,' I try to explain. 'Someone found out somehow and they're trying to wind me up.'

He's already marching to his office. I don't have any choice and slowly climb the steps behind him.

He closes the door. He clicks his fingers and I'm to sit in the old creaky chair on the wrong side of his desk. There's a pile of drawings done on art card on his desk and the one on the top has the name Chloe Pryor in one corner. Her again – I don't know who she is and yet there's something that seems to be tying us together.

Dad puts the balls of crumpled posters onto his desk in front of him, straightens his tie and sits. He gently folds his hands one over another. After eighteen years I've learned that when he acts calm he's not.

'I think it's about time we had a conversation,' he says. 'Don't you?'

I nod.

'Yes, Dad.'

'So?' He's waiting. 'Why did you do it?'

'The posters?' As I say it the image of Brad Marston bursts into my head as he grinned at me from his car yesterday. Was it him, tormenting me still after all these years? And why do I feel sure his little brother Gary has something to do with it too? 'That wasn't me, someone's just trying to—'

Dad slams his hand onto the desk. I jump in the chair.

'I don't mean these juvenile bits of paper, which I dare say my staff is probably whispering about already. It,' he says. '*It*. Why did you do *it*, you imbecile child?'

I swallow. He must mean about me with Dorfmann. Not anything else. Please don't let him know about anything else.

'I wasn't trying to be cruel.' It still doesn't make much sense to me, but I try. 'That is, I was – kind of – but I'm not. Cruel, I mean.'

If anything, that makes him worse. He comes forward until he can't come any nearer.

'I don't care about who you did or didn't hit. In fact I'm pleased about that part, at least now I can sleep better knowing you might actually have a spine. What I care about is that you were stupid enough to get caught, because now you'll have to explain to the academies how you managed to get thrown out of one of the best sporting schools in the country so close to your crucial exams, and poor discipline's exactly the sort of crap they won't tolerate, no matter how many runs you can score.'

He waits again for me to say something but I really don't know what he wants, so I act like he's making a bit of a joke and hope that he is.

He's not. The balls of ripped-up posters explode and fly into my face.

'You might think playing with your future is funny, but it's not. Not one bit. Do you have any idea of how many boys dream of having a talent like yours?'

They can have it, I think, but say nothing, which only pisses Dad off more.

'Do you have any idea how much I've invested in you? How much time and money I've spent on your future, which you now treat as nothing more than a joke? I can't abide waste, Karl, but what you've done goes beyond understanding. You've acted like a spoiled brat with no thought whatsoever to the consequence of your actions, and that's not the behaviour of a son of mine, so I'll ask you again: why did you do it? Tell me. Explain it in your own words, because despite what you think I really, really *want . . . to . . . know.*'

He shouts and hammers each of the last three words into the woodwork with his fist.

I look at him. He's waiting. He can wait like a rock, Dad can. My brain trips over itself as I try to find an answer he might accept, but there's nothing. Not one single thing.

And anyway, what's the point? Seriously. What's the bloody point?

'You want to know why I did it?' I say.

He rolls his eyes.

'Didn't I just say that?'

'I did it because I *wanted* to get expelled.' For a second I think he's going to hit me but to my surprise he pulls back. This is my chance. 'It's true, Dad. I wanted to do something so bad they wouldn't have any choice but to kick me out.'

'Don't be absurd. You did no such thing.'

'It's true, Dad. I did.'

He throws out a joyless laugh.

179

'Why would any sane person on God's green Earth do a thing like that? I don't have time for your obtuse attention-seeking, Karl, there's enough silliness going on in the school as it is and you're a headache I could do without.'

He means all the talk about the UFO, of course. I know, because he jabs his finger at the stack of drawings on his desk, and the top picture – the spacecraft, the dark figure in the trees, those strange, hypnotic almond-shaped eyes – suddenly sucks me in. What is it? I wonder. It's nothing more than a child's imagination on paper. An eight-year-old's figment in crayon. Any sane person would see that, so what is it about Chloe Pryor's picture that makes me unable to look away?

Then I see it.

'Go.'

Like Mr Jefferson said, her picture is different to all the others I've seen. Only a small thing, nothing much. In fact, most people probably wouldn't even notice it, but different all the same, because in her drawing she's drawn herself. Everyone else drew the one alien, or sometimes two, but she's added a small human figure that's clearly herself, and she's put her right in the shadow of the creature.

'Get out.'

I stand and begin to leave.

'But I'm telling you now, you will obey me. You will find an academy that will take you, however long it takes. You will attend and exert yourself. And you will fulfil your potential. That isn't up for debate.'

He whips me with his eyes. As far as he's concerned, the conversation's over, only I stay on the spot because that picture is still telling me something. I don't know Chloe Pryor, and she doesn't know me, but she seems to be telling me that it's OK to be different. While everyone else put the same story onto paper, she broke away and did her own version.

Suddenly the words are rising up my throat and gliding over my tongue and out past my lips like they've got a will of their own. And now they're just there, filling the air between us.

'I'm gay, Dad.'

He says nothing for so long that I tell him again.

'I'm gay. That's why I did it. I'm gay, and I had to get out of that school – for good, and at any cost – because I was terrified about what the other boys were going to do to me when they found out, and I didn't know what else to do. Only my plan didn't really work because I'm still scared. I don't know why people have to hate someone just because they're different, or because they don't understand what it's like to be them, but all I ever wanted was to hear that it'll be all right, and that it's OK to be the real me, not least because it's impossible to be someone I'm not so I shouldn't ever try.'

His mouth twitches.

He looks down at the floor like he's dropped a pen.

He pushes his chair back and stands.

Slowly, he walks around to my side.

The next thing I know is the front of his fist crunching into my nose. I hit the floor and see stars mixed in with the weave of the rug, and I taste blood in my throat.

I cough. Or perhaps it's a sob. Tears blur everything.

I hear him leave.

I'm so weak I just stay on the floor, right up until the point I hear the blast of a horn, and the grind of tyres doing their best to stop on dirt, and the sickening bump. And the *miles* of horrible silence afterwards that yell at me something far more terrible than what I've just been through has happened.

'Karl.'

I'm back in Dad's office now. There's blood on my shirt. I look at it as if it isn't real, but it is.

It is.

There's a strange ringing in my ears.

'Karl.'

I'm holding a child's floppy toy rabbit tightly in my hands, and there's blood on that too.

'Karl?'

I look up. Mrs Greenacre's face floats inches in front of me.

'Are you OK? You're OK now. Are you all right?'

'Dad . . .' I say. But Dad's not here. And despite everything he said, and what he did, I wish he was, because if nothing else he's good at forcing things back into order. I wish I hadn't told him anything and that everything was normal.

'He's kind of busy at the moment,' Mrs Greenacre tells me. 'My husband's gone to find your mum and she'll be here soon. Poor thing, you've had one hell of a shock. Would you like some tea? I'll get you some tea, that's what you need. Some nice, sweet tea.'

A cup of tea appears. She holds it, steaming under my nose. It smells surprisingly good but I can't let go of the rabbit and the ringing just won't stop.

'Is that for me?' I say.

She puts the tea down.

'Karl? You do remember what happened, don't you?'

I do. I just don't want to.

Mrs Greenacre sits next to me.

'Outside the school. Little Chloe Pryor ran out into the road and one of those *blasted* army trucks hit her and . . . and . . . you were the first to get to her. Do you remember? Your father is out there now. The ambulance will be here soon to take her away.'

Take her away.

Chloe Ravioli.

Liar Pryor, pants on fire.

'So she's all right? She's all right. Is she?'

Because maybe she is. Maybe . . . maybe it only *seemed* like she was . . .

Mrs Greenacre holds me.

'No, my dear, she's not all right at all. Oh Karl, this is such an awful day. Just awful. You poor thing. You poor, poor thing. Don't you worry, have a good cry. I'm here for you. Let it all out if you want.'

Only *she's* the one who's crying. Quietly, trembling against me. I can't. All I can do is listen to the damn ringing in my ears. Staring at Dad's desk. Remembering the moment before Dad hit me and Chloe's picture. Just an ordinary picture, of something childish and silly that most people don't even believe, but not to me.

I ease away from Mrs Greenacre and stand. I cross the study. More than Mrs Greenacre's sweet tea, or having Dad here, or turning back time, I want to see that picture again. I *need* to. I want to see the thing that proves Chloe was alive. Be near something that she created.

Only the picture's gone. Just . . . gone. The others are there but there's no sign of hers. It's gone, and Chloe has too.

Through the net curtains I see a cloud of children outside. Not playing, not singing, not doing anything. Ghoulish spectators milling in silence and looking to where I am even though I know they can't see in. And I see Gary Marston amongst them, and I swear to God he's grinning, just like his big brother used to each time he beat me up, and just like Robert Dorfmann did before he started telling the whole school about me, and somehow I know with absolute certainty that *Gary's* the one who took Chloe's picture from the desk, just like I know he had something to do with all those home-made posters about me. It's *his* fault. *He* did it. It was *him*.

I tear out from the office, into the sunshine, and launch myself onto Gary Marston until someone pulls me off.

The crickets are louder tonight. Mum and I sit together at the table.

'That poor girl,' she says at last.

She holds me. Then, a bit later, she says it again. 'That poor girl.'

I still have Chloe's toy rabbit with me. I know I should get it to her parents at some stage, and I will, but for tonight I want to keep it. I don't know why.

'Your father will be back soon,' Mum says.

A friendly warning? Or a hope that for once he'll do or say something to make things better? I can't tell. I'm too exhausted to think.

Dad comes in through the front door and we eye one another in a silence that screams. Then he slips past, careful not to get too near. He undoes his tie – World War Three could break out and Dad would keep his tie on until he got home – pours himself a whiskey and downs it like it's Mazowe orange juice. He pours himself another and sits with it while I just sit there and watch. His hands are trembling. His lips are trembling. His whole *body's* starting to shake. I've never seen him like this before.

'Dad? Are you OK?'

I wait. And wait.

'Don't worry,' he says at last. 'Everything will be all right.'

Words I've yearned to hear yet thought I never would. At last. My heart pounds.

But then he says, 'There'll be an inquest, but as long as we all stick to the same story, we'll get through unscathed. The main gate was locked. You got that? The gate was locked, because we lock it every day between drop-off and pick-up. I'll give Elijah a pay rise to help jog his memory, he won't be a problem. You know blacks, they'll swear the sky is green for a bit of extra cash.'

His laugh isn't even a laugh. Then he stops, but he still won't look me in the eye.

I shake my head.

'You're pathetic, Dad.'

First, shock, and he jumps to his feet to protest. Then, outrage, and he comes like he might hit me again. Mum yelps.

'Who are you to tell me anything?' He struggles to hold his voice level. There are tears in his eyes. 'Who are *you* . . . you vile . . . you disgusting . . . you . . .'

Only nothing he says or does can scare me, because I've stopped being frightened of him.

The early morning is so fresh and so clean that I wonder if it rained last night without me hearing. The sky is a faultless blue, pale and promising for a typical African day, but one that hasn't been created yet. Because none of them has been created yet, I think, as if only just realising that.

I carry my bag to the front and Mum is waiting for me in her dressing gown outside on the veranda. Has she been here all night?

'Where will you go?' she asks.

'I'm going to stay with Toby for a while in town. You remember Toby, don't you?'

'Of course.'

'You probably wouldn't recognise him though, last time we hooked up I think he was growing a goatee.'

'Little Toby Scott? But he had the face of a cherub.'

'Yeah. Well, by now he probably looks like Doogie Howser got kidnapped by *ZZ Top*.'

I laugh. She laughs too. It doesn't last long.

I put my bag on the floor and shuffle it with my feet. This is hard.

Mum holds herself.

'What are you going to do?'

'Right now, I don't know.'

'Are you scared?'

'Terrified.' I laugh nervously. 'But it's a good fear. I'll find something, and if that doesn't work I'll find something else. Whatever it is it'll be my decision, though.'

'Karl?'

'I can't stay, Mum, you know I can't. Please don't ask me to.'

She smiles sadly. She's really struggling now.

'I wasn't going to, your mind's made up. I just want you to know I'm sorry.'

'You didn't do anything.'

'And I should have done. I know why you did what you did to that horrible boy – why you really did it. I've always known somewhere deep down. I used to tell myself that it would be OK, because there's nothing wrong with being gay, and that you'd find your way through it or come to me if things ever got too much. The truth is, life gets too much for everyone at some stage, so what I should have done is talk to you about it. And listen to you. But I didn't, and I'm sorry.'

I don't know what to say.

'I also think what you're doing is right,' she says. 'I wish it wasn't, but it is.'

'But you're crying.'

'That's because it's hard being a parent. I thought I knew that, but no one could have prepared me for just how hard it is.'

'Thanks, Mum,' I say because that's what I think she's saying. 'For everything you've done for me.'

'I don't mean that, darling,' she says. 'I mean now. The letting go. This is the hardest bit.'

We hug.

'Promise me one thing, Karl.'

'I'm not going far, Mum, it's not like I'm not going to see you.'

'Promise me you won't hold onto these feelings about your father. He has enough anger inside to last ten lifetimes and I don't want you to have to endure the same sentence. Don't waste the one life you have fighting hate, because hate will always win. Trust me, it's not worth it.'

We let go.

'Sure, Mum. For you.'

'No. Do it for you.'

'You OK?' Toby says as I climb in. 'You look like crap.'

He notices Chloe's toy rabbit in my hand.

'I have to deliver it to someone on the way,' I tell him. He doesn't ask who, he's already guessed. 'Can we just go?'

'Sure,' he says.

He crunches the car into gear, and as we drive I look back at the house I grew up in, and the only home I've ever known, until it vanishes behind the dust. And I think, Letting go *is* hard, even though this is what I want to do. What I need.

We move down through the school, past the car park, out the main gate and on to the road. At this time of the morning I expected it to be clear, but as we pick up speed I see another car parked on the verge, very near to where the army truck that hit Chloe sits in shame with one skewed wheel still stuck in the ditch. It's a grey Peugeot estate. There's a man nearby, staring at the place on the ground where the dirt is stained with brown red.

We roll slowly past. He doesn't move. I don't think he knows we're there. And we've got the windows right up but we can still hear the unbearable sound of a grown man crying.

'Who's the guy?' Toby asks.

'Mr Stamps,' I tell him. 'One of the parents.'

'Jesus Christ. *Serious?* Man, no wonder he's suffering.'

'I don't mean one of Chloe's parents. Another girl's.'

'Oh. But he's seriously cut up.'

'He helps around the school. He gets on great with all the kids, and they all love him.'

'Jesus.' Toby glances into the rearview mirror and squirms again. Grief is uncomfortable at any distance. 'Poor guy, he looks in really bad shape.'

'Chloe was one of his Lift Clubbers too, apparently.'

'Jeez. He's a complete mess.'

And I think, He is.

Then I turn to face the road ahead.

'It was a silver thing that flew past really slowly. At first all I saw was a flash that went like that, then I saw a shiny thing on the top. It landed in the trees.'

'Did you see this man you drew?'

'Yes, I saw him. But it wasn't a man.'

'And he looked like this?'

'Yes.'

'The eyes were pointed as they came into the centre?'

'Yes. And they were all black, there was no white in them.'

'And was he near the craft?'

'Yes, but then he came towards me.'

'Did he look at you?'

'Yes. It made me want to run away only I couldn't.'

'One of the other students said he thought it could have been someone from the workers' village. Was it?'

'No.'

'Are you sure?'

'I'm sure. It wasn't a person.'

'Do you think he was anyone from around here?'

'No.'

'From somewhere else, then? Another country in the world?'

'No.'

'Where do you think he was from?'

'Up there.'

'And what do you think his reasons for visiting Earth might have been?'

'It was about something that was going to happen.'

'He told you this?'

'Yes. And it's true, isn't it? A bad thing has happened. A terrible thing.'

'Yes, it has. But are you only saying all this in hindsight?'

'What's hindsight?'

'It's when we can say something about the past because of what we know now, in the present.'

'No. They told us but we didn't listen.'

SIXPENCE

we have many types of *mbira*, and this *mbira* we name *madan-danda*. it is special because it calls the ancestors.

this is what Baba Elijah sayed.

he sayed, the music is very very important. he sayed, it is very very important because it is the music that summons the spirits. we do not go straight to God, we have to go through our ancestors because they are the ones who died and are nearest to God. we are not nearer to God. we are the living ones.

and i was thinking, i do not care about calling the ancestors. i do not care about talking to God. i care only about the singing. i care only about the dancing. and so i care about the music that *mbira* makes.

usually i steal because it is my father who wants something. but this – this *mbira* – i wanted it for me, so i stole it from Baba Elijah when he was not looking, easy as a pie.

but when the spirits came down from the sky they were bad. and it was me that summoned them.

mbira is made of very many teeth that are metal, and they are attached to wood from a tree that bleeds blood when it is cut. some teeth are long-big and some teeth are short-small, and when Baba Elijah has *mbira* in his hands it is like magic fills the air because the music that comes is from heaven.

when i plucked the metal teeth with my fingers the music was not good and not smooth and the sound was like *plonk* and *plonk* and *plink* and it cut the air like broken glass. i am not good *mbira* player, so the spirits i called cannot be good spirits. they are the bad spirits. they are *Tokoloshes*.

so now i am scared and i do not play it any more.

the dogs are barking outside. sometimes they bark because they fight, and sometimes they fight because men in the village like my father make them, because the men are drunk and they want to bet for money for beer. but now they are barking because someone is coming and the person that is coming is running a stick across our house and it makes a noise *tack-a-tack-a-tack-a-tack* across the bumpy metal walls.

i wrap the *mbira* in the old towel quick-quick and i put it into the hole under my bed and pull the earth over with my hand to hide it but the light in the room goes dark and someone is standing in the door. the mist and the morning sun are behind him and bright so i cannot see his face and he is black as shadow, just like the spirits who came from the sky, so i think it is one of the *Tokoloshes* again.

mwana!

but it is not a *Tokoloshe*, it is my father who is here. it is Dhedhi.

mwana means baby. he calls me this always because he thinks i am a baby still. he is wearing the clothes he was wearing last night. he wears this green jacket all of the time, every day and every night. it is the jacket he used to fight in during the war and he wears it still even though the war ended long time ago.

what are you doing, *mwana*?

he sees how dusty my hands are. i must speak quickly or he will know the truth because Dhedhi can see a lie like he sees lost coins in the dirt.

i say to him, i am looking for a thing that i have lost.

but he does not believe this either and he pushes me out of the way and he looks under the bed to find the *mbira*. i think he will be angry. he will not be angry because i stole it, he will be angry because i stole it and i did not give it to him so that he may sell it for money for beer.

Dhedhi looks at it. once upon a time he used to make music, and when his fingers touch the keys of the *mbira* i think maybe he will play and he will be happy again like he was then, and the bad spirits i called will hear the good music and leave. but when he makes just one note he throws the *mbira* into the corner like it is a snake that has bitten him and one of the keys is falling to the floor because it is broken.

this is not music, he says.

no, Dhedhi? i say.

no, he says. it is not.

Dhedhi did not come home last night. he cannot stand in a straight line and i smell beer coming from him even when he is not talking. i hope he will leave me now and sleep but he does not. he is pulling his arm from his jacket and now i am more scared because he is showing me the skin there that is pink because it is where the bullets went into him when the white men shot him in the war. he takes me by the hair on my head so that i am near him and i scream a little bit and he is putting my face next to the pink skin.

do you think you know music better than i know it, *mwana*? he says.

no Dhedhi, i say.

do you think it is right to bring the music like this into my house?

no Dhedhi, i do not.

i am the one who knows music. during the struggle i am the one that took music from corner to corner in the whole country, and i am the one who gave music to the freedom fighters in the bush because i knew we were conquering and that the colonisers were definitely losing.

yes, Dhedhi.

i was not afraid in the war, i did not hide.

and then Dhedhi sings the song that i have heard so very many times from him.

they came from britain,
from america and france
to take our land.
let us fight them now.

Dhedhi is pushing his teeth into my ear and his teeth are biting me hard, and soon my arm will break like a stick in his hand. but if i ask him to stop he will say it is because i am on the side of the white man and that i want to be their slave.

forward with war! Dhedhi sings.

so i have to sing, forward with war!

down with the white man, he sings more.

his hand hurts me even more.

down with the white man, i sing back to him.

i cannot hear you.

down with the white man!

now at very long last he releases me and pushes me and i

fall back onto my bed and my head hits the wall with a loud noise.

good, *mwana*, he says. very good. you see how my music is better than your silly spirit music?

yes, Dhedhi.

i want to leave now but he says, come with me, *mwana*.

why? i say. but i know this smile on his face, so i know why.

i have seen a nice watch, he says, and i would like it. you must get it for me.

Dhedhi says it is OK to steal from the white man because they stole from us. the *murungus* took our land, our food, our cattle, our gold. the animals that cross the land. our jobs. our homes. the rain. the moon, the stars. everything. the *murungus* took it. but now the power belongs to us, not them, so we must take it all back.

we walk for some minutes. then Dhedhi stops and sits low in the grass. he pulls me hard so that i am sitting too and we are looking at the gate to the school now. the shadows are long but when they are short it will be hot.

why are we here, Dhedhi? i say.

he looks at me with angriness that makes me want to run away.

do you not listen to me? i would like a nice watch. wait and i will show it to you.

so we wait, and soon we hear the sound of feet running along the road and we hide more into the grass. then there is a boy who is coming to the school gates who is older than me and he stops with big breathing and he looks at the time closely on his wrist. he carries a bag on his back that says the word *NIKE*.

there, Dhedhi says and he is licking his lips. do you see? it is a very fine watch, i think.

indeed the watch is very fine. i have not seen a watch like it. it is black and big and it sings. it has many many buttons that i do not know how they work, but they give the screen blue light when the boy asks it for the time and it is very very bright so that i can see it even in the day.

the boy wipes sweat from his head and runs into the school. Dhedhi stands and i am standing too.

this is the watch i would like, he says.

i do not tell him anything so Dhedhi hits me on the head.

do you not think i should have that nice watch?

but Dhedhi, i say. it is not a *murungu* watch. he is an african boy, not a white boy.

Dhedhi hits me again.

is he rich? he says.

i do not know, i say.

does he not have fine clothes and a fine watch? and is he not a pupil in this very fine school?

yes, Dhedhi.

then he is rich. and if his father is rich then he must be working for a *murungu*. so it is still OK to steal from him.

i do not understand but i am afraid to say so, because now Dhedhi's hand is biting me on the back of the leg and it is stinging so much that i jump into the air.

we cannot steal what already belongs to us, he says. do you want the *murungus* to keep what they have taken? the colonisers came to our land, pretending only to hunt, but they did not go. we have defeated them now. do you think we should remain their slaves? do you think that it is right that they imprison us?

no, Dhedhi, i say quickly.

then go and get me my watch.

he pushes me out.

and hurry! bring it to me before the end of the day.

i know this boy with the nice watch. i have seen him before. every day he is running to school carrying the bag on his back that says the word *NIKE*. he has fine clothes but i do not ever see his mother or his father driving him in a car so i wonder if they are poor. maybe Dhedhi is wrong, and he is not rich. he does not ever arrive to school with any of the other children, he is always on his own, and always he has many rivers running down his face. even when he is not running he has rivers on his face that i think must be tears from crying.

he arrives to school. he washes in the pavilion. he dresses in his school clothes and puts the clothes that he was using to run into the *NIKE* bag with his watch. every day it is the same.

today it is the same.

so when it is later and the children are eating the lunch i can walk to the back of the classrooms and i can pull myself up quickly and climb in. cool as a cucumber. i find the watch. it is right at the top of the bag and i take it and put it into my good pocket without the holes. the boy has many others of things that i know Dhedhi would like, he has the *NIKE* shoes and the *NIKE* shirt and the *NIKE* shorts, but i do not take these because even if his father does work for a *murungu* i do not think it is fair. i do not want to take the watch either but Dhedhi will hurt me if i do not.

i want to leave by the way i came in but i hear a whistling outside the window, and it is Baba Elijah digging the earth at the back of the classrooms. maybe i can wait, but also i know that this is the classroom that belongs to the teacher with the scar on his face who i do not like, so i leave through the door.

today there were four *murungus* who came to the school who are from america. i know this because i heard their voices when they were walking to the rocks with young mastah Hyde at the breaktime, and they were looking out to the trees where i saw the *Tokoloshes* come down from the sky. now i see the young american *murungu* again with the fire in her hair coming towards me on the grass, and she sees me too.

hey! she shouts.

and i think, maybe the girl knows it was me that called the bad spirits here, and that is why she comes after me now. so i run.

come back! she shouts some more.

i do not. i run quick-quick away from the classroom as fast as i can go. but then i see another teacher ahead, so i am running from the path and into the chapel where it is cool and quiet. i will hide in here until they have all gone. it is safe in here.

while i am waiting i take the watch from my pocket. maybe i should leave the watch here, i think. i do not care what Dhedhi says, it was wrong to take it so i will leave it here, and then i will run away to somewhere i will always be safe, because i do not want to steal for Dhedhi any longer. but where? where can i go?

i press a button. the watch makes a noise and shines so blue and so bright that i drop it to the floor. further down the chapel the door is opening.

i pick up the watch again and i hide deep-deep into the corner, because i think it is the spirits who have come again, but it is only a white girl from the school who is coming. she has a toy rabbit in her hands. i think she must be coming here to pray to God because she is going over there to the big cross at the end and i see she has left something behind on the bench. it is a small toy made of plastic with hair the colour of fire, like the american girl i have just seen outside, but when i pick it up and hold it in my hand it looks at me with eyes that are black as night. and i am sure it is telling me something . . . like something bad is going to happen . . . just like the *Tokoloshes* did when they came.

the girl hears me cry out and sees me. i hide the plastic creature into my pocket next to the watch. i expect she will tell me to leave, because everybody tells me to leave when they see me – everyone except the american girl who just shouted at me to come back. only like the american girl this girl does not tell me to go away either, so then i wonder, why is she here? is she hiding, like me? maybe she is hiding from her teachers. or maybe she is hiding from the *Tokoloshes*.

when she speaks to me she says, i am not hiding, i was praying. are *you* hiding?

Baba Elijah tells me that sometimes praying and hiding are the same thing because a church is a place of safety, and Baba Elijah is very wise because he is old.

i say, yes, i am hiding.

well, you don't have to hide from me, she says. i won't get you into trouble.

i smile at her. no one has ever said this thing to me before.

it is someone else that i am hiding from, i tell her.

from the star people? she says.

so she *is* hiding from the bad spirits. she saw them come from the sky too.

but i am afraid to even think about the *Tokoloshes* because they may hear my thoughts and find me again.

so i tell her, no.

but you do believe they're real, don't you?

no.

neither do i, she says. and they've gone now anyway. i was actually hiding from meg and stamps.

what is this *meg and stamps*? i say.

megan stamps, she says. she was my friend but she's not any more. she's mean. her daddy does lift club for us on tuesdays and thursdays and one time he . . . he . . . he let me sit in the front on my way home and i think the reason she hates me now is . . .

i do not understand, but i do know she is telling me a truth because she is seeming so sad, so when she asks me, why are you hiding then? i must tell her the truth also.

because i have been *ve-ry* very bad, i say, because i have stolen things.

like what?

like this, i say, and i take her plastic creature with the orange hair from my pocket to give to her back. i think she will be angry.

but she is not.

that's OK, she says. i don't mind really, you can keep it.

i say, no. i cannot.

but she says, it's OK. i want you to have it. besides, i have another orange one at home. what's your name?

i am Sixpence Chaparadza, i tell her.

hello, Sixpence Chaparadza. i am Chloe Pryor.

Chlo-weeee?

she laughs a little bit.

no, not Chlo-*weeee*, she says. because that sounds sort of rude. just Chloe.

she puts her other little toy people on the bench, with yellow hair, and green hair, and purple hair – she has so many – and writes the letters in dust on the floor.

there, she says. like that. Chloe. see?

i do see, but now i am afraid that Chloe will find out that i am a thief, because i know the letters of her name. i have seen them before, written in a hat i found one day before the *Tokoloshes* came up near the trees. and in a cardigan. and in some shoes. i found them all just lying there on the ground. there was no one around but i know i should not have taken them because they were not mine, because they all had this *CHLOE* written on them, but i did take them. and now she is giving me her toy as a gift . . .?

and Sixpence?

yes, Chloe?

hakuna matata.

these are not words that i know.

what does this mean? i say.

it means, no worries for the rest of your days, she says. it can be our own special thing. a secret. you know, to help us when we're scared. that's what friends do.

are we friends?

of course we are, that's why i gave you my orange troll. and i don't have any friends at the moment so you can be my best friend, if you like.

and i don't have any friends either, so i tell her, yes, i would like that very much.

i am scared all the time, but i do not say this *hakuna matata* as i run to the madondo bottle store. i think maybe i should, because when i get there Dhedhi is waiting outside with very serious lines on his face. he is sitting in the shade because it is very hot already and he has a drink of chibuku beer that is almost empty. i smell it from where i am standing. a man is sitting with him who wears the uniform of a policeman and i wonder if Dhedhi is in trouble, or if i am in trouble, but the policeman is drinking chibuku too.

iwe!

Dhedhi moves his arm like he is shooing flies and drink spills onto his shirt. he is annoyed. he is also drunk. he is smiling at me but it is a smile that shows only teeth and cruelty, it does not have happiness in it.

this is my son, Dhedhi says to the policeman friend. my only son. look at him. i know i must be a bad man because truly i have made the spirits angry, because they have given me . . . *this.*

the policeman and Dhedhi laugh together.

Dhedhi stands.

this child, who thinks he knows music better than me, he says. dance, *mwana.* if you know music so well, dance for us now.

i do not move.

you say you love the music, so dance, he says. *dance!*

but even though there is no music there is also no joking in his voice, so i dance.

faster, he says, clapping his hands. *faster.*

i go faster.

the laughter is louder and the clapping is faster, so i must go faster too.

soon he is tired and i am glad.

he stands, waiting for me to give him the watch, so i take it to him. he looks at it like it is treasure, drinking more chibuku and licking his lips but some of it is falling over his chin.

i am right, *mwana*, this watch is very fine, he says. *ve-ry* very fine, because now i can see when you are late.

he raises his hand to me so that i jump. he laughs once more again.

did you know, my little *mwana* here thinks the spirits come to see him? he tells his friend. i hear him talk in his sleep. he thinks the *Tokoloshes* come to his room.

he puts his new watch onto his wrist.

but today it is me the spirits have come to see, and today they like me very much, because look at what fell from the sky.

then he holds me with unkind fingers.

and who knows? maybe tomorrow they will come again, and maybe they will bring me a . . . a *radio*. a nice radio, to listen to the music while we drink, and you shall dance for us some more. yes, that is what they shall bring me. do you not think, *mwana*? a *fine* radio. now *go!*

the other children in the village are playing football in the dry dirt. i wish i could play football with them but i cannot, because they do not let me. they do not like me because they all know i steal, so i must watch them running and scoring goals and pretending to be like the David Beck-ham and the Ryan Giggs.

how much i would like to play with them too. instead, they shout at me to leave, so i leave.

it is true what Dhedhi told his policeman friend, i see the spirits every night. but it is not in my dreams that i see them. i *see* them, just like the ones in the ship that landed in the trees. they come into my room – as real as the toy with orange hair that Chloe gave me, and as real as her clothes i found and stole in order for Dhedhi to sell – because i am bad. i took the *mbira* from Baba Elijah, i played the notes in a bad way, and now they are here.

i wish these bad spirits would not keep coming, but they do, because i am bad too.

and i think, but if i am good, will they go?

if i return the *mbira* to Baba Elijah, and if i return the watch to the boy, and if i return the stolen things to all the other children, and if i never steal again, will the bad spirits not see that really i am a kind person and leave me alone?

i think they will. i think that this can happen. happy as a Larry!

then i think, but Dhedhi is still wearing the watch, so how can i return it to the boy?

and i think, Dhedhi took Baba Elijah's *mbira* today for money so it is gone for ever, and i do not know where all the many other things i have stolen are now so i cannot give them back either. if i am to keep the *Tokoloshes* from coming to me in the night i must do something that is good . . . but what?

i feel the toy Chloe gave to me today like it is burning in my pocket. i remove and hold it up, and its hair is as orange as the late afternoon sun – before today i would not believe such hair could ever be real but then i saw that american girl who came after me, and her hair was as orange as this.

no one has ever given me anything before, so this toy makes me very happy because truly Chloe is my friend, the best friend i have ever had. then i think, but what kind of friend am i to her in return? because i have stolen from Chloe too – her hat and her cardigan and her shoes, even though i did not know they were hers at the time – and this makes me very sad.

i put the toy with the orange hair back into my pocket.

that is when i have my good idea.

Dhedhi has not come back to the house but he will come for his supper soon so i go quick-quick back outside and to the place where the school puts its bags of rubbish. i hunt to find many pieces of wire and bottle tops and tins of nugget shoeshine polish, and with them i make a fine car. Number One! i run with it and the wheels all turn smooth-smooth, and the steering is mushi-mushi. but i did not make it for me, this car, because that would not a good thing to do. tomorrow i will give this car to Chloe because she gave me her toy so i shall give her a toy too. i hope she will like it and i hope it will make her happy as she made me, because that will be the *good* thing to do that will make the bad spirits go away.

the sun is disappearing down, and when i get back home once more again it is so dark i cannot see my feet. Dhedhi is home so i must make his sadza and gravy, and when he is eating inside i sit outside even though it is cold, and the sky is bigger than i have ever seen it before. so big. and it is like the stars are all eyes and they are watching me, just watching. they are the spirits there and they are waiting and watching what i am doing.

a brown castle lager bottle comes out of the house. it is

flying, and it hits me in the foot. then it is Dhedhi who is coming.

mwana! he says. i have no beer. get more beer, he says.

yes, Dhedhi, i say.

i put the food that i have not eaten onto the ground and go inside. he gives me some coins from his pocket, but when i try to leave he grabs my wrist.

and while you are fetching me beer, he says, you can fetch me the fine radio i would like. eh, *mwana*? i have seen mad-em Hyde with a radio i would like very much. it is very very dark, she will not see you, it is a good time to get me this thing.

but Dhedhi, i say.

you cannot steal what has been taken from you, he says. remember this.

but no one has taken a radio from us, i say, we have never had a radio before.

when he squeezes his fingers together, Dhedhi is able to fit his hands right around my neck.

mad-em Hyde works in the tuck shop, and also she works in the library, and that is where she keeps her radio. i have seen it many times before.

it is late and the gate into the school is locked now, but i know a place where the trees on this side and the trees on that other side are very very close. i wait for a line of army trucks to drive by and then i climb over. my feet find the path and i am running to the main part of the school.

it is dark everywhere, and very very quiet when the children and the teachers are not present. i like it like this because it is much better to get into the places where i should not be. the library is easy. i do not think headmaster Hyde believes his books are valuable because the windows do not close well and i am inside.

i cannot see properly and i must put on the electricity. i search in the cupboard where mad-em Hyde puts the library cards and the books that have pages that must be fixed, but i find no radio. i will have to go home without it, so i had better get some extra beers for Dhedhi to make him happy, but first i shall stay in the library for a while because i like it here, it smells full of clever paper. i wish i was clever because then i could get a job and leave Dhedhi.

sticking out from a shelf i find a book with a picture of the stars on the front that some student has not put away properly. i wonder if it will show me where the spirits are coming from, so i take it out and put it on the table, and as i turn the pages they are full of pictures that show me the stars and the planets and the space. there is a picture of the world, and i see that the world where we live is big because there are many many many kilometres around it, more than there are from here to the madondo bottle store. and yet it is not big because next to the sun the world is like an ant next to a football, so it is the sun that is big.

and yet the sun is not big either because on the next page there is a picture of another sun that makes our sun look like a football on the very edge of the rufaro stadium, so that *other* sun is big.

and yet it is not big, because there is a picture that shows me all the suns are a part of many many many many suns that live together in a place that is a whirlpool of stars, and our world lives in this place also but it is so small in the whirlpool you cannot see it.

so the whirlpool of stars is big.

and yet it is not big.

because there are many many many many *many* of these whirlpools of stars in the universe of space, so many that they do not end. the space goes on for ever and they are in it.

is this where the spirits live? amongst all these stars that are so very far away? there are so very many, so there must be so very many spirits, and how can i make these so many spirits stay away?

a sound is coming. there is a *something* outside.

i move to switch off the electricity, then i hide back into the corner and i am sitting with my back against the books and hoping the *something* will just go away because perhaps it is headmaster Hyde. but the thing has heavy feet that is making a scrape sound that is not like a person, so now i am scared that it is the *Tokoloshe*. it has found me. i can hear it moving behind the wall very slowly so it knows i am here. it stops. everything is quiet, but i know it is still out there so i close my eyes and i think of my true friend. i think of Chloe. i know she would help me, and i know what she would tell me to do.

hakuna matata, she would say. *no worries for the rest of your days.*

so i say it too.

hakuna matata.

the moving sound moves away. it has gone. i do not hear any sound at all. i think it is safe to go home now and i start to move.

but it is not safe.

the *Tokoloshe* bumps against the window that is right above me. it has gone *around.* i lift my head and i see the stars outside, and i see the *Tokoloshe* as it blocks the stars with the shape of a head, and a neck, and hands, and it is making breathing clouds against the glass that come and go, come and go.

i run to the shelves where i came in, and before i climb i turn and see the *Tokoloshe* standing at the window still in the dark. there is a bright light that comes from it and the light is sniffing the floor like a dog, and i know that if that light finds me i will be dead.

hakuna matata. hakuna matata. hakuna matata.

no worries. for the rest of my days. Chloe told me this.

hakuna matata.

and then . . . there . . . on mad-em Hyde's desk. it is the *mbira* that belongs to Baba Elijah. today Dhedhi took it to sell for money, and yet now it is here on the desk in front of me. was it there before? i did not see it, but maybe i did not see it because i was looking for the radio.

i take it in my hands and it is very very cold, like it has been in ice. one metal tooth was broken because Dhedhi threw it and broke it but now it is fixed again. i hear a whisper and i realise it is the *mbira* talking to me. it is waiting for me to play it again. it wants me to play it like i played it before, because if i do i will call many more of the bad spirits to come from all those many places in the universe.

i drop the *mbira*.

when i climb the shelves again it is like there is a lion at my feet and soon i am right at the very top, and i am pushing through the window.

i jump onto the grass.

and a hand falls on me to hold me in place. the eyes are so close they are all i can see.

gotcha this time, says a voice.

but it is an american voice. it is the american girl with the orange hair, it is not one of the spirits after all.

she says, what are you up to, little fella? kinda late to be returning your library books, isn't it?

and she smiles, because she has caught me now. she has caught the thief and soon everyone will know what i have done.

i pull away so that i am free.

hold your horses, cowboy, i only want to ask you something, she says, even though i am not a cowboy, i am a thief. she does not want to ask me anything. she does not even know me.

i do not stop running until i am home, like the bat out of the hell.

when i am home i see Dhedhi is asleep with a bottle in his arms.

he does not hear me come, and he does not move when i take the watch from his arm. tomorrow i will give it back to the boy, and tomorrow i will give Chloe her present. i must do these good things, because only then the *Tokoloshe* will leave me alone. i do not want to hide any more.

hey! what the hell are you looking at?

in the morning a white boy is calling to me as soon as i walk through the school gate. he is carrying his school bag that i see his name on, and each letter has been made many times with an angry pen. i have seen this name on something i have stolen.

i tell him i am not doing anything, but now the boy is coming forward and he is putting his foot on the car that i have made specially for Chloe, and he does not stop until the car is flat and broken, and when he has finished he gives me the smile of a fat man who has eaten the starving man's food.

there, he says. now bugger off.

does he know i have stolen from him? i think maybe he does. or is it because Dhedhi is right, and this is really how cruel all the white people are?

when he walks away none of the teachers shout at him for what he has done because they are not watching, just as they were not watching on the day the spaceship landed. they did not see it. they will not believe me if i tell them what this boy did, as they do not believe about the bad spirits coming from the sky. only the american girl with the orange hair has seen what he did, from way over there by the classrooms, and she calls me over with her hand. but she does not care about me, only that i am a thief.

i pick the broken car from the ground and move so she cannot see me. i try to fix the car but when i do the tins that are for the wheels fall off. i wipe tears from my eyes, and when i look again i am surprised to see Baba Elijah standing in front of me.

he says to me, the consequences of bad behaviour are not immediate, but they will come.

so i say, i am glad, Baba Elijah, because that boy should not have done that to me.

i am not talking about that boy, he says. i am talking about you. i know that you have been stealing, Sixpence.

i cannot find words to say.

he says, come, let us sit in the shade to talk. no african person is good without the shade of a tree.

Baba Elijah is not my father. Dhedhi is my father, but

everyone in the village calls Baba Elijah *baba* because he is old and he knows many things because he has worked at the school for many many years. i follow him and we sit on a large rock. he has long fingers and they move slow, and they start to take the wires of my toy car apart.

he says, so.

then he is waiting, but i say nothing.

he says, so what is it that you have taken this time? he says. i saw you yesterday. i saw you here in the school, and i saw you climbing into that window and that classroom. it was to steal again, yes?

yes, Baba, i say. it was this watch.

i show him the watch from my pocket but he does not take it, he just looks.

and is it for your dhedhi that you are stealing this?

yes, Baba.

why?

because Dhedhi sayed he needs a watch.

but when i say this thing Baba Elijah looks at me with sadness in his eyes, and sadness is worse than any angryness.

Dhedhi says it is OK to steal from the *murungus*, i tell him. the white man stole everything from us, it is not stealing if it is already ours, i say.

i do not tell him it was from an african boy that i stole this watch.

and tell me, Sixpence, what do all your friends say about this? do they think it is good? he says. you do have friends, do you not?

of course, Baba, i say. i have many.

but you are young, and yet here you are telling your problems to an old man, Baba Elijah says.

214

i want to say, i have Chloe, she is my friend. but he is pulling more wires from my car so i am thinking that soon my car will not be here and i will not have anything to give to her.

he makes a song under his breath. it is a sweet sound. i look at him with great surprise.

you sing, Baba, i say. you sing very well, i did not know. how do you sing so well and i did not know?

he says, when you are musician, the wind is always carrying notes and you just have to listen. i am very much happy about that.

did you sing in the war?

yes. and sometimes i would sing with your dhedhi, he says, and now i am so very surprised that i do not know what can i say because this is like a different Baba Elijah.

he says, during the struggle, we used to sing all over the country to the freedom fighters in the bush, because music did a very vital role. our songs gave us strength, like this: *let's march together, let's push together.*

Baba is pulling a last nugget shoeshine tin away, and now there are no wheels on my car. the *Tokoloshes* will come back for me tonight for sure.

Baba says, when you are not free you cannot think of anything else other than your freedom. but, when the war was over and we attained our independence, we had to make a different direction. we used to advise people for war, but when the struggle was over our songs had to change.

now Baba turns the car upside over, but even though he is old his hands are strong because he is pulling the wires from one another and it is like the car is breathing again.

we are a musical nation, and our music is very different from overseas music. overseas music is to entertain, but our music teaches people how to behave. our songs are revealing the bad from the good, so after the war we needed to show we are now a team, to show that those who had been enemies now are friends and that we flow together like water and river. but your dhedhi did not want to change the songs to songs of peace, he still wanted to sing the songs of war.

Baba points to his heart.

he says, you see, the struggle is not just the fight for freedom with guns and bullets. it is also here, inside. but this is not something that your dhedhi understands.

but i am not like Dhedhi, i say. and i do not want to be like him.

then i am very much happy about this also, he says.

i am watching as Baba Elijah is replacing the wheels, and my car is a car again.

but Baba Elijah? i say.

yes?

if your music was to teach the people what to do, why did you not change the words to your songs at the beginning of the war? if you changed the words at the beginning to say that people should not fight then surely we would not have war.

Baba Elijah looks at me.

if there was no sun, would we have eyes? he says. if there was no wind, would the trees grow strong roots into the ground?

i look at him. i say, i do not understand.

Baba Elijah turns to the sky.

a teacher cannot teach without pupils, he says. you cannot feel happy without first being sad. you cannot have peace without the war. you cannot have one without the other. no one thing exists on its own, or acts by itself. everything is connected, from here to the stars. this is what i am saying.

he passes me my car made of wires once more. it is like when i made it. no, it is better than when i made it.

now this is fixed, he says.

he stands and is starting to leave.

Baba?

yes?

the *mbira* you showed to me.

do you know where it is, Sixpence?

i do not say anything at first.

then i tell him, no.

does he know that i do know where it is? does he know that i am lying?

then what about the *mbira*? he says.

you sayed it calls the ancestors.

it does.

so if someone plays it, the ancestors will come?

they will. spirits to give us wisdom and advice.

but what if someone plays *mbira* in a bad way? will only bad spirits come?

Baba Elijah smiles like he is finding this funny.

have you seen the spirits? he asks me.

i do not answer.

there are bad spirits, yes, he tells me. we call them *mashave*. they are spirits who make trouble because they were not buried in the right way when they died. you must take care with these.

i feel sickness in the very bottom of my stomach.

but how will i know the bad spirits from the good spirits? i say. will they tell me?

bad spirits will always tell you they are good to trick you, he says.

then how will i know if they are bad? i say.

217

Baba Elijah pulls the air into his body and it makes his old bones stronger, like he did with my car. he is a young man again.

problems come when we ask the right question in the wrong way, he says.

i do not know what this means. he is wise, but sometimes wise words make no sense.

Baba, i do not understand, i say.

and he says, Sixpence, if you are worried about calling the bad spirits here by mistake, then i am telling you that this is not possible to do.

i am surprised and happy about this.

i say, no?

he says, no, you cannot call the bad spirits. i know this because they are already here. they are everywhere, all around.

after a long moment i say to him, then who did i see come out of the ship that came down from the sky?

Baba Elijah just touches my head, like that is an answer. like he does not believe i even saw the ship.

he stands. he looks over to the classrooms and says, i think the american girl is still waiting for you. why do you not go to her?

i stay sitting on the rock.

because she saw me take the watch, i say. she knows who i am.

really? well, i am thinking we are none of us who other people think we are, as i am not who you thought. and she is not even from here, she cannot know you at all, so why do you not tell her who you are?

but who am i? i ask.

he looks at me.

you are Sixpence Chaparadza, of course, he says.

then he turns to leave. when he has gone, i see the american girl has gone too. i stand and walk the other way to look for the only friend i have instead.

i find Chloe in the chapel again, hiding. she is not at all happy, crying and wiping her nose on her arm.

i offer her the present i made and i tell her, *hakuna matata.*

she does not answer, so i say, it means no worries.

i know what it means, she says. i'm the one who told you it.

no worries for days, i say.

for the rest of your days, stupid, she says.

i feel she does not like me any more. i thought she was my friend. my best friend. i brought her the car.

but you have worries? i say.

loads, she says.

i made you this, i say. a boy tried to break it but it is fixed again – Number One! – but Baba says i should not be angry with the boy who broke it because *chisi hachiyeri musi wacharimwa.*

what?

it is meaning, *the consequences of bad behaviour are not immediate, but they will come,* i tell her. but when i say this Chloe is making many more tears that are flowing down her face.

is that true? she says.

it is, i say.

when? if someone is bad behaviouring, when will the consequences come? soon?

i cannot give the answer to this because i did not ask Baba.
maybe soon, i say.

i hope so, she says.

why do you say this thing? i ask her, but Chloe is hiding her face behind her knees.

so i ask, why are you here, my friend?

i told my mummy i didn't want to come to school today but she made me, she says.

but why are you *here*? in the chapel again?

i wish now i hadn't done that silly drawing, she says.

what drawing? i say, because there is no drawing here that i can see. then i ask her, are you here because you are scared?

yes.

of the big ship that came from the sky?

yes.

so you did see them?

yes.

but you must not be scared, i say. they are not the bad spirits.

how do you know?

because Baba told me, i say. he says the bad spirits are already here.

i am starting to think she will not answer and she will call me stupid again.

then she says, he wants to hurt me.

my friend Chloe starts to cry again, and i hold her by the hand. could Baba Elijah be wrong?

i say, are you sure?

yes.

did he tell this to you?

no, but . . .

then how do you know? how does he want to hurt you?

she moves like she is sitting on stones.

i don't know, she says.

Baba says problems come when we ask the right question in the wrong way, i tell her.

she makes a cross face at me.

that's silly, she says. it doesn't even make sense. who is this Baba?

she is right, it does not. it made much more sense when Baba sayed it.

i try to remember what else he told me.

if there was no sun, would we have eyes? i say.

that's silly too.

if there was no wind, would the trees grow strong roots into the ground?

stop it. i thought you were my friend.

a teacher cannot teach without pupils, and you cannot feel happy without first being sad.

you're being mean, she says.

why does she say this? i am only wanting to be her friend.

the spirits who came on the ship do not want to hurt you, Chloe, i tell her. maybe they want to help.

help?

from the struggle.

the what?

the struggle. the thing that is inside you and inside all of us.

i point to my heart and i say, so you see, you do not need to be afraid.

i am making her cry fresh tears, and now i wish i had not sayed any of these things to her.

but it's not the aliens i'm afraid of, she is sobbing-and-shouting at me. i never saw them. i never saw the spaceship either, i just said i did because if so many others saw it and the grown-ups believed them then maybe the grown-ups would believe me too. i knew you wouldn't get it. no one gets it. leave me alone.

many many tears are spilling from her face. for a long time i do not know what to say.

then i ask her, if it is not the sky people who are making you scared, who is?

she says, someone else.

who?

it's Megan's . . . it's Megan's— leave me *alone*.

and now she is running from the chapel, and now she is gone.

when i go outside already she is not in any place that i can see. i run around the chapel.

Chloe, i say. *Chlo-weeee*.

then i can see her, and she is running and vanishing around headmaster Hyde's office block like she is going there so i chase and run and it is hot. i hear a *bang-bang* in my ears, it sounds like it is coming from the road. it is not a good sound, but it is Chloe that i must see so i do not go to look.

when i arrive at the office there is someone inside but coming out in a big rush and it is not her, it is young mastah Hyde, so i duck behind the secretary's desk until he has gone. now i can go inside the office to look for Chloe but Chloe is not here, there is only me and no one else. where can she have gone?

on the desk there are drawings made by the children of the ship that came from the sky, and of the creatures that walked out of it and through the trees towards us, just like i remember them. many many drawings, because so many children saw what i saw too, but the one on the top has the letters that spell Chloe's name and immediately i understand that she was telling me the truth – she did not see the creatures, because the one she has drawn is different to the one that i saw and the ones that everyone else drew. the figure she has drawn has a mouth, but the one i saw that day did not, it spoke to me without talking. and the figure she has drawn has a nose, but i did not see one of those on the creature either. and then there are the stars . . . and also she has drawn one of the children standing in front of the figure, which no one else has done, and i realise then that it is herself she has drawn . . .

i hold Chloe's picture in my fingers. i will take it to her, because this must be the one she wants back. she sayed. i shall take it and give it to her and she will be my friend again, and it will be a good thing to do because you cannot steal what belongs to you already . . .

from outside, there is screaming.

Dhedhi is angry because he believes his policeman friend has stolen the watch from him, so he throws bottle tops at me from the table. when i begin to cry he thinks he has made me do it so he laughs and throws more. his eyes look like they are bleeding and he has a comb still in his hair from the morning.

iwe! he waves the bottle in my face. i want food, *mwana.* get me food.

tonight i feel the cold more than i have felt it before so i go to lie on my bed. i have Chloe's drawing there that has the sky men and the sky men's ship and the small person that must be her in it, the drawing that i was going to give back to her. in my hand, i am holding one of her small plastic toys with the black eyes. it is like the one that she gave me yesterday, but this one has hair like a *green* flame, not the orange, because now i have two. i found this other toy on the road near the school gate after i could not find Chloe in headmaster Hyde's office. at first when i saw it i could not understand why it was there. then i could not understand why an army truck had stopped on the side of the road when always they rush by so fast. and i could not understand why so many of the children and teachers had come into the road. more than anything, i could not understand why young mastah Hyde was there too, and who was that person he was kneeling over, and why he had blood all over his clothes.

now, i cannot understand why Chloe is gone and why she is not coming back. i know that this is true, but i do not understand why it must be so.

food, *mwana,* Dhedhi tells me one more time. food and beer.

i tell him, no.

he turns like i have struck him with a fist. he is standing, and he is coming over to my bed, but then i think maybe he is scared of me because he raises his arm to whip me.

he takes the toy with the green hair that i found in the road from my hand.

what is this? he is laughing. a toy for little *mwana*?

i jump from my bed.

i say, give it to me, it is not yours.

i try to take it and he holds it above his head, so i push

him and now i can take it. i return to my bed but Dhedhi is angry and he holds me by my shirt, but this shirt is very very old and it has many many holes and it makes a big tear so that i can get away from him and he has only the shirt in his hands.

come here, *mwana*, he says.

i say, *no*. and i say, i will not steal for you any more. i say, it is wrong. it is wicked and bad and i will not do it again.

he is coming towards me but i move quick-quick and he falls into the ground and he hits his head on my bed so that he looks at me like i have just woken him up. he tries to stand but he is too drunk.

he is shouting, get out. go.

and i go, so then he is shouting at me, if you leave you can never come back, and how will you like it then?

i do not want to come back, i shout in return, and i run from the house and disappear into the wood smoke that hangs over the village. but where can i go? i run faster and faster, and soon i am not in the village any longer but i am at the fence that is around the school, and i am climbing this fence and i am running some more and i am close to the end of the playground and near the trees where those creatures landed in their ship. it is too dark, i cannot identify where it was, but i continue past the rocks and into the trees and through the grass and now i am in the place where the grass is not long because it has been burned.

when i look up to the sky i can see through the gap in the trees and see all the stars in the sky.

and i cry.

and i call up to the spirits, wherever they may be. i say, please, bring her back. and i hope they will hear.

225

because if they are not the bad spirits after all, as Baba Elijah tells me they cannot be, then they must be good spirits who came, and good spirits always help us. so they can fly high and fly fast to heaven in their ship to save Chloe's spirit from there.

i cry some more.

then i hear some footprints treading in the burned grass, and there is a shape coming to me. i think the spirits have heard me and they have come. there is a light, and there is small fire, but in it i do not see the face of the creature with the big head and the big, black eyes, i see Baba Elijah.

he sees me.

when he is close i ask him, how did you know that i am here?

and he says, i did not.

i say, then how . . . ?

he says, just because i did not know you were here does not mean i should not come looking.

Baba takes his best jacket and puts it around me. he collects wood from the ground and lights it with the matches in his pocket.

come, Sixpence, sit with me by the fire, he says. no african person is good without the warmth of a fire.

when i stop crying i tell him, i wish that i am no longer able to remember Chloe.

why do you wish this? he says.

because remembering her hurts me so, i say, i do not like how it feels. she was my friend. she was my best friend. my only friend.

i did not realise, says Baba, that you knew her for so long.

i did not, i say, and i take the small toys from my pocket to show him. i show him the green one.

i say, this one i did find in the road when Chloe . . . yesterday. it is hers.

then i show him the one with the orange hair.

but this one she gave to me because i was sad. i am nothing more than a thief but still she gave this to me. it is mine. no one has ever given me anything before.

she was a very good friend indeed, Baba says. and it is good that you feel this way. it shows you will be happy again.

i will never be happy again, i tell him.

a person is a person because of others, he says. death does not end them. if we bring them into our homes and our hearts we keep them alive, so talk to her, and you will feel happy again.

but where has Chloe gone, Baba? i say. is she in heaven?

do you believe in heaven?

i do.

then that is where she is.

can she come back?

Baba Elijah smiles to me in a sad way.

no, she cannot come back.

not even if the spirits go to the stars and get her?

why do you keep talking of the spirits? he says.

because i saw them. in their ship.

Baba stops. he is bringing his face closer to me.

you saw the spirits?

yes.

when?

i saw them in the school when they came down from the sky.

but Sixpence—

i did. i saw them. i thought they were the bad spirits, and

that i had called them here because i took your *mbira* and played it badly. but then you told me that the bad spirits cannot be called because they are already here, so they must be the good spirits come to help us. are they not?

Baba Elijah is thinking for a long time.

i know that it was you who did take my *mbira*, he says. i have always known this. i know also that you are sorry.

i am, i say.

he is thinking for a while more longer, making his fingers warm around the fire. when he speaks, he speaks very slowly.

i tell you again, it was not bad spirits that you saw. but it was not good spirits either. these were not spirits of any kind.

then . . . what, Baba?

he lifts my chin so that i am looking at the stars.

that is your answer, he says. there. tell me what you see.

i see just the space, i say.

and what does it mean, this space?

i think for a long-long time.

it has no meaning, i say. it is just there.

he says, everything has meaning, Sixpence. just because we do not understand it does not mean it is not so.

then he says, we are the humans, and the humans believe that everything is separate. we believe everything is its own thing and that they have been put there for us because we are better than them all. worse than that, we think we must fight them. always, we think we must fight. the humans against the animals. the humans against the nature. the humans against the humans. why? because we are foolish, and we are feeling that if we do not fight we will not survive.

Baba Elijah takes my face to look at him again.

what we humans cannot ever remember, he says, is that the

universe created us, as it created all things. every one of us is part of everything, because when we are born we do not come *into* the world, as a stranger comes into the room, we come *out of* it, as a leaf comes from a tree.

Baba sweeps his hand across the night.

that, he says, is us. all of it. we are not separate, we are to-*geth*-er. nothing exists on its own, and nothing acts on its own, and that is why i say to you, if there was no sun we would not have eyes, and if there was no wind the trees would not grow strong roots into the ground. and if we are here, in this place, do you not think that others have been made out there, in space?

but the space is too big, i say. how are they able to come so far?

problems come when we ask the right question in the wrong way, he says. the question is not, how can they come? the question is, how can they *not* come?

can this be true? i am thinking to myself. what Baba is telling me. that it was not spirits that i did see, it was creatures from the space?

then why do they not talk to us? i say.

Baba does not answer this. instead he says to me, tell me the things you saw on the day the ship came.

so i think.

and i remember.

there was . . . a shining object in the sky, i say.

yes?

with many many lights, going around and around, and it was floating above the trees, and the shining object came down to the ground and it grew very very bright so that it hurt my eyes and i had to look away. when i turned again i saw a

229

creature coming out of the trees. i saw it. he was black as a shadow, and when he talked he did not talk with sound but with pictures that he put in my head. i did not put them there, he did, and i was very afraid.

Baba asks, what did he tell you with these pictures in your head?

that there was something bad coming, i say. and it was true, Baba, because it has happened, has it not? something bad happened today.

it did, says Baba. and now, Sixpence?

and now what? i say.

now what do they tell you?

they do not tell me anything, i say to him. why would they need to talk to me still? the bad thing has happened. Chloe is dead now and they have gone.

maybe, he says, they are talking to you – to all of us – all of the time, only we are not listening.

i think about this thing he has sayed. i think about it so very very hard, and i remember the picture that Chloe drew. because on her picture the figure was different, he was not the same. he had a nose, and a mouth. and the *stars*. but i do not know what these things mean.

in the end i say, Baba?

Baba Elijah is looking at me like he has been waiting for me to speak.

yes, Sixpence?

i think the badness that the creature was talking about has not finished. because you are right, Baba, the bad spirits are already here. they have always been here.

yes, Sixpence. i believe this is true.

but i do not know where. or who. so i must speak to someone

about it. i must tell them about this thing so that they may find it.

yes, he says. you must.

but who can i tell? i say. i am a thief and i have no friends. who can i tell when no one will believe me?

again, you ask the right question in the wrong way, Baba says to me. do not ask, who can i tell if no one will believe me? instead ask, who is it that wants to talk to me?

but Chloe was the one who wanted to talk to me, i say. there is no one else.

Baba looks into my face.

is this true? there is also the american girl. *she* would like to speak to you. do not be afraid to look to those who are outside your world, Sixpence, for sometimes it is only they who can help.

'I saw something silver and we ran to the edge of the playground really quickly. I saw an object hovering with little ones all around it, and it was scary but exciting at the same time.'

'A silver object?'

'Yes. We saw the silver thing, and there was a man standing at the bottom of it and there was a man standing nearer in the trees. They were just looking at us. They didn't move their heads like we can, and their eyes looked at me . . . no, into me as if to say, Who are you?'

'Were you frightened?'

'A little at first, although they weren't frightened of us and the near one actually came nearer.'

'So you actually felt safe being so close to him.'

'I think so. Sort of. Yes.'

'Do you think you might see him again?'

'I don't know. Maybe not.'

'Does that make you feel sad?'

'Yes.'

'And if you did see him again, what would you do?'

'I'd talk to him this time, because I didn't do that before.'

'And if someone were to say that this was just your imagination or a wild fantasy or mass hysteria, what would you say?'

'Well, it's not any of those things because I saw it. I did. We all did. I know it was real. It happened.'

'How can you be so sure?'

'Because I know what I feel inside.'

HOLLY

Africa doesn't have a single cloud in the sky and the sun's so strong I just want to cut it out with a knife. I didn't know it was going to be like this. As in hot. I mean, I did, but not so hot *and* cold, because when we got off of the plane it was freezing but now I'm sweating under my Green Day sweatshirt in the back of the car and my stupid skin's already pinking, and I *know* my stupid freckles are gonna come out angry, and who the hell likes freckles?

'The aliens came just after the children had gone to the playground for their breaktime.'

Well, I sure as hell hate freckles and so does everyone else, and that includes Denver Johns. He *said* he liked them. He *said* he liked everything about me – Denver *Johns,* who's sixteen, with the coolest room above his parents' garage *and* just about the biggest Nirvana T-shirt collection in the world, which must be worth a fortune now that Kurt Cobain's dead. But it was all a lie. He digs Courtney Shapiro, not me.

'There was much screaming and noise, and at first I did not know why it was so.'

I *know* Denver digs her, because I caught them at the shopping mall outside Norney's one day, smashing their retainers and eating each other like hungry pigs in a cornfield. Courtney'd even pulled her T-shirt off of her shoulder to show off her bra strap, the skank. She's older than me and has kissed loads of guys. Plus she's got tits and knows guys like a girl who shows a bit of bra strap. Guys like a girl even more if she lets you *feel* her bra, any magazine will tell you that. I don't even have a bra yet, at least not a proper one. I haven't kissed a guy either and now I probably never will.

When they finally realised I was there Denver looked all surprised with this dumb expression dripping off of his face, while Courtney just stared at me, like, Can I help you? I didn't know what to say, so I wigged out at them both pretty good but that just made Courtney laugh at me like I was this hysterical little *kid*.

I wanted to go home and obliterate Denver Johns from the inside of my pencil case with the blackest pen I could find. But I'm thirteen now, only kids do stuff like that, so instead I went out and bought myself this deep-red lipstick called Viva Glam. Denver was going to see that I wasn't just a stupid kid, that I'm just as good and cool and beautiful and willing as Courtney Shapiro any day of the week. I was going to knock on his door, and he was going to answer it, and after he'd gazed at me, like, for ever, he'd take my hand – which would feel a lot less like rushing to get front-of-stage at a Guns N' Roses concert and completely like being Meg Ryan at the end of *Sleepless in Seattle* – and lean in until our faces were nearly touching, and then say something like, 'I thought you'd never come,' before leading me inside . . .

I wrote it all down, just to make sure it would happen, but it never did because my stupid mom only went through my room when I wasn't there – again – and busted the lipstick *and* my diary. She and Dad didn't just freak out, they hauled my ass out of school and made me come with them on this stupid trip. Bam! There went my first two-week parent-free vacation, traded in for a crazy story about UFOs and aliens landing in the middle of Nowhere, Africa. I didn't even try to tell them the truth, that nothing had actually happened with Denver, because they wouldn't believe me. They're my parents, of course they wouldn't.

The car bumps off of the main road and onto dirt.

'But later some of the children said they did see something land in the trees. It lands in the trees, and there was this person there, and after it leaves there were some burn marks in the ground.'

The guy who picked us up from the airport's called Elijah, and I swear he must be a hundred at least. He talks sort of . . . well, different, because he's an African, I guess. Mom and Dad are riding up front with him, and Dad's fish-hooked on every word while Mom's already inking something down in her notebook. Jason's in the back with me and he's got one of his cameras out of the bag to get Elijah in shot. He notices I'm watching and puts the camera on me.

'Enjoying the ride, Freckles?'

I cover my arms. He's a jerk, because it's like he can almost see what's going through my head and he's trying to yank my chain. Who needs an older brother when you've got him around?

'You OK?' Dad turns round.

'Fine. I was just having a bad dream,' I tell him, and push my head back into the window. 'And I'm still in it.'

Africa's nothing like what I expected, just a load of tall grass and these huge, balancing rocks – no animals.

Soon we're slowing down and Jason turns his camera out his side.

'That's great. Can I just get a shot of that?'

Yeah. Real great, I think, as we drive through a high metal gate that says LEDA SCHOOL on it. I could be back home right now, staying at Mandy's, making plans to hook up with Denver after class . . . But oh no, I've got to come to a nothing, deadbeat little school in a country no one's ever heard of. I've got two more weeks of this which might as well be eternity. I bet Denver's already forgotten me and he and Courtney Shapiro are sucking face right now.

Jason zooms in on the sign, then out, then in again. While we wait for him to get his shot a big truck rushes our tail and the whole car shudders.

Leda's the weirdest school I've ever seen. We head up the driveway that's just more red dirt, between these flat-topped trees, and then there's the school at the end. But it's not one big building full of classrooms and hallways and lockers like back home, instead it's all on one level and you get into all the schoolrooms directly from outside. This guy who's a bit older than Dad's waiting for us at the top of three steps, and he looks like something out of an ancient movie about British colonies because he's wearing a shirt and tie with short pants and long socks.

'Good morning, and welcome to my school.' His accent's all funny, like it's been squashed but with spikes sticking out.

He steps forward and shakes Dad's hand, like up and down really fast, then Jason's. Mom and me are invisible.

'I'm George Hyde, headmaster of Leda. I can't tell you how privileged we are to have you here – Elijah, stop standing like an idiot and take their bags to Mrs Greenacre's house at once. Please, come in out of the sun. Would you like a tea or coffee? Karl, for goodness' sake, go get our guests some tea.'

Forget George Hyde, though, and his weird accent. And forget Denver Johns and Courtney Shapiro, too. Even Kurt Cobain doesn't feature on this chart because *Karl* is this guy who's *so* Johnny Depp in *Edward Scissorhands*. You know, dead cute but sad, and way more exciting than anyone else I know because you have no idea what's going on under the hood.

Suddenly I'm thinking being stuck in Africa might not be so bad.

'Of course.' Karl talks looking at the ground like a lost dog – *so* cute. Just the way his brown hair hangs in front of his eyes makes my stomach swirl. 'Sorry. Some tea. Yes. Or coffee. Sorry. I mean, which would you prefer, tea or coffee? I'll get it at once.'

Man, he's adorable. *And* he's about eighteen. Imagine if I made out with him, because *then* who'd be the kid, Courtney Shapiro?

I plant my sunglasses into my hair, real slow so he notices how cool they are, but then Mom notices how I'm looking at him and fishes a stick of gum out from her bag.

'I know exactly what you're thinking, young girl.' Talking to me like I'm still ten. 'And, by the way, when were you going to tell us about Denver Johns?'

Actually, that's a complete lie, she doesn't say that at all. What she really says is: 'Want one? I don't know about you, but my breath could knock birds out of the sky. Long flights taste pretty lousy.'

But it's there, I swear it is. Prying. Wanting to know. I can hear it in her voice.

I take the gum and turn to Karl before she can say anything else.

'I'll come with,' I say.

'Good idea,' I hear Mr Hyde behind us. 'A woman should be in charge where kitchen duties are concerned, Karl's so hopeless he burns boiled eggs.'

Jeez, this guy's a real jerk.

I follow Karl into the staffroom.

'Your dad's a real jerk,' I say.

You remind me of Johnny Depp.

I can't *believe* I said that. I'm such a schmuck. The cuter they are, the more of an idiot I turn into. That's the rule, isn't it? That's me. I thought Denver Johns was the one to finally break that stupid rule, and maybe he was, but I went ahead and blew that one too. Now I'll never have a boyfriend, at least not one I like. Karl's probably already calling me a dumbass in his head.

We all walk out across the schoolyard to see the place where these aliens are supposed to have landed. The yard's actually just dry grass, and I guess the recess bell must have rung because all the kids are hanging around and staring at us like we're animals in a zoo. Haven't they seen Americans before? Actually, probably not, this is Africa after all. I hear one guy say something about my hair and crack up like it's funny. Agent Orange, Fanta Head, Rust Brush, Ginger Ninja . . . You name it, I've heard it before, but I'm so mad with myself for ruining it with Karl I shoot that kid a look anyways, like *putz*, only he's all, what-are-you-going-to-do-about-it?, and he must be all of twelve, which makes me even madder.

Mr Hyde stops at a boundary line of rocks and points to the trees where the spaceship apparently came down. Mom and Dad are giving him air time because they always do, but even I can tell they don't believe that he believes any of this crap, he might be a jerk but at least he's not stupid, I've got to give him that.

'Excuse me, sir?'

Karl wants to ask my dad a question. I don't care what, I just want to listen to his voice. I could listen to it all day. I move closer until I swear he can hear my heart hammering. God, I hope he never finds out how much I'm sweating under this shirt.

'Holly?'

But of course Mom has to interfere again.

She takes some dollars from her bag and points to a door back near where we've just come from.

'They sell candy in there,' she says. 'It's called a tuck shop. Go on. My treat.'

See what I mean? Always on my back.

But I go, because the airplane food was something you wouldn't give to your dog and I am actually quite hungry. Only when I'm inside this tuck shop place it's all Mint Crisp and Jub Jubs and Jumping Jack popcorn. There isn't a single thing in there I recognise, and suddenly I feel even further from home.

The woman behind the counter doesn't know I'm there, she's on her own planet just playing an invisible piano on her knees. I start to leave.

'Hi, Holly,' she says before I hit the door. Then: 'You are

241

Holly, aren't you? I guess you must be. I was hoping to greet you when you arrived but Mr Hyde is . . .'

I turn, and she's smiling in a way that says she knows exactly what I think of that jerk because she thinks it too.

'Well, let's say he wanted to do all that himself,' she goes on.

'Yeah, I get that. He sure likes the sound of his own voice.'

Sometimes I think I should count to a thousand before I open my mouth.

'What can I get for this?' I slide the three dollar beans Mom gave me across. They don't even look like real money to me.

She picks out a chocolate candy from the shelf. 'So? What do you think?'

I shrug.

'I've never had one of those before.'

'Not this.' She points straight up. 'About the spaceships! Here, in our little school! Would you believe it? Pretty exciting, hey?'

'I don't know,' I shrug again. 'Was it?'

'I'd say. Having a story that's big enough to travel all the way to the United States? Us? It's the most exciting thing to happen around here in years.'

Which is another way of saying this place is more of a dump than I thought.

'At first we were . . .' She leans and pulls a face to show me what she was – like in a car going too fast around a corner. 'But the children, they all stuck to their story and made all these drawings, so now we're . . .'

She comes closer, as if I've offered to tell her the secret of some buried treasure.

'I don't know what you folks are going to make of any of this, but you believe what you want to believe, don't let my husband tell you what to think.'

'Your husband?'

'That's right. My husband is the headmaster, Mr Hyde.'

She's his *wife*? And Karl Scissorhands' *mom*? Man, I could die.

She's still smiling. Maybe she didn't get that I called her husband a big-mouth, or maybe she's just a little crazy. Either way, I think I'm safe.

'Why, what does he think?' I ask. Although I already know because Karl kind of told me.

'He thinks it's just their imaginations taking advantage of the fact that there were no adults around at the time, that someone's told a tale and got everyone riled. A belief that I don't share, I hasten to add.'

'But don't you think it's a bit strange that out of two hundred kids . . .'

'. . . only a quarter of them actually saw something?' she says.

'Well, yeah. Don't you?'

'I'm fully aware of how children love a tall tale,' she says, 'but I've seen the pictures those kids drew. I've heard them talk about it, and looked into their eyes. And I'll tell you this for nothing: after over twenty years of living in this school I know kids, and they saw something, Holly. They did. I don't know what it was, but they saw something that day and it really got under their skins.'

Her eyebrows jump up and down. No, not crazy. She's something else, though, I just can't figure out what.

She slides my money back across the counter.

'This one's on me. A small welcome gift. I reckon your parents are going to be pretty busy over the next few days, so if you need anything I'm always somewhere around, even just for a chat.'

Now I'm suspicious all of a sudden.

'About what?'

'Whatever you like. About the school, what happened here . . . boys. Anything.'

So *that's* why Mom was so keen to get me up here. She thinks if I won't talk to her about Denver, and what she thinks happened, then I'll tell this lady instead. It was a trick.

I hear a snigger, and the guy from outside with the attitude and the oh-so-hilarious ginger jokes is right behind me. He's probably been there the whole time. He may be younger than me but he's taller than I am, which bugs me even more.

'What are you laughing at, *space* boy?'

'Your tan.' He snorts. 'Anyone tell you that you look like a matchstick on fire?'

OK, I haven't heard that before. I slide my shades down so he can't see how much it stings.

'Ha ha, that's real funny. Where d'you steal it, from your alien friends?'

I think I've got him with that one, but quick as a middle finger, he digs out a Native American voice you only ever hear in crappy old cowboy films.

'Much sorry, White Feather, me not see ship in sky like um heap big morons in school.'

'Are you sure? Cos you sure look like a moron.'

He checks himself up and down and acts surprised, but like all sarcastic.

'Oh yeah, you're right! I am a moron. Thanks for pointing

that out, beautiful.' Then he puts on a Lloyd face from *Dumb and Dumber*. 'Suck me sideways.'

It's not even a good impression, but for some weird reason I start to blush because I've never been called beautiful before, and he didn't even mean it.

'You just think you're all that and a bag of chips, don't you?' I snatch my chocolate bar.

I want to go home.

Recess is over. Dad's already started his interviews in a classroom and Mom's talking to a bunch of young kids under a tree, and the staffroom's empty again. I wish Karl would come back because I'm bored and homesick and I could do with something tasty to distract me, but I've listened to Boyz II Men until the batteries on my Discman started to fade and read my *YM* magazine twice and I still haven't set eyes on another soul.

When the bell rings some teachers come and go, and Mr Hyde's secretary brings me a sandwich for lunch, which is nice if you like eating meat only I don't. Jason comes back for a fresh videotape and fakes surprise when he sees me.

'Where's your new beau, Holly?' Now he acts looking around – he thinks he's so funny. 'Dumped already? That must be some kind of record.'

'Quit with the jokes, already, my sides are hurting.'

Which is the wrong answer completely because now he knows he's bugged me. He smirks and digs into his camera bag.

'Hey, you want to hear how our first morning went?'

'No thanks.'

He's going to tell me anyway.

'Some of those kids . . .' He stops. For once he sounds almost serious. 'Man, if I didn't know better, I'd swear they were speaking the truth. You know?'

'Not really.'

'That bunch your mom was talking to . . . there was something real about the way they spoke to us. How old are they? Eight? Eight-year-olds don't lie, at least not that well. Besides, the lens can spot BS a mile off and so far I haven't seen any. Want to see?'

He slots the tape into his other camera and squints into the eyepiece until he finds the place he's looking for.

'Here, this girl's called Chloe, she's great. Real sweet. When I have a daughter I want her to look like her.'

Jason with kids? Jason with a wife to have kids with? Total gross out.

'When she started telling us how evil she thought the creatures were I swear I got goosebumps all over,' he says. 'It was real to her, you know? Like, really real. She was genuinely scared. Plug in your headphones, take a listen.'

I ignore him and pretend to carry on reading my *YM*. He puts down the camera.

'What's the deal? I thought you were interested in all this.'

'Who says?' Wrong answer, Holly, but it's too late to take it back.

'Your dad, for a start. He told me you were desperate to come and find out more, he said you said you didn't want to miss it for the world.'

'Yeah. That's right, I did.'

I sit up to take a look and try to act like it's no big deal, but now he pulls the camera away.

'You think I'm a fool, Holly?' he says. 'Your parents are

246

good folk but I didn't believe them for a second. They wouldn't take you out of school for *this*.'

'Why not?' I say, and straight away his victory grin jumps back onto his face. When will I learn?

'Because you're thirteen, and yet you ditched the chance of a two-week freedom ticket staying with a friend to come watch your parents work? Like, what thirteen-year-old girl would ever do that? You don't give a damn about their work.'

'Maybe I do,' I tell him. 'Maybe I want to be a psychiatrist too, one day. Help kids who need it.'

'Help kids? You?'

'What's wrong with that?'

'What makes you think you can help anyone?' He laughs to himself. 'I'm right, aren't I? You're not the slightest bit interested in this story, I bet you reckon that lot are crazier than a bag of raccoons. So why are you really here? No, don't tell me. You're in trouble, right?'

I pick up the magazine again but I'm blushing hard and I can't make it stop.

'You get caught going through your dad's liquor cabinet?' he says.

'You have a big mouth, you know that?'

'Get busted stashing a packet of smokes in your bedroom? Or some pot?'

'Bite me.'

'That's it, isn't it. You smoked some weed.'

He thinks he's got me and looks pretty pleased with himself, so the next thing I know I'm reaching out and zinging his ear hard. He jumps up with a yelp and I feel pretty pleased with myself, but *man* is he pissed. I kind of wish I hadn't done it.

'Are you sure you're not adopted?' he says.

'Everything OK, you two?' a voice comes from the door. It's Dad.

Jason backs off to his camera. I get up. I want to tell Dad how much of an asshole Jason is – no, how much of an *asshole's* asshole – but that's not how the rules work.

'Fine.' I grab my shades off of the table and head out.

'Where are you going? I've got a bit of time, I was hoping we could have a chat.'

Not him too. I thought they dragged me here to get me away from Denver Johns, not bring him up every chance they get.

'Sorry. I gotta bounce.'

'Have you put cream on? The sun here's much stronger than at home.'

'Whatever.'

Everyone's at lunch and the school feels deserted. It is hot, but there's a covered pathway that runs in front of the buildings so I stick in the shade until I'm outside the library. The principal's wife's inside sorting books. I'm about to say hi only I don't, because she's got this weird-looking instrument thing on the desk that has long metal teeth fixed to a piece of wood, and she's staring at it as if she's about to play it. Slowly, she plucks one of the shorter teeth and it makes a sound like *plink*. She plucks one of the longer ones and it goes, like, *plonk*. She checks she's alone, then tries it again but a bit faster and with both hands.

She looks up and I pull back from the door like I've been caught smoking or something.

I walk away quickly.

There's another noise comes from somewhere else, and I see

this little African kid inside one of the classrooms over the grass. He can't be a student here because he's not wearing the uniform and the clothes he has got are, like, rags, yet he's digging around in a bag like he's trying to find something in a hurry and when he comes out he's got this real nice, fat, dollar-sign G-Shock hanging off of his thin little fingers. I know I've only just got here, and I don't know anything about anything in this place apart from the fact the principal's son's dead cute, but *no way* that watch belongs to him.

Finally, someone *real* to talk to.

'Hey.'

His head snaps up like he's wired up to the mains and looks ready to fill his pants.

Then, quicker than I can say Carl Lewis, he's off.

'*Hey*! Come back.'

I follow him through the bushes.

He should be right in front of me but already he's gone, like he was never there. How did he do that?

I follow the way and run past a swimming pool and a chapel, then stop. There's a sports building on the edge of a field. Maybe he's in there, maybe he's not, but either way I need to get out of the sun quick because it's slapping the top of my head like a pillow full of headache and my skin's already starting to burn.

I go over and push the door open, and inside it's dark but I can just make out bags on hooks and balls in buckets and funny-shaped baseball bats against the wall that must be for that British game that no one understands. The place stinks like boys' armpits.

Someone's in a restroom at the far end with the door wide open, sniffing like he's trying not to cry.

'Hey,' I say, but softer than before because I must have scared the crap out of the kid. He thinks I was chasing him.

I bump a chair and the sniffing quits in a flash.

'I wasn't trying to scare you, I only want to say hi, is all.'

Now he's running again, right at me and in a blur. But it's not the little African kid, it's a white boy, and as he rushes out into the bright daylight I see it's that jerk from the tuck shop again.

'What's the matter with you?' I yell after him when I stop being frightened.

He doesn't even look round. Not so full of it now, is he?

I feel better, but as usual it doesn't last long because out there the sun's still falling like lava, and it's not like I've suddenly become miraculously olive-skinned in the last two minutes. It's the middle of the day, I'm going to fry. Want to know the one thing worse than someone teasing you about how you look? When you know they're right.

I stay in the shade of the doorway and dig my Viva Glam lipstick out of my jeans to cheer myself up. Mom and Dad would kill me if they knew I'd fished it back out of the trash that day. Well, they wouldn't *actually* kill me, because that would be murder, they'd want to sit down and Have A Talk which is far worse. It's like they stopped knowing me all of a sudden and are always trying to find things out. But they should know me, right? They used to, so how come they don't now?

Running in the heat's made me tired plus my jet lag's kicking in. I slide down the wall, and it's like sinking into a bath. I pull my shades on and close my eyes. The cicadas screech.

I role-play what it would have been like if Mom hadn't read my diary, because then they wouldn't have freaked out and brought me here, and I'd be staying with Mandy like we'd arranged. Maybe Denver and I'd be going steady by now. Even if Denver is a total dork, it's better to have a boyfriend than not have one, right? Everyone has a boyfriend, I don't want to be the only one without.

I hear a distant rustling noise. Leaves swaying, or footsteps through dry grass. I'm too tired to open my eyes but I guess it's that jerk coming back, but I don't want it to be him so I twist the half-dream and imagine Karl instead. Well, I can dream, can't I? He's coming to find me, and when he does he'll wake me with a light kiss and say something like, I've been looking for you . . .

Then it's not Karl, it's someone else. Well, a figure of some kind. Not human. Short, and thin, and the nearer it comes the thinner it gets, all dark like in a skin-tight suit with long arms and legs and a huge oval alien head. Black hair, and eyes the size of footballs, but no mouth. Closer and closer, coming in until it's face is an inch from mine, peering like it wants to know what I am . . .

My eyes fling open. The creature vanishes instantly because it was only in my dream. In the real world, I can tell it's a while later because it's not as hot as it was, and it's a little girl who's actually watching me, with blonde bunches and her head on one side.

I push my shades up, but she's already gone.

I go outside and she's on the path that heads back to the main part of the school. I catch her up easily, and when I move in front of her she jumps like I've got snakes in my hair. I can tell she's been crying.

'Hey. Did you want something?' She doesn't say anything, just shakes her head, which I guess is a lie because I can tell she did. 'It's OK, don't be frightened. What's your name?'

She doesn't want to give it to me at first, but in the end she says, 'Chloe,' in a voice I almost can't hear. She squeezes a cuddly animal into her chin.

'And who's your friend?' I say.

'This is Ignatius Rabbit.' She holds it out.

'Well, it's nice to meet you, Chloe. And nice to meet you too, Ignatius. I'm Holly, the freak from another planet – at least, that's how I'm starting to feel because everyone else around here's either an idiot, or thinks I'm an idiot, or just runs away. Guess it's my accent and my stupid hair that does it. Suppose you don't see many redheads round here, do you?'

'I like you. And I like your hair,' Chloe says. I don't know whether to laugh or give her a hug.

'You do?'

'It's pretty.' She blinks her big eyes. 'You're pretty. When I'm older I hope I'm as pretty as you.'

Man, this kid is the best. Who the hell would want to do anything to make her cry?

'Did you see a little African boy around here? About your height?'

She shakes her head. 'No.'

'Skinny little guy. Had something in his hand. I think he might have stolen it.'

'He didn't steal it because I said he could have it.'

'You did?' The surprise must be dripping off of my face. That watch was hers?

'Yes.'

And she gave it to him?

'No way. Really?'

'I gave it to him, I did. I have a spare one at home so I said he could have it. He didn't do anything wrong.'

'*Really?*'

I laugh, which I guess is kind of a dumb thing to do because now her face's starting to break up.

'Why don't you believe me?'

'Hey, easy, Chloe. I never said I don't believe you.'

'But it's true, you don't. Do you?' All I can do is give her a big, stupid shrug – she's right. 'No one ever believes me.'

Tears are leaking out all over the place. I only came after her to be nice and I end up making things worse. Nice going, Holly, real cool move. I go to put an arm around her but she won't let me, she just goes rigid like a statue and says something I almost don't hear.

Hakuna matata.

I swear that's what it was. You know, that song from *The Lion King,* but it sounded more like a cry for help. Am I that bad?

'What did you say?'

She doesn't answer, I guess because of the teacher that's walking up suddenly from behind us. Heavy black hair cut straight over his eyes, a stuck-on smile, and when he gets to us he spiders his hand onto my shoulder even though I've never met him before in my life. Teachers back home wouldn't *dare* do that because they'd get sacked or sued, or both.

'Chloe.' He gazes down at her. 'Why aren't you in class?'

His words are all fluffy on the outside but hard as stones underneath, kind of as you'd expect for someone skipping class but Chloe cowers like she's done the worst thing in the world.

JASON WALLACE

Man, how serious can that be here? Her poor rabbit's getting the life squeezed out of it.

'Mr Stamps, I was only . . .'

'I'm not really interested in the *I was only*s, Chloe. Now off you go. You're in enough trouble as it is, don't make it worse.'

The guy stares at her, and her eyes fill up again.

'Anything wrong, Chloe?' he says.

I think there is. And I think he knows there is. But instead of telling him, Chloe looks to me.

She opens her mouth to speak. But then the guy turns to me too, like he's daring me to listen to what she has to say. Like when Courtney Shapiro seemed to be daring me to say anything when I caught her with Denver Johns that day at the mall, only this time I'm a lot more scared than I was then. Whatever's going on here I don't want to get involved, it's got nothing to do with me, so before Chloe even has the chance to make a word I give her another dumb shrug and straight away she shuts her mouth again.

She wipes her tears with her toy rabbit, then gives me one last glance as she walks quickly down the path.

See? is what that glance says. Told you no one believes me.

I feel like a total bitch, though I have no idea what I've done wrong.

The guy stares at her until long after she's out of sight. When he faces back to me he swivels like he's on wheels.

'You must be Holly,' he says, suddenly a mouthful of smiles.

'Yeah. How did you know?'

'Because I know everything about everyone.' He winks to show me it's a joke. Oh sure, he's a real scream. 'I watched you arrive this morning. Mulder and Scully. That's what everyone's calling your folks – our very own X-Files. "The truth is out there", and all that.'

'Yeah? Well, there's only one truth, which is that this trip is a total waste of time.'

I don't like this guy and don't plan on sticking around, I wish I hadn't taken his side now, but when I start to bug out he steps in the way. Like, right there. Easy on the coffee-breath, dude.

'Are you wearing lipstick?' he says, and *bang!* It's like I've slammed into a wall. I'm already tucking my lips in and trying to rub it off with my teeth. I am going to be in such *shit*.

The spider at the end of his arm comes out to give my shoulder another squeeze.

'Don't worry, your secret's safe with me,' he says. 'Besides, it suits you.'

And suddenly I forget what I was just thinking about him and grin.

'Hey, why don't you come with me?' he says. 'There's something I reckon you and Mulder and Scully would love to see.'

'Yeah?'

'Don't sound so worried, it's actually really cool. I bet you won't have seen anything like it.'

'What is it?'

'I'm going to show you the exact point they say the flying saucer touched down.'

'The trees? Already seen them.'

'Not from amongst the trees themselves you haven't. And not the burn mark that's on the ground. Mr Hyde doesn't like anyone going up there – that's his rule for the kids but he really means everyone – but how are you ever going to enjoy life if you don't break a few rules, hey?'

He flashes his eyes, like Denver Johns used to flash his at me whenever we first used to pass one another in the school hall. I laugh. Maybe this Stamps guy's not so bad.

'And don't worry about Chloe,' he starts walking, 'everything you just heard was me blowing hot air for her own good, she won't be in trouble. I'm not a teacher, I'm one of the good guys.'

And to prove it he puts his hand onto the back of my neck.

OK, enough already!

Mr Lego Hair's bugging me now because his fingers *keep on* touching my neck. Like, all of a sudden we're best buddies. Like, just because he did it once and I didn't say anything he thinks he can do it all the time. He's starting to creep me out. I don't want to go with him to see the burn mark, I really don't, only I can't find the right excuse to make or the right time to make it.

But then again, he's still being pretty nice about me, so am I busting his chops for no good reason? Because how bad could he be when he looks after the kids in the school like he does, not for any money but because he likes it? How bad could he be if he's *allowed* to look after the kids like he does? They all love him – Chloe included, he swears it – a lot of the teachers here are pretty strict while he wouldn't discipline the pupils like that even if he could, because he wants to be the one person in the school the kids can turn to.

At least, that's what he keeps telling me.

And anyway, turns out his own daughter is one of the students here too, so what's he going to do?

He shows her off to me by digging his wallet out of his

top pocket and flipping it open, and a picture of her's on the inside. She looks real normal, too, kind of sweet in a grumpy sort of way, in which case I figure I'm totally being a paranoid ass.

'That's Megan, there,' he says. 'As you can see, she and Chloe are best friends, they do everything together. That was them a few weeks ago playing *The Lion King* down at the bottom of our garden.'

He chuckles and stares at the photo for a little while longer before putting the wallet away.

So Chloe *must* like him, in which case I've gotten him all wrong. Like maybe I've gotten that dork with all the ginger jokes wrong too, because when we bump into him on the way to the trees it turns out Gary – that's his name – has good reason to be such an idiot.

'There's no need to be like that,' Mr Stamps tells him. 'Look, I heard about your mother. I can see why you'd be angry. But you're also inches away from leaving this school with a dark mark against your name just like your brother, so you really have to watch that temper. If you ever want to talk about how you're feeling, I'd be more than happy to help.'

So now I feel bad for thinking about Gary the way I did as well as Mr Stamps, if my mom left me and Dad I'd be a mess, no wonder he was crying. Jeez, nice going, Holly.

'You want to hear a small piece of advice?' Mr Stamps goes on. Like, real genuine. 'Just because you think something today, doesn't mean you'll think it tomorrow. Nothing in this world is for ever, not even how you feel, so don't do anything you'll regret.'

Then he unbuttons the top of his shirt and opens it up to show Gary something on one side of his chest, and it's these three stars. Which is kind of weird – not the tattoo itself, because Kurt Cobain had them and Johnny Depp has them, just the fact that he's showing Gary and me at all – but then I remind myself he's not a teacher and already it sort of seems OK.

'When I was in the army I got inspired by the night sky while on recce out in the bush once and I thought this was the best thing in the world. When you see your first African night tonight, Holly, you'll understand why.'

His eyes land right on me as he says that last bit. Like, real intense.

'Now when I look at them I just see a bad idea.'

I get what he means straight away, because the tattoo is pretty faded and uncool, and it's not like he can just take it off or anything. But that's also when the creepy feeling comes rushing back to me without any warning. Out of nowhere, just like that. *Wham!* I don't understand why. He's being nice and all but it's just this bad feeling in my stomach that I can't make stop and I can't make go away.

Finally, Mr Stamps peels his eyes off of me and paints them back over Gary. Thank the Pope.

'Right, time for me to shut up before I start sounding like Headmaster Hyde. Have you had your interview with Holly's dad yet?' he says.

'I'm not having an interview,' Gary tells him.

'How come?'

'I didn't see the spaceship.'

'You sure?'

'Positive. And, if you ask me, no one did.'

Gary definitely can't be a total idiot if he hasn't bought into all that alien crap. In fact, right then I decide Gary's OK, and wish more than anything he'd stick around. I don't want him to go. Or maybe it's more like I just don't want to be left alone with Mr Stamps. I don't know. He seems to genuinely care about everyone like he says – Gary, his daughter, Chloe – and they all genuinely seem to like him back, so why do I feel so bad as we move on and head, alone, across the schoolyard and towards the line of rocks?

'Are you all right?' Mr Stamps asks.

Even the smile on my face feels weak.

'Sure. Why?'

'Maybe it's the heat,' he says.

Maybe it is. It is real hot.

'It's tough on everyone,' he tells me, 'but especially if you're not used to it. It'll be nice and shady in the trees, I promise.'

I think that should make me feel better but it doesn't. In fact, I feel worse with every step, and it's more than just the heat hitting me, I swear. It's as if there's something I should be scared of, only I just don't know what it is yet. And it's up in those trees. I don't believe in any of that garbage about the aliens, I really don't, but it's as if something happened there and it was so bad it left a part of itself behind. Just this *sense*.

And now we're in there, under the dim umbrella of leaves, and it is cooler like he said. But when we walk through to a clearing and the sky opens up again the feeling in me is so strong I think I'm gonna barf over my Converse All Stars, because on the ground the grass is short and charred and it runs around us in a big and perfect circle. And I can *feel* it, as if it's still burning. Like it must have been when it got like this. And a smell is filling my nose that's like burned toast only thick and sick and looking for a way inside.

JASON WALLACE

Suddenly I realise Mr Stamps is standing right in front of me.

'It's true what I said to Gary, the African night really is a wonderful sight. You wait. It's like nothing else. So pretty . . . it leaves you mystified how anything could be so beautiful, and you wish you could capture it and bottle it and keep it in a secret place that only you know about, no one else. Because you don't want anyone else to have it. They don't appreciate it like you do. They don't deserve something so special.'

And for a moment, I swear, without me ever realising he got there, he's so near I can't find air.

From somewhere else amongst the trees, a voice calls out. 'Hello?'

Not close, but close enough for Mr Stamps to look round, and I hot-foot it out of there and just *run*.

Dear Diary, I've changed my mind: this place is full of *freaks*.

I stand outside on the grass, watching Dad through the window of the classroom he's using for the interviews, going through the pictures he asked the children to draw. It's night now, so I can see him but he can't see me, he doesn't even know I'm here. I came down to talk to him but something's holding me back from going in.

Is it the sight of all these stars? I guess that weird Mr Stamps was right, because I never knew there could be so many. So, so many, exploding across the sky without moving. Stars're all I can see. I feel . . . no, I am small under them. *Less* than small.

Or is it because I suddenly think, just from since I went up to the trees, Dad seems a bit older and moving around just a little bit more like Grandpa? I don't ever want Dad to get old – he's my dad.

I carry on watching. When Dad finally sees me he comes over.

'Holly? I didn't realise you were going to follow me down. Everything OK?'

I spray the grass with my torch.

'I wanted to ask you something.'

'Fire away.'

'What if . . .' I stop and start again. 'All those kids you've been talking to, what if what they say they saw was true? What if a ship *did* land here, and an alien *did* come out to make contact?'

He opens his mouth and at first nothing comes out. Clearly it's not what he expected me to ask.

'I thought you didn't believe in any of that.'

'I don't. I didn't. But this afternoon I started to wonder if things aren't always as they first appear to be.'

He laughs. 'Maybe there's a bit of the psychiatrist in you after all, because that's pretty switched on. Things are hardly ever how they first appear. What specifically do you mean?'

'Like the burn mark.'

'Ah yes, the burn mark. You saw it too.'

'It could have been made by a fire, I guess, but surely not in a circle as perfect as that, and if it had been a fire why has no one talked about seeing any smoke?' Plus there's Gary, I think, and weirdo Mr Stamps, because they're not what they appear to be either. But I keep them to myself. 'So? What if the aliens were really real? As in, if everyone saw them, not just the kids but the adults too? What would that mean?'

'Well, first off it would mean normal wouldn't exist any more,' he says, 'because suddenly we'd know for sure it wasn't just us. It would change everything. And it could never go back to how it was.'

'Why not?' I say. 'And *why* would it have to change everything?'

'Because by knowing we're not alone in it, our place in the universe would take on a very different meaning. We might feel threatened, or comforted, or something else altogether. But we'd feel something. It would be huge, it's all we'd talk about.'

He strokes my hair. It feels like when I was young and I like it. Things were easier then because I never had to think about things like this.

'Is that what's bothering you?' he says.

Is it? Things changing when I don't want them to, things not changing when I do . . . ? I thought I liked all that but now, when it actually might be happening, I'm not sure.

It all seems so complicated, but how can I put that into words?

'No,' I tell him.

Dad kneels down to my level.

'Holly, shall I tell you why we took you out of school and brought you here with us?'

Here we go again. I'd start walking away if it wasn't so dark.

'Dad, do we have to talk about this now?'

'I think it's time we did.'

'But Denver and I never did anything. I swear. Not even a kiss. Sure, maybe he would have done sooner or later if I'd let him, or maybe he wouldn't. Maybe I wanted him to, I don't know, but it was just a dumb diary. Nothing actually happened.'

I think he's going to tell me he doesn't believe me.

'I know it didn't,' he says.

'You do?'

'I worked it out pretty soon after Mom read what she shouldn't have read – for which she is eternally sorry, by the way. The reason we made you come has nothing to do with Denver or any other boy. Well, not directly.'

'Then, why?'

'Truthfully? Because we realised you're growing up. And fast. You're changing.'

'But Dad, everyone grows up. And I stopped being a kid, like, centuries ago.'

'We know that, but it didn't stop us freaking out a little, I guess we just panicked and tried to find a way to hold onto our baby for a while longer.'

I look at him. I'm not sure what he's getting at.

'Why are you telling me all this? Are you saying you believe in the alien story?'

He smiles and strokes my hair.

'I'm telling you because I want you to know *everyone* is scared of change, even grown-ups. But to answer your question, if you're asking me, do I believe the kids saw something? Absolutely. We've only spent a single day with them but already I know they're too credible to be lying. If, however, you're asking me, do I believe they saw the flashing lights, the ship, the figures coming out . . .'

'So you *don't* think they saw a ship?'

'I'm not saying that.'

'You think they did.'

'I'm not saying that either.'

'So what *are* you saying?'

Dad drives me mad sometimes.

'I'm saying, you're right: not everything is as it seems to be. There's always a reason, and it's easy to rush to the obvious conclusion, but the real answers are harder to find. That's my job. And yours, because we're all psychiatrists really, you don't have to have a degree to work out what's going on with people. You're a very clever girl.'

He stands.

'You know what?' he says. 'It's getting late, and this work can wait till the morning. Give me two minutes to lock up and we'll head back and see Mom at the house.'

I wait for him and look back at the stars.

Suddenly a light blinks on somewhere. The library, I think. I watch and see a small black head darting between the book-shelves before the light goes back off. It's that little African kid again.

I go over and try the door. Locked. But I know he's in there, only why would he be hiding in there, at night, in the dark? Why?

I go to a window round the back and peer in. It's too dark to see anything so I fire up the torch, but still nothing, just that weird instrument thing I saw Mrs Hyde playing earlier today, only it's lying broken on the floor with a load of books that have come off of the shelf somehow.

There's scuffling further down the library wall, and I swing the beam just in time to catch the kid drop from a high window.

'Gotcha this time.' I grab his arm. 'What are you up to, little fella? Kinda late to be returning your library books, isn't it?'

Is he here stealing? If he is, why hasn't he come out with anything?

He looks at me and his eyes go wide and white. I don't

want to scare him so I relax my hold on him, and he rips away.

'Hold your horses, cowboy, I only want to ask you something.'

I sprint after him over the uneven ground behind the classrooms and run straight into Dad.

'Oh, it's *you*,' he says.

I'm not sure who I thought he was for a second, but I'm so relieved I could scream.

So what's the deal with that Mr Stamps, then?

That's what I was going to ask Gary next morning. Kind of to break the ice, because now I know about his mom I feel sorry for him, but also because he looked pretty weirded out when Mr Stamps showed us his tattoo yesterday. Does he creep him out? He does me, only I still can't say why. Everyone seems to think Mr Stamps is this really cool dude who's nice to everyone – and he is, as far as I can tell – but as Dad says it's easier to rush to the obvious answer.

When I see Gary, though, he's marching towards his classroom like he's going to start a war, and when I follow him in he's already writing the words KARL HYDE USES THE E— on the blackboard, so my first thought is that I'm wasting my time because he really is just a dork after all.

'What're you doing?'

He spins, and when he realises it's me he gives me a what-the-hell-does-it-look-like? face and flips me the bird.

'Leave me alone, Yank.'

I stay right where I am and think what Mom or Dad would say.

'Whatever it is, I don't really care.'

'Good, because I wasn't going to tell you.'

'But I am interested in why you're doing it. You know, it would be much easier for everyone if you talked about what you're feeling instead of being such an asshole the whole time? I bet you're quite a nice guy underneath all that crap.'

The words hit him. I think he's surprised . . . and I am too, they sounded pretty good.

He takes a step forward, then aims a finger at my head.

'How the hell do you know anything about how I feel?' he says, real angry, and suddenly I wish I hadn't come. I can't even remember why I did.

'Easy, dude, I'm just saying . . .'

'You don't know anything about me.'

'I'm just saying' – *what* am I saying? He's right, I don't know him at all – 'if you want someone to talk to, try me. It might be easier with a stranger.'

He laughs, though not in a good way.

'I told you, Copper Top, I didn't see the spaceship.'

He really hasn't got a nice word to say to anyone.

'I'm not talking about that.'

'Tell your dad I wasn't anywhere near the trees. I was in the tuck shop when it came, but I wouldn't have seen it anyway because there *was* nothing. No spaceship, and no aliens. Nothing. If he thinks there was he's as crazy as the rest of them.'

'Stand down, soldier, what bug's crawled up your—'

'It was just a light. A reflection, that's all. That's what it looked like.'

I stare at him.

'I thought you just said you didn't see anything,' I say. 'Because you were in the tuck shop.'

I wait. He has no idea what to say next.

'Don't be scared,' I tell him.

'I'm not scared.'

'Everyone's scared of something.'

'Shut up, Yank,' he yells. And that's when I know I *should* have shut up because he's running at me and pushing me to get out – again! – only this time it's hard enough to knock me off my feet. As I go down my head thuds against a chair and for a couple of seconds everything goes black.

It's not serious, but a teacher called Mr Greet takes me up to the nurse's office and goes to fetch Mom along the way.

'What happened?' she asks.

'Some guy,' I say. 'It's nothing.'

She looks at the shades in my hand – one of the arms is broken.

'You sure?' she says. 'That doesn't look like nothing.'

'Really. I can fix them, it's no big deal.'

Of course she's not convinced, because moms never are, but while we wait outside it turns out Mrs Hyde's the school nurse too as well as all the other stuff she does, and she takes one look at me and nods like that's all the explanation that's needed. She convinces Mom and Mr Greet that she'll take care of me from here, then gives me a huge hug as soon as they've gone that makes me want to cry.

'Let me guess,' she says. 'Gary Marston?'

'How did you know?' I say.

'Everyone knows Gary Marston, he's been making quite a name for himself recently. His brother was an awful bully and he's the only role model he has. It's terribly sad. What did you fight about?'

'We were arguing about whether he was in the tuck shop that day,' I say, because Gary will be in enough trouble as it is. 'You know, when everyone saw the . . . thing.'

'The spaceship?'

'Yes.'

'I see.' She looks closely at my head. 'Well now, Holly, I've got good news and bad. Which do you want first?'

'The bad.'

'OK. It doesn't look like you'll need stitches, and that's no use for getting lots of sympathy.'

'And the good?'

'It's less work for me.'

Mrs Hyde's funny, too. I like funny.

She gets me to sit by the window and touches my head like we're friends.

'Mrs Hyde?'

'Yes, Holly?'

'I wasn't spying on you. You know, when I saw you in the library yesterday. I hope you don't think I was.'

'Of course not. You're not from around here, everything must seem very strange to you. It's only natural to be curious.'

'What was it, by the way?'

'The thing I was playing?' She dabs cotton wool and warm water. 'It's a traditional instrument called an *mbira*, I dare say you won't have any in the States. I found it in the middle of the road near the school gate and thought I should rescue it before one of those ghastly army trucks smashed it to dust. I don't know how it got there but I did see a man weaving up the road on a bike so I think he may have dropped it, and he was obviously drunk even at that time so I decided to keep hold of it for a while.'

'Can you play it?'

'The *mbira*?' She laughs and shakes her head. 'You heard

me for yourself, I think you know the answer to that. Usually if I hear music my fingers will happily make the same notes on a piano, I'm pretty good at that, but the *mbira* is a lot harder. It just came out in a mess.'

'What, you can play anything just by listening to it?'

'On the piano, yes, but that's less to do with freakish talent and more to do with endless practice and strict parents when I was young. I got pretty good, even played a few concerts of my own.'

'Wow, that's totally cool. You should play in a band. Or an orchestra. For money, anyway. Back home you could make good money being able to do something like that.'

'You're very kind. I used to dream I *might* do something more with music, only something always managed to get in the way. Marriage, baby, work. Life. There was a time I used to get upset that I didn't try, but now . . . now I find it hard to even remember what it felt like to have ambition, just that it was there.'

She takes in a deep breath and gazes at nothing out of the window.

'Listen to me, I must sound such a dusty bore to a young thing like you,' she says eventually. 'Shame about the *mbira*, though.'

'How do you mean?'

'Well, I left it on the library desk and locked up as usual, and when I opened up this morning it was broken again. In pieces, this time, all over the floor and yet there was no way anyone could have got in. Spooky, hey? Who knows, maybe one of the aliens came back and got in.'

Not an alien, I know exactly who it was. But breaking into

the library to smash up a musical instrument makes no sense and I don't want to get the kid into trouble for no reason.

She pats my back and I stand.

'Right, I've got good news and bad again. Which do you want first?'

'The bad.'

'The bad news is, I've loved our chat, Holly, but I'm all done so I'll have to let you go.'

'And the good?'

'The good news is, for what it's worth, you won the argument with Gary Marston. He wasn't in the tuck shop when the spacecraft came. And even if he had been he still would have seen it because there's a clear view of the exact spot where it landed from as far back as the counter.'

She winks at me.

'And actually? There were *two* of the bigger spaceships that day, only the other one stayed quite high up, I'm not sure if anyone else spotted it or not.'

I have to remind myself to breathe.

Is she having another joke?

I go to ask, but when we get to the door there's this piece of paper blowing across the ground outside. She picks it up, and on it there are the words KARL HYDE USES EDELVALK BOYS FOR TARGET PRACTICE.

Gary.

But when I turn to tell Mrs Hyde, she's gone paler than the paper itself.

'Sorry, my dear, can you make your own way back? I need to . . . I should probably . . . see to my husband . . .'

Then she's gone, walking quickly towards the main part of the school.

*

There's another piece of paper lying on the path. Then another. Then one at the bottom of a storm drain. I stop to pick this one up, only it says something different: KARL HYDE ISN'T WHO YOU THINK HE IS. Whatever *that* means.

Did Karl do something to Gary? Or has this got something to do with Gary's mom leaving? I can't think what.

I carry on walking, then stop again when I see Mr Stamps drifting about down near the parking lot. He looks round so I step into the bushes. Did he see me? I don't know, but he's not in any hurry to move on, like he's waiting for someone. For me? To show me around again, or ask why I ran off yesterday? The pavilion where I went looking for the African kid and found Gary instead is just over there, so I back up around the corner and head up to sit it out.

I think I'll be safe here, but a few minutes later I hear the crackle of crisp grass as someone takes, like, for ever to walk around the building. I move to the johns right at the back. The footsteps stop and come back again, but a bit lighter than before, and they end up by the door, and then the door opens, and someone sticks in their head. I don't have a clue who he is, but I've never felt so relieved to see anyone as I feel seeing him.

'You're Holly, aren't you?' he says.

'That's my name, don't wear it out.'

'I'm Tendai. I saw you up in the trees yesterday. Were you checking out the burn mark?'

'That was you?'

'Yes.'

'In that case I owe you. Thanks.'

'For what?'

I check over his shoulder. 'Has he gone yet?'

'Who?' he says.

271

'That creep.' How many can there be?

'Gary? Yes, he's gone. He left this on the door, though.' He holds up one of the home-made posters, then looks at my head. 'Does it hurt?'

'I'll live.'

'If it makes you feel better, Gary pushes lots of people around these days.'

'Yeah, he's a real jerk all right. But he's not a creep, I wasn't talking about him. I was talking about that guy.'

'Which guy?'

'You know.' But he doesn't. He really doesn't.

I think I'm beginning to understand what it must be like for those kids who say they saw the spaceship only no one will listen to them.

I slide down onto the ground and itch around my cut. I must have it all wrong after all. And Dad's wrong too, maybe everyone rushes to the obvious conclusion because the obvious conclusion is always right.

'Never mind. It doesn't matter,' I say. 'So tell me about Gary. Was he a jerk before his mom left or did he become one overnight?'

'I was his friend,' he tells me. 'His best friend.'

'Was?'

'We fell out. He started calling me names.'

'Oh dear, you poor baby. So what? Kids slash each other with names all the time.'

Man, one of these days someone's going to stitch my mouth shut with a staple gun.

My plaster's bugging the hell out of me.

'Not any old names. Bad stuff. Racist stuff, like *kaffir* and *munt* and *nigger*.'

I stop scratching.

'I take it back. That's pretty bad.'

'We've hardly spoken since.'

'Since when?'

'Four weeks yesterday.'

'Not that you're counting or anything. That's pretty specific, he must have really gotten to you.'

'I know it was then because it was the day the aliens came. We were down near the trees, and we'd just finished arguing when I saw the ship hovering above. It was coming down.'

I only just realise what he's saying.

'Hold up.'

'What?' he says.

'Gary said he was in the tuck shop when the aliens were supposed to have come.'

'And . . . ?'

'Well, he wasn't, I know that for a fact. He lied. But now you're saying he was right there by the trees? Why would he make up a lie like that if all those the kids who saw the aliens were just making up a stupid story?'

My heart's beating in my throat. Because what if they *did* see something, and Gary saw it too?

What if things really *aren't* always what they first seem.

But before Tendai can say anything a sound rushes around the building that's like the world's ending. Not my world, though. Someone else's.

Oh my God, it's Chloe. She's the one it happened to. Ran out into the road and . . . and I can't believe it. She can't be dead.

I was only talking to her yesterday so she can't be. She was so sweet. Not her.

Please don't let it be her.

Mom cries, Dad holds her and looks tired, and even Jason doesn't look too pretty as he sits staring at nothing on the floor.

'That poor girl,' Mom keeps saying. 'She was so sweet. Such a dear.'

And it's almost like I hate her for reminding me as it only makes this horrible, horrible feeling worse. As though the more she says it the truer it becomes, and the more my chest wants to burst. Because maybe there was some mistake, it didn't happen and Chloe's actually OK.

Then, like Mom's only just realising, 'And her parents.'

At which point she and Dad pull me in and hold me so tight I almost can't take a breath. I want them to hold me tighter and not let go.

'That poor girl,' she says again. 'Poor, poor, poor Chloe.'

Teachers are lost spirits drifting around the staffroom, and everything about this place and everyone in it is suddenly so grey, like colour never existed. I don't want to be here.

It's the next day, and no one seems sure if the school's even open. Some of the kids turn up but the class bell doesn't ring and they mostly hang around in groups and cry. At some stage Mr Hyde calls them together for a special assembly on the grass and tells them they're to go to their classrooms and treat the day as normal, but how can today ever be normal? After Chloe, how can anything in the school ever be normal again?

Mom and Dad offer to speak to some of Chloe's class. I wish someone could speak to me too, so when I spot Mrs Hyde walking slowly across the grass to the tuck shop I go in after her.

'Mrs Hyde?'

She looks, but her smile doesn't quite work. Now what do I say? I want to talk about Chloe but for some reason I can't.

'I was just wondering, how's Karl? You know, after yesterday. I heard he was the first one to get to . . . after she got . . . Is he OK?'

For a moment I think she doesn't even realise I'm here and I follow her stare out of the tuck shop. She was right, a faraway bit of me thinks – the bit that doesn't want to be anywhere near this school any more – you *can* see the place where the spaceship was meant to have landed from here. But she's not looking that far. She's looking at where Mr Hyde is still standing on the grass. All alone, tie flapping in the hot wind as he gazes emptily at big clouds in the sky.

'They've gone now,' she tells me and sighs.

I'm not sure who she means.

It's like I have to see Chloe's face again, because maybe that'll make her less dead. Like if there's something to prove she was here she can still come back again.

That doesn't even make sense to me, but long after the school is closed for the day I still sneak into the classroom where Mom and Dad work and dig Jason's camera out of the bag to watch the recording he made of her. I skip through the tapes until I find Chloe. Dad spoke to the older kids one-to-one or in pairs, but the Year Threes were interviewed in a group like they didn't matter as much. Did Mom and Dad mean to do that? If anything Chloe's *more* important than the others, or maybe I just think that now because she's dead.

I squint through the eyepiece. The shot pans around her group as they sit out on the grass, zooms, blurs, and then there she is, sitting with her legs crossed with her back almost touching the tree, her floppy white hat making shadow over her eyes. She's hugging her toy rabbit real hard. Just a shy eight-year-old kid being a shy eight-year-old kid, I tell myself. Then her mouth starts to move and her eyes flick to the camera, but it's like she's looking right at me. Talking to *me*. Only she's dead, trapped wherever it is dead people go, and that's why I can't hear her.

I pull back and almost drop the camera.

But that's stupid, I'm just freaking myself out. I plug in my headphones and look into the eyepiece again.

'*Were you close?*' I hear Mom's voice.

'*Yes,*' says Chloe, in a time when her life had been full of tomorrows – that thought makes me so sad I could cry and never stop.

'*How close?*'

'*Very.*'

'*Were you scared?*'

'*Yes.*'

'*Why? What made him scary?*'

'*The eyes.*'

'*What about the eyes?*'

'*The eyes looked evil.*'

'*What was evil about them?*'

'*He looked evil because he was just staring at me as if he wanted to hurt me.*'

'*Why would he want to do that, do you think?*'

'*I don't know, he just did.*'

She's scared. She believes what she's saying.

Jason wasn't wrong about that.

Then I notice the girl by her side. Her face dips into shot, and her hand scratches something down Chloe's leg that hurts enough to make Chloe jump. Mom doesn't spot it because she's talking to one of the other kids now. Chloe looks like she's about to break into tears, but I don't know if she does because the camera pans away onto a boy who's asking about Jason looking like a rock star.

I rewind and watch it again, and the girl who scratches her is just as cruel the second time round. You can see her thinking about it just before she does it. I want to cry again, but when I watch it for a third time I suddenly stop feeling sad and get angry instead, I want to give that little bitch a slap to make her stop. And there's something familiar about her, too. I know I know her from somewhere, I just can't remember where.

Is that why Chloe wasn't in class when I caught up with her on the path the other day? Was she hiding from that butt-head? Certainly hiding from someone. Chloe's last hours alive were spent running away because someone was being mean to her, and right now that makes me so mad I could explode.

But why were they being so mean? To *her*?

Forget about the stupid aliens, that's the answer I want to find.

I rewind the tape to watch one more time, and that's when I remember where I've seen that girl before. It was in Mr Stamps' wallet. He showed me, just after I spoke to Chloe on the path. It's his daughter, Megan. He told me she and Chloe were best friends, they'd been playing *The Lion King* together, so if that's true I'd hate to see what she's like with people she *doesn't* like.

Dad's coming, carrying a pile of drawings he's collected back from Mr Hyde's office. I quickly switch off the tape and drop the camera back into the bag.

'I was wondering where you'd got to,' he says. 'Night's almost on us, you know, and neither of us has a torch.'

Then, when I don't answer, 'You OK?'

I nod.

'No,' I tell him.

He comes and puts his arm around me.

'Pretty horrible couple of days, huh?'

'The worst.'

'Come on, let's go. You shouldn't be sitting all on your own in the dark, it'll only make you feel worse.'

He leaves the drawings on the desk and we start to head out, but then he stops. He looks round and frowns.

He goes back to the drawings and pulls the first one off the top of the pile. When he doesn't find what he's looking for he pulls off the next, then the next, then the next, until he's down to the last one. When he gets there he shakes his head and goes through them all again.

'Well, that's plain weird,' he says.

I hover by the door.

'What is?'

'Chloe's picture. It was here, I know it was. I took these to show Mr Hyde yesterday morning before . . . before . . .' He swallows hard. 'Right here, with all the others. Now it's gone.'

He pinches the top of his nose. His eyes are raw.

'Like you say, the worst couple of days. There's probably a perfectly good reason, I'll look for it tomorrow.'

He leads me out onto the grass. The sky's getting darker by the second, stars are flooding through and I just stand there, gazing, while Dad locks the door, but when he comes back for me I don't want to move. I can't.

Dad comes closer. He doesn't say anything, just kneels and pulls my head onto his shoulder.

'It's so unfair,' I manage to say.

He holds me tighter.

'I know.'

But he doesn't. He can't do, because he doesn't understand what I mean. I'm not totally sure if I do either.

'Why did it have to happen?' I'm trembling all over. 'Why her? Why?'

'That one I can't answer, I'm afraid. I don't know why. I don't even know if there *is* a why.'

He pulls away and tilts his head up to the filling sky. I see his eyes glistening in the dim light.

He says, 'Where I grew up you could really see the stars.'

'You've told me, Dad. Like, a million times.'

'So rich, like a pool. And so much brighter than what you can see at home.'

'Yeah. And candy was cheaper and streets were cleaner and kids respected their elders, right?' I laugh because it's funny, but before I realise I'm doing it I've finally started to really cry. Tears waterfall down my face.

Dad thumbs them away.

'But they were still the same stars as these, not different. That's what I'm saying. The same stars that have been there for thousands, millions of years, and will be there for millions and millions more to come.'

If Dad thinks he's making me feel better, he's not.

'What are you telling me? That stars hang around for a long time? Everyone knows that.'

'No,' he rubs my arms. 'I guess it's my clumsy way of pointing out that everything – out there and down here, and as sad as it can be – has a cycle, because death is the most natural, most inevitable part of life. Because one day even all these stars, that have sparkled over every human that's ever been, will be gone.'

'But why?' I say.

'Because nothing can live for ever.'

'But *why*? What's the point in living if all we do is die? What's the point in anything?'

'I don't think there is a point, not in the way you mean. The stars, the planets, the galaxies. Us. They just are, as we just are.'

'That's stupid. They have to have meaning. Life has to mean something.'

'Really?' he says. 'You believe that?'

I nod. 'Doesn't everyone? Otherwise there'd be no reason for living.'

'Well, I don't think that. But I still think there's *plenty* of good reason.'

'What is it, then?'

He holds my face in his hands.

'When you listen to music on your Discman, do you skip through just to hear the end?'

'No.'

'Of course you don't. Because the beauty of a song is in the song,' he tells me. 'Just as the beauty of life . . . is in living. *That's* the point. Isn't it?'

*

Is it?

Truth is, I don't know what to think now. When I was a kid we were told God created everything, and that the point in living was to be good so that when we die we can go to heaven and live for ever. My grandpa died last year, but if he's in heaven who is he exactly? Is he still the old man I knew, or the young man I've seen in Mom's old black and white photos, or a kid even, because he was one of those too.

And if God created everything, why did He make us so small in a universe that's so stupidly big? Is it because we're not the only ones in it? In which case when we get to heaven we'll meet the spirits of all sorts of alien creatures too, not just us humans. But *are* there aliens on other planets? Because we were also always told God made us in His image, only the aliens those kids drew in their pictures didn't look anything like us, so if they are real maybe God didn't make them because He's the one who doesn't exist and humans just made Him in *our* image.

I used to pray to God because we had to. Now, alone in my room in Mrs Greenacre's house, I sit on the bed and wonder if I should pray now. You know, just in case. For me. And for Chloe. The only problem is I can't actually remember any prayers.

I close the curtains and the stars have gone. And good, because I've had enough of thinking.

I close my eyes.

A tap at the window has me sitting back up like a pole.

Already I'm telling myself I imagined it, it wasn't there. Then it comes again, more urgent this time.

I stare at the faintly glowing curtains and scare the crap out of myself by imagining it's Chloe on the other side of the glass, floating in fog to haunt me. But who's being a jerk now? Ghosts aren't real, and why would Chloe come haunt me even if they were? Because I didn't believe her about the watch?

I flick the bedside light on and count to ten, then grab the curtain and tug it open. See? No one there.

I move closer all the same, and then have the crap scared out of me again when a face emerges out of the dark. Not my reflection, it's a black face with big white eyes. I almost scream.

'You!' I say.

The little African boy just stands there, shivering in the cold. He's holding something in his hand.

I open the window. This time he doesn't run away.

'What are you doing here?'

'You are not like the others,' he says. 'I do not know you, and yet you are nice. You do not tell me to go away,' he says.

He steps closer and pushes something through the window. It's a sheet of stiff paper, folded in half.

He says, 'Chloe was not scared of the people from the sky. She did not even see them.'

I expect him to finish that with, Because they were never here, but he doesn't. Instead, he says, 'She was scared, though.'

'I know,' I say, remembering how she was on the tape. 'Of who, though?'

'The bad spirits.'

'Bad . . . *spirits*?' I laugh. I can't help it.

'They are here already' – he's dead serious – 'They are all around. Look. See.'

He shoves the paper at me again, harder.

It's a drawing. A kid's drawing, done with crayon, not pen,

and in it are the spaceship and coloured lights and one figure coming out of the trees that all the kids who say they saw something drew, but the name in the bottom corner tells me this was done by Chloe.

'I don't get it. How do you know she was scared?'

'Because she told me.'

'She told you what? Who she was scared of?'

He shakes his head, and says, 'I saw the stars.' Then, 'But I am not clever and I do not understand.'

He touches my hand.

'Nothing exists on its own,' he says. 'We are *together*. Everything is together. That is why I come to you.'

A rustle of bushes and he's gone, and I'm left looking at empty night shadows.

I stare at Chloe's drawing, and the spaceship in the trees, and the alien coming out of them, and the figure I guess must be her just near it – I think she was the only kid who drew themselves in their picture. And I wonder, why did she draw this if she didn't see any of it?

The little African kid said he saw the stars. I look up and I see . . . well, stars, because that's all there are, so what is it about them that he doesn't understand? As far as I can tell, no one understands them – least of all me – so what does he mean?

I lie on the bed with the curtain open and look up at them for hours, until eventually I fall asleep.

Over breakfast, Dad says he's cutting the project short and that we'll find a hotel in town for the rest of our stay. He says it wouldn't be right to carry on with the interviews, and we should let the school grieve. He also says he's going to try to bring our flights home forward. A couple of days ago I would have done cartwheels at that news but now it makes me feel kind of empty.

Mom comes to my room as I finish packing.

'There are no lessons again, but Mr Hyde has arranged a service in the chapel today,' she says. 'For Chloe. He says we're welcome. I think it would be nice.'

I close the lid of my suitcase on Chloe's alien picture because if Dad finds out I've got it he might think I'm the one who took it.

'Sure,' I tell her. 'I'd like that.'

It's not a service just for the school, though, it's for everyone, the chapel's already full and we have to sit outside on school chairs and listen to the reverend there. He's using a microphone connected to speakers on the grass so we can hear him fine, although I kind of wish we couldn't because when he talks about Chloe his voice is so sad. Everyone just stares ahead, Mom and Dad included, and even Jason stops using the camera he brought to film it all.

I scan around. Loads of people have come. Parents, workers, and I reckon the whole local village is standing at the edge of the grass. I spot that nice old guy Elijah who drove us from the airport, and he's standing with the African kid – I really want to go over there right now and ask about the picture he brought me but I'll have to wait.

I spot Tendai a few rows ahead of me, and it's like he feels me watching because suddenly he turns round. We nod.

Then my heart stops when I recognise Chloe's *jackass* of a best friend Megan Stamps near the front. I watch her closely. Is she upset about Chloe? Guilty? Or just embarrassed because her dad is so busy trying not to cry that his shoulders are jumping like rabbits in a sack.

The reverend says, 'Let us pray,' over the loud speaker and everyone bows their head. I sort of bow mine, although I'm actually peeking too, and I can't bear it because now everyone looks even sadder. And I start thinking, Maybe we shouldn't be looking down for Him all the time, and for the answers to life, we should be looking up. That's where heaven's supposed to be after all.

So I tip my head, and the sun on my face is like breathing fresh air. And when I open my eyes I catch the first star twinkling way, way in the clear blue sky, the first of all those billions of stars shining through.

But it's the middle of the morning. Stars don't show at this time.

Do they?

I look again, only now the star's vanished and I can't find it. Maybe it was a plane, although it didn't look like one because it didn't move, it was there in one place.

Did anyone else see that?

When the service is over there's tea being served at tables on the grass. Everyone walks slowly and stands in small groups with cups in their hands and talks in suitably low voices. I look for the little African kid but I can't see him any more. I want to speak to him. I want to know what I'm supposed to do with Chloe's picture. I tell Mom and Dad I'll be right back, but while I'm looking I practically bump into Gary and he turns and tries to glare me down only it doesn't quite work because he doesn't scare me one bit.

He's chewing on his lip like a dog with a bone, and when I start to go he suddenly reaches out and touches my arm. For a few seconds neither of us says anything, I think he's more surprised than I am.

I look at his fingers – his grip is surprisingly gentle – and he lets go.

'I heard you're going back to America,' he says at last.

'Word gets around quick.'

I eye him up. If I didn't know any better I'd say he was trying to be nice. His face is on fire.

'I just wanted to say sorry, that's all. You know.' He touches his own head then points to mine. 'For that.'

'You broke my shades, you know. They were real expensive ones.'

'Sorry for that, as well. I'll give you some money.'

'And for the names?' I say. 'I don't actually care about the sunglasses, they're only sunglasses. But the names hurt just as much as the cut. More.'

'And that. I'm sorry. I am.' He licks his lips, then decides not to say whatever he was going to say and gives me a phoney salute. '*Ufambe zvakanaka.*'

'What? I'm American, remember? I don't speak African.'

'It means, Have a good trip. I hope you do.' He turns to go, then stops. 'And just so you know, there's no such language as African. Africa isn't a country.'

Then we both glance across the way because there's this wail from over by one of the serving tables that has everyone looking. Mr Stamps is still crying only much worse than before. I guess that's his wife trying to ease him but it looks like she doesn't really know what to do, and his daughter's just staring like she doesn't know him. Eventually he goes quiet and everyone huddles back, as if their tea cups are the most interesting things in the world.

'Poor guy,' says Gary. 'I guess he liked Chloe more than we realised.'

'Yeah, poor guy,' I say. 'But a bit weird as well, don't you think?'

'Who, Mr Stamps? He's not weird. Everyone thinks he's great.'

'Sure. Except you don't.'

Gary doesn't know if I'm joking or not. Should I have shut up? *Is* it just me?

'No . . . But he's OK.'

'He gives me the creeps.'

'I wouldn't know about that.'

'And what about that tattoo?' I say, and I finally manage to crack a smile from him.

'OK, I'll give you the tattoo,' he says.

'I mean, who wants to see that?'

'Not me.'

I laugh. 'Yeah. A bunch of stars next to a nipple – who'd want to go near that? Totally gross.'

Then I stop laughing.

Because that's it. The stars. Not in the sky, but all in a row, just like on his chest.

Gary's frowning at me.

'Oh my God,' I say, and I dart quickly through the crowd to where Mom and Dad are. And the whole way I'm thinking, I've seen them. Have I?

'Holly?'

I have. I've *seen them*.

'You OK?' Dad's voice, from a million miles away. 'You don't look so good. Do you feel ill?'

'Quick.'

'What?'

'You have to come with me, quick,' I tell him.

'Where?' he says. 'Why?'

'You have to come now.'

And then I run. Faster than I've ever run before. Away from the classrooms and up the path, back past the chapel and the playing field, around Mr Hyde's house and to the house where we're staying. I open the door, sprint in and skid down the polished hall floor. Into my bedroom. I fling open my suitcase. And there . . . there is Chloe's picture of the alien.

But she didn't see the alien, or the ship. That's what the boy told me last night. She didn't see any of it. And yet here's the alien she drew, like all the others but different because Chloe drew herself in the picture too. The alien's up close and leaning right over her.

Like all the others, but not.

Because hers has a nose.

And a mouth.

And on the creature's chest, just to one side, are three small stars. Blue biro on top of black crayon. They're there. All in a line, and what are the chances of an alien having the same tattoo as Mr Stamps? What are the chances of an alien having a tattoo at all?

Dad rushes in, all out of breath. Mum right behind.

'What is it?' he says, sounding scared. 'Tell me.'

Then he sees the picture in my hands.

I hand it to him.

'Chloe didn't see an alien. That's not who she was so afraid of. It was him,' I say, pointing.

I start to cry, but there's something good about these tears. 'It was him.'

'. . . I think they're good people because they're showing us things that other people don't believe in. That not everyone can see.'
'And what happened next?'
'The ship went a couple of metres off the ground and then it just vanished.'

TENDAI

My name is Charmaine.
I come from Spain.
I eat sugar cane.
What sugar? Brown sugar.
What brown? Sand brown.
What sand? Sea sand.
What sea? Blue sea.
What blue? Sky blue.
What sky? Up high.

'Girls' games are so gay.'

I'm sitting in the shade outside the classroom with my feet dangling in the storm drain when Gary comes and sits beside me. I hadn't seen him coming. I shuffle slightly but it's too late to get up and leave so I stay where I am and pretend I don't care. It's hot. Real hot. Only a week before the end of term – and the year, and Leda School for good, at least it is for us seniors – and I thought I'd managed to get through the rest of it without having to really speak to Gary again. I was wrong.

Out of the corner of my eye I check him looking across the playground.

'But hey, if they seem to enjoy it . . .' he goes on.

I turn to him, not sure if he's having me on or not. He keeps his gaze ahead.

'I thought school would never be happy again after what happened,' he says, 'but it is. Have you noticed? Singing's come back and now hardly anyone sits at the edge of the grass and just cries any more, and nearly everyone plays at breaktimes. It's almost like it used to be. You know?'

He turns and checks right at me. Is he waiting for me to say something back? In the end, when I don't reply, he gives me a punch on the arm. But only light, like when we used to be friends.

'But that makes me sound like a complete poof, so don't tell anyone I said it. OK?'

'OK.'

We go back to checking the playground in silence. Man, it's hot. Too hot to run today. Only sensible runners will make it to the top. That's what my coach says, and he's pretty good so I listen to what he says. I wonder if Chloe's grandpa knows I'm training properly for the nationals now? I think he'd be pleased. And I reckon he'd be even more pleased to know it was my mum and dad who said I should do it, and that they drive me there and even stay to watch me train, and tell me I'm really good.

Mum and Dad and I do lots of things together, now. They were really sad when they heard about Chloe, of course, but for the first time they saw I was sadder. They saw *me*. It's weird, but even by not being here Chloe is somehow looking out for me, and that just makes me miss her more. I'll never forget her.

And Nelson? I don't see him or hear him like I did, and Mum doesn't cry anywhere near as much as she used to when anyone talks about him. He's still there, somewhere, but like Chloe is, so it's in a good way.

I fiddle with my watch. Not long after Mr Stamps got arrested for all that stuff with Chloe, Sixpence's dad got arrested too, only for thieving – he got caught breaking into a house in town and that house happened belong to a Government minister. Every so often stuff he stole comes out of nowhere and onto Mrs Hyde's desk in the library during the night. My G-Shock was one of the first things, which I was pretty pleased about, but on it I see there's still a few minutes of breaktime left and I'm not sure what to do.

'It's weird, don't you think?' Gary says eventually.

'What is?'

'To think that next term we won't be here. We'll be somewhere else.'

I find myself nodding.

'St John's for me. All the way down at Appleton for you,' I say back.

Maybe I shouldn't have said it quite like that. As in, I'm glad Appleton's such a long way because it'll keep him away from me. I wouldn't want to have to go to boarding school either.

So I ask, 'Nervous?'

'Of course not.' He gives me eyeballs. 'Maybe. A bit. So what if I am?'

I wish he hadn't come over. Why did he have to come and sit next to me?

Then he swallows hard, like he's trying not to cry.

'I don't want to leave. I never thought this would ever actually happen.'

And all of a sudden he's the Gary Marston I met on our very first day at school: scared, shy, sitting in his sun hat and hiding in the tall grass down by the rocks. It's like it's that time again and we never changed, only I know we have.

'I guess everything ends eventually,' I tell him. 'It has to, because new things can't start unless other things finish, can they? Next term the Year Sixes will be the Year Sevens and sitting at our desks, and all the other kids will move up, and a class of brand new Year Ones will come who we won't ever know and they won't know us.'

Then I laugh.

'Well, they'll know you all right.'

'You reckon?'

'After what you did? Definitely. The younger kids will be talking about it for years.'

To my relief he laughs too, and when it's not funny any more we sit and watch our feet as they swing over the edge of the drain, just like when we were little.

'They'll probably talk a lot about what happened this term. The alien stories, the Americans coming, Holly, Mr Stamps . . .' I pause. 'Chloe.'

Now the smile's slowly fading from Gary's lips.

'Which is a good thing, right?' he asks, and checks my face to make sure. 'If they talk about her, if she's part of the school history, she'll be kind of alive even though she's not. Won't she?'

We look at each other. The insects hum loudly over in the tall grass.

Gary points to my wrist.

'Hey, you got your watch back.'

'Yes.'

'Did you get your camera back, too?'

'Yeah.'

'Can you maybe show me how to use it one day? Perhaps I could come to yours in the holidays.'

I'm not sure I've heard him right.

'Why?' I say.

'No reason.' I can tell it's a lie, though. 'OK, well promise you won't laugh?'

'Promise.'

'I want to make a film when I'm older. Lots of films, actually, but there's this one idea I've got in particular, so I figure I'd better learn how to use one of those things first. It's going to be really good.'

'What's it about?'

He shrugs.

'About what happened. You know. Here.'

'All of it?'

'All of it.'

'You mean, everything? Even the aliens?'

Straight away I wish I hadn't mentioned them. It sounds so stupid coming out of my mouth now – lights, flying saucers, creatures from outer space . . . no wonder Gary thought we were idiots. And he was probably right. We can't have seen all that, can we? We saw something, but maybe it was just something we didn't understand.

'The whole thing,' he says. 'Right down to Mr Stamps going to jail.'

He pauses, but I'm not really listening now because suddenly I remember something.

'Gary?'

'But some things sound crap when you let them out of your head,' he talks over me, 'so don't ask. That's all I'm going to say about it.'

'I wasn't going to ask that.'

'What, then?'

'It's something Holly told me.'

'The stupid Yank who thinks Africa's a country? What does she know?'

'Well for a start she knew what Mr Stamps was really like even though she wasn't even from here. Maybe it's *because* she wasn't from here. I guess, sometimes, it needs someone from somewhere else to show what's right in front of us.'

He shuts up. When he does that you know you're right, so I carry on.

'Why did you say you were in the tuck shop when the aliens came? Because you weren't. We were near the trees just before and no way you could have got up to the tuck shop that quick. If all us lot were just making up a stupid story, why did you lie about where you were?'

'I said I don't want to talk about it.'

'Why not?'

'*Because I saw Chloe!*' he shouts out of nowhere.

He turns sharply, warning me with a finger.

'I saw Chloe hiding near the trees that day, and she was scared of something. Really scared, like terrified. And I didn't do anything to help her, and now I wish more than anything I could change that because if I had stopped to help her she might still be alive. OK?'

'OK,' I say after a long pause. 'OK.'

So, him too. He's feeling what I'm feeling. We're the same.

Eventually he backs down. He turns away from me and goes quiet to watch a line of ants. He interrupts them with his finger, but the ants find their way around it and keep on going. Ants always do.

Across the way, Mr Greet starts chewing some poor kid's ear off for an undone shoelace. Gary gives me a nudge.

'"You know something? That man is in more dire need of a blowjob than any white man in history."' He turns and sniggers, while I've already started to laugh. 'Robin Williams says that in *Good Morning, Vietnam*. I've got it on video, I can bring it round.'

'Afternoon, boys.'

Mrs Hyde is standing right behind us.

Gary and I jump up quicker than a cat off a hotplate.

'Hi, Mrs Hyde. We didn't realise you were there.'

'I know. Gary, I've got something for you waiting in the library. A calculator with your name scratched into the back. Can you collect it before the day's out, please?'

'Mine?'

'It is unless you know of another Gary Marston, Supremo of the Universe.' She shares a smirk with me. Gary's gone real red. 'And don't leave it too late, I have a home I want to get back to as well.'

Seconds later, the bell rings. The girls in the middle stop their clapping game, the juniors stop running around, and everyone starts drifting back to class.

'Are you scared?' Gary asks me suddenly.

He must still be talking about starting at a new school.

'It'll be strange,' I tell him. 'I'd rather stay here but we can't. Anyway, being scared's also kind of exciting, but if it gets to be too much I just open my curtains at night so I can look at the stars. They make me feel closer. You know?'

'To what?'

'I don't know. Just close.'

'That's not what I meant. Are you scared of . . . you know . . . them? Are you worried they might come back?'

Them.

Is he taking the piss?

I turn but he's not laughing. He's not even smiling. He won't look at me.

Did he see them?

I take a deep breath.

And I say, 'Gary . . . ?'

ACKNOWLEDGEMENTS

For their invaluable help during the writing of this novel, I would like to thank Andrew Shoesmith, Anele Moyo, Matt Cleveland and Oriana Fenwick.

As always, I am indebted to my editor, Charlie Sheppard, for her wisdom, patience, encouragement, foresight, unwavering enthusiasm, humour and professionalism, not to mention her brilliant editorial eye – thank you. Equally, a huge thank you to the whole team at Andersen Press: you are a fantastic team, I feel privileged to work with you in my small way.

Lastly, a bottomless thank you to Carolyn Whitaker, who first got me on the road. You are much missed, and fondly remembered.

Out of
Shadows
Jason Wallace

**WINNER OF THE COSTA CHILDREN'S BOOK AWARD,
THE BRANFORD BOASE AWARD AND THE UKLA BOOK AWARD**

Zimbabwe, 1980s
The war is over, independence has been won and Robert
Mugabe has come to power offering hope, land and
freedom to black Africans. It is the end of the Old Way
and the start of a promising new era.

For Robert Jacklin, it's all new: new continent, new country,
new school. And very quickly he learns that for some of his
classmates, the sound of guns is still loud, and their battles
rage on . . . white boys who want their old country back,
not this new black African government.

Boys like Ivan. Clever, cunning Ivan.
For him, there is still one last battle
to fight, and he's taking it right
to the very top.

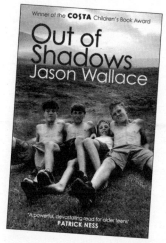

'Honest, brave and devastating,
Out of Shadows is more than just
memorable. It's impossible to
look away.'
*Markus Zusak, author of
The Book Thief*

9781849390484 £7.99

The Absolutely True Diary of a Part-Time Indian

SHERMAN ALEXIE

A NEW YORK TIMES BESTSELLER
WINNER OF THE NATIONAL BOOK AWARD

*'Son, you're going to find more and more hope the farther
and farther you walk away from this sad, sad reservation.'*

So Junior, a budding cartoonist, who is already beaten up
regularly for being a skinny kid with glasses, decides to go
to the rich all-white high school miles away. He'll be a target
there as well, but he hopes he'll also get a chance to prove
everyone wrong. This is the incredible story of one Native
American boy as he attempts to break away
from the life he thought he was destined to live.

'Excellent in every way'
Neil Gaiman

'Overflows with truth, pain
and black comedy'
New York Times

9781783442010

JUNK

MELVIN BURGESS

**WINNER OF THE CARNEGIE MEDAL AND THE
GUARDIAN CHILDREN'S FICTION PRIZE**

With an introduction by Malorie Blackman

Tar loves Gemma, but Gemma doesn't want to be
tied down – not to anyone or anything. Gemma
wants to fly. But no one can fly forever. One day,
somehow, finally, you have to come down.

Junk is a powerful novel about a group of teenagers
caught in the grip of heroin addiction. Once you take a
hit, you will never be the same again.

'Everyone should read *Junk*'
The Times

'Ground-breaking . . . remains the
best book about teenagers and
drugs to this day'
Guardian

9781783440627   £7.99

EVERYBODY JAM

ALI LEWIS

Shortlisted for the Carnegie Medal

Danny Dawson lives in the middle of the Australian outback. His older brother Jonny was killed in an accident last year but no one ever talks about it.

And now it's time for the annual muster. The biggest event of the year on the cattle station, and a time to sort the men from the boys. But this year things will be different: because Jonny's gone and Danny's determined to prove he can fill his brother's shoes; because their fourteen-year-old sister is pregnant; because it's getting hotter and hotter and the rains won't come; because cracks are beginning to show . . .

'What an incredible debut. Lewis brings rough poetry and raw poignancy to this coming-of-age tale. I loved it.'
Keith Gray, author of *Ostrich Boys*

9781849392488 £7.99